The Place We Went to Yesterday

Lisa Mauro

Heartless Press
Whitesboro, NY

Heartless Press
Whitesboro, NY

ISBN: 978-0-9862419-0-1

Chapter 1 5
Chapter 2 26
Chapter 3 36
Chapter 4 48
Chapter 5 72
Chapter 6 89
Chapter 7 103
Chapter 8 110
Chapter 9 128
Chapter 10 141
Chapter 11 160
Chapter 12 190
Chapter 13 202
Acknowledgments...211

For those who wish they had been forgotten.

My dearest Chris,
Thank you for giving me a comforting place to remember.

Lisa Mauro

Chapter 1

"Welcome to your new home," the woman said. Her voice sounded flat. A smirk stretched her chapped lips. I wanted to peel the outer layer of them off, like an onion, but decided against it. She pointed to a bunk at the end of the room. "The top one is yours. There's a chest at the head of the bed for your things."

She turned to face me. Her eyes looked dead. "I'm Ms. Kole and I run the home. You'll be up at 6:00 AM. Breakfast is at 6:30 AM. You will need to leave by 7:00 to get to school and will be expected back no later than 5:00 PM. Dinner is at 6:00 PM and lights out is at 9:00." Ms. Kole crossed her arms over her chest. "You will sign in and out each day so we can account for you, and we do bed checks throughout the night, so I suggest you not plan on going anywhere once you're here." She paused. I chewed my lip in the hope she would subconsciously get the message. She put a hand to her mouth but did nothing else. "Any questions?"

I shook my head, knowing my vocal chords were going to refuse to give way to sound.

"Good. If you need the staff, we'll be at the front desk. There's no call button here and we don't like having our time wasted. Dinner is in ten minutes. I suggest you get ready."

What does she mean by 'get ready'? My worldly belongings amounted to a small bag of personal items and certainly not many clothes. In addition to the fact that I came from nothing, I was always reminded how difficult it was to find clothes in my size. Well-intentioned people donated items, but most of them didn't fit. Sometimes, I would take them and throw them in the nearest dumpster, mostly out of disgust.

I scanned the room and my eyes darted back and forth, taking in every detail. Ten sets of bunk beds lined the walls, enough for twenty girls to a room. We had passed a large restroom with shower stalls on the way down the hall, but I had no idea how many girls would fit in there at a time, or if we had assigned times we needed to 'get ready'. The beds were simple.

All of them were made. It was all militantly meticulous.

The floors looked like poured concrete and had a glossy finish to them. I could imagine children roller skating on them, bouncing themselves against the edges of the wooden bunks, giggling. All of the chests had thick locks on them, but there would be no semblance of privacy here. This wasn't the place for it. I made my way down the length of beds and found mine. *At least*, I thought, *I am near a window*. It could be worse. I could be surrounded only by other girls and the concrete block walls, which were a shade of green that was probably meant to be soothing, but instead looked cold and institutional.

At 4'11" and well over 200 pounds, there really wasn't a way for me to get myself in and out of the top bunk. I sighed and sat on the bottom bed, looked out the window, and hoped for nothing and everything all at once. Then I leaned down and opened the chest, and set the lock to my own combination, 4-1-9-7. My birthday. I was an April Fool's joke of the greatest proportion.

People judged me as lazy and slow. I was sixteen and couldn't climb into a bunk bed. And while I had no real use for math or science, books were my escape. I had been tested years ago at school and my mother was told that I read at least three years beyond my grade. She had pursed her lips and said nothing. I supposed she only read at an elementary school level and would just use this as another thing for which to resent me. I shook the memory off, shoved my bag into the chest and locked it, and pulled hard on it to make sure it stayed shut. I didn't have much, but what I had was mine. And it was everything.

I visualized the path we'd taken to get to my room and reversed it in my mind, so easily found my way to the cafeteria. Already, a long line had formed. Everyone talked to someone. A tall girl punched another in the arm, and I hoped they were joking. I watched the steam rise from behind the sneeze guard. I wasn't hungry for a change, as I was too nervous to eat. Also, my habit was to skip a meal and then binge later when no one was watching. *Maybe I could take a few rolls back to my room and stash them in the wooden chest*, I thought. *No. I will get caught, and I do not need any more attention drawn to my weight. I am already one of the biggest girls here*. It was difficult not to notice.

I made my way slowly through the line, and kept my eyes focused on my feet. I was wearing mismatched socks. Although I knew it, no one else could tell. The woman with the hair net asked me what I wanted and I just pointed in a circle. I wanted everything. I wanted nothing. I wanted out. There was nothing she could do for me except scoop mashed potatoes, corn and what I think was supposed to be meatloaf into a compartmentalized paper tray, and shove it beneath the thick sheet of plastic that separated us. I didn't thank her. No one else did either.

I reached for a carton of apple juice. The pickings were slim, and I don't like water. *Apple juice it is*, I thought, and made my way to the only empty table I could find. The possibility of a friend was going to be too much to ask for. Not only was it too soon, but girls like me don't trust anyone easily. I shrugged like it didn't bother me to sit alone, but I felt every pair of eyes on me. The metal seat creaked when I put my weight on it and I worried that without someone sitting across from me, the entire thing would tip over and I'd be covered in what I could only imagine was mediocre meatloaf.

"You're new," a voice said, hovering above me. I didn't bother to look up. Thick thighs leading to a small waist covered in denim, invaded my space. "I said," she moved closer. "You're new."

"Yeah."

"Then this is your first and last warning: get up from my table."

I looked up at her and saw a burning fury in her eyes. I knew it wasn't personal. This was just the type of person who felt like they had to control everyone. "Here you go," I said, and picked up my tray and walked away.

She laughed, cruelly. "Somebody ain't got no backbone," she shouted after me.

I knew better than to fight about it. Instead, I took my tray near the window, held it in one hand and ate with the other. *Let them think I am weak or crazy,* I told myself, *none of it matters anyway*. Deep down I didn't believe it, but I also figured that if I just kept telling myself it didn't matter, eventually it wouldn't. I practically inhaled my food. I did *not* like standing. It hurt my back. I dumped my tray in the garbage can near the door and walked back to my room. I sat on the lower bunk for a few minutes before I heard a voice next to me.

"That's my bunk," the voice said.

I craned my neck to see her. "Yeah, sorry about that. I was just resting for a minute."

"Where's yours? Did they assign you one yet?"

"I'm above you."

Her eyes widened as she took in the size of me. "You're . . . *above* me?" she asked, confusion clear in her voice.

I nodded slowly. "Yep."

She bit her lower lip. "I don't see that happening," she said. "Ms. Kole was just being a bitch. She had to have known you couldn't get up there."

"Thanks," I said, with as much sarcasm as I could muster, and then I rolled my eyes for good measure.

"Well, I just assumed," she paused. "I mean . . . *can* you?"

"No."

"Well, no offense, but I don't even think I'd feel comfortable with you above me. Do you want to switch bunks?"

"Sure." I eyed her up and down, full of suspicion, and took in all the details. In sixteen years, this was the kindest thing anyone, let alone a stranger, had done for me. "Do we have to switch lockers?"

"Nah," she shrugged, "don't worry about it." She climbed up to the top bunk with ease. I heard the wood creak and realized her offer to take it was really in both our best interests. "Oh, by the way," she said in a chipper tone, "Don't use your birthday for your code. It's practically public knowledge and anyone can find it in a file. The staff sucks at keeping anything private."

"Too late," I said, dejected.

"Do you have a name?" she asked.

"Ella."

"Ella? That's pretty." I heard her whispering it repeatedly. "What are you?"

"Human."

She laughed. "No, I mean, what's your background?"

"Hispanic."

"Oh, me too," she said. "Ella, huh?" She paused and I waited for her fill the silence. "Wait, it's not Ella at all, is it? Your parents just named you 'she'?"

"Yeah."

"That's awful."

"Isn't that why we're all here?" I asked rhetorically. She didn't respond. Eventually, the room filled with the other girls. They created a lot of noise, but I was in my own world. I had my ragtag copy of *The House on Mango Street,* and despite knowing every word and placement of punctuation, I clutched it in front of my face, reading it anyway.

I'd stolen the book years ago from the shelf of one of the string of psychiatrists I was forced to meet. I liked the cover, but that was all I knew about it at the time. The first few visits, I'd read it quietly while I waited. Sometimes, I would bring it into the office with me and flip the pages rather than talk.

Eventually, I got the sense they were going to assign me to someone else, since they often did if we had four unsuccessful sessions. By this they meant that they couldn't garner participation. Unable to part with the book, I'd shoved it between a textbook and notebook and carried it out with me so it wouldn't be noticeable.

My mother found it later, beneath my pillow, and demanded to know where I got it. I lied and told her it was from the library, and she never caught on that it didn't have the library information anywhere in or on the book. Other than food, which I justified as needing to stay alive, that book is the only thing I ever stole. Well, that and an item I kept to remember someone that meant something to me at one time. Sometimes, I felt badly about it, but most of the time I didn't bother wasting the energy to feel anything at all.

I hadn't asked that girl her name. I tried imagining what it could be, but decided to give up. Names are important to most people, I suppose. My mother, Malda, was named for her mother and her mother before that. My younger sister, Maria, was named after my aunt. My youngest sister, Yvette, was named after an aunt on my father's side of the family. This is the way it goes for most of the people I've met.

Not me. I'm a personal pronoun. I spend a lot of time with this fact because most people don't find themselves in this predicament, and have no way to relate. "Ella" seems like it could be short for something else, or maybe I could be a mysterious Italian girl. But I am not. I am simply *She*. My parents couldn't even be bothered to name me. I often think about what that exchange might have looked like in the hospital; my mother covered in sweat, legs still spread in stirrups, a pool of human tissue between her legs. In my mind, when the nurse carried my wrinkled, crying body to my mother—swathed in a standard-issue hospital blanket—she must have just looked at me with utter disgust.

"What is it?" I imagined her asking the nurse.

"It's a beautiful, healthy baby girl," she squealed with excitement. "Look at those big, brown eyes and full lips. She's going to be a handful!" I pictured the nurse handing me over to my mother without a shred of suspicion. "Have you picked out a name for her?"

"For who?"

"Your daughter."

"She."

"Well, yes, her. This little bundle of love, right here," she said as she pinched my cheek, and my face instinctively shied away from her touch.

"Yeah, that's what I said," my mother repeated. "*Dame el papel*," telling the nurse to give her the paper. As she scrawled the letters, E-L-L-A, she gave the correct pronunciation. "Eh Ya."

Ella. She.

"Oh, *Ella,* that's a pretty name."

My mother looked at her furiously, and then she wrote S-A-N-T-I-A. "Ella Santia," she said simply.

"That's a beautiful name," the nurse said, and then whisked me away to the neonatal unit. I imagined that my mother gave her typical scowl before rolling over and going to sleep, pain medications coursing through her body.

The sound of people speaking snapped me back to reality. So much for my imagination. "Who's the new kid?" someone asked no one in particular.

"Looks like just another bitch," another one answered.

I went back to reading my book and eventually, as I predicted, the harassment stopped. About a half hour later, I saw waves of jet black hair streaming over the side of my bed. "Want to go up to the roof before they lock the place down?" the girl in the top bunk asked.

"Do you have a name?"

She smiled. "Lara." I found her crooked teeth endearing.

"How long have you been here?"

"About a year."

"They haven't placed you in a foster home?"

She tumbled over the side of the bed, landing hard on her feet on the concrete floor, and did a small curtsy as though she was in an Olympic performance, and then shrugged. "I'm a runner. They finally realized it was better for everyone if I just stayed in a group home."

I eyed her suspiciously. "Why are you being so nice to me?"

"Well," she said, "someone has to be."

I shook my head. This just did not register with me. "Actually, I could really use a shower."

"Let's go to the roof for five minutes and then we'll head to the showers. It's not exactly something you'll want to do alone."

"I didn't figure it would be." I eased myself off the bed.

My back ached. It was my weight, but these shoddy state-issued beds weren't going to improve the situation at all.

Lara watched my slow movements. "Are you up for this? We're going to have to take the stairs."

"How many flights?"

She looked upwards and appeared to be counting on her fingers. "Five," she paused, "well, five and a half if you count the landings, or whatever they are."

I rolled my eyes and muttered, "Let's go." We made our way past the curious looks in the room. The hallway was far too bright, and the fluorescent lights bounced off the shiny floor. The sickly walls absorbed most of it, but if you held your head at a specific angle, it felt quite possible to be blinded. We walked past the staff office. I was surprised no one asked where we were going, since most of the other girls were either in the community room or already in their own bunks. Loud arguing came from the communal lounge as we passed. No one ever agreed on television shows in places like this, and it always came down to whoever was the most physically intimidating.

"So, how old are you?" I asked.

"Fifteen." Her distorted teeth peeked through a smile.

"I thought you were younger."

"I'm used to that." She flipped her hair over her shoulder and added, "People usually only think I'm thirteen."

"Do you think that works to your advantage?"

She faced me and her look turned serious. "It absolutely does. People discount everything about me. I'm small for my age. I know that, but there's a lot of power in here." She pointed to her forehead then to her heart.

I smiled. I'd never felt a connection like this with anyone else, certainly not my family, and I couldn't say I'd had many of what you could actually call friends. This was a new experience for me, and I found myself conflicted between racing to tell her everything about me, and maintaining my guard. I opted for the latter, only because I had enough experience with the things people could do to others by using their most intimate secrets against them. Preying on weakness was an art form in which many were well versed.

We trudged up the bleak stairwell. Lara didn't seem impatient with my frequent need to rest. I held onto the railing, and by the third flight, felt like I was pulling myself up by my arms and that my legs were just weighing me down.

"Do you want to go back?" she asked.

"No, we're more than halfway there. Let's see this magical roof of yours." We climbed the next two and a half flights in silence. Well, relative silence. My breathing became labored and my heart pounded in my ears. I was self-conscious, and supposed she could hear every heartbeat along with the wheezing.

"We're here!" she exclaimed, and pressed the metal bar of the door and shoved it open, making sure she replaced the rock which held the door ajar so everyone could get back in. We made our way onto the roof, and I noticed that a few girls were hovering in small groups. Some of them were passing cigarettes back and forth. Some were passing joints. A few loners crouched on their haunches, staring blankly in front of them.

We made our way around to the other side of the building where there were less people. "Hey," she said while tapping me on the shoulder to get my attention, "if you look past that water tower towards 125th street, you can see where I grew up. My birth family still lives there." She pointed outwards and my eyes followed her delicate fingers.

"It's nice up here," I said.

"I come up here a lot. I like to watch people. I imagine entire lives for them: routines and conversations. I watch women juggle shopping bags and strollers and toddlers' hands. I watch men sit outside *bodegas* for hours drinking *coco jugo* and smoking cigars."

"You said 'birth family'," I interrupted her. "Were you adopted by another family?"

Her eyes narrowed. "No." We stared off in silence for a while. I listened to the sound of taxis and men cat-calling women on the street—it wasn't a tall enough building to make this a silent movie. I watched the lights of the city ebb and flow, and looked for the familiar dark patch of nothingness at the end of Central Park, but it was completely out of sight, just as expected. "Can you see your place from here?" she eventually asked.

"No." I said nothing else about it. The truth is, I was physically too far away to see anything from my past. Mentally though, it never left me. I could never escape it. I drifted off around the other side of the building, despite knowing I would never see The Baruch Houses from here, and I didn't even want to face that direction. Next, I moved to the west side of the building and craned my neck to see if the Hudson would come into view. It didn't.

"We should head inside," she said. "Showers are a commodity around here."

"That doesn't sound very reassuring."

"I mean, we'll get one. It's just a question of what misery we'll need to put up with, and of course, whether or not there will be any hot water left." We made our way back down the stairwell. My knees hurt, but we did it in much less time than the initial climb. I counted each set of stairs; they alternated between eight steps and a landing for each floor. I thought about why the architects could have made it such a strange number. If they bothered to count eight stairs, why not just round it up to ten? Clearly, my obsessive-compulsive disorder was in overdrive.

Lara showed me where to get toiletries. Most of the girls didn't bother to have their own. The little bit of money anyone seemed to have went towards drugs, liquor and cigarettes. If the state provided shampoo and conditioner, that was just fine with everyone else. "We only use towels once," she said and handed me two of them. I looked at her quizzically. "Trust me, you'll want two."

She took items off another shelf and placed them on top of the towels. "We reuse the other usual stuff and just store them in our lockers. But really, no one bothers with the towels. That's part of the reason you need to get in here before the crowd. I've seen new girls go days without a shower because there weren't any towels left by the time they got around to wanting one."

I followed her lead. "Do you have *chancletas?*" she asked. I shook my head. Despite it being summer, I had very few belongings, and flip flops had been the least of my concern. "It takes a few days for the staff to figure out what new girls need, but when they come around, make sure you add them to the list." She looked down at my feet and sighed. "I'll shower first and then lend you mine. At least you know where my feet have been."

I laughed, "Do I?" She punched me lightly in the arm.

We made our way to the showers and they were far better than I expected. I once had to shower at a YMCA and the flimsy curtain, paired with my size, meant the majority of my body was exposed. It was beyond uncomfortable. I remember dodging in and out of the way of the shower nozzle as quickly as possible. I didn't even bother washing my long hair because of the time involved.

Rather than standard-issue half-walled stalls, these were fully enclosed and had frosted glass doors. I hung my towel over the inside of the door for additional privacy. You could never be too careful in places like this. I balanced the small bottles of shampoo, conditioner and the bar of soap on the small curved shelf and made the water as hot as I could stand it, as the knots in my back unwound themselves. If I were a different person, I may have even hummed a tune. But I am not.

The water squished between my toes and ran off the sides of Lara's *chancletas*. She had propped herself up on one of the sinks and was waiting for me to finish, but she didn't seem to be in a hurry either. I heard her talk to a few other girls as they went by. She appeared to be friendly to everyone. Maybe that was her survival tactic, but whatever it was, it worked for her.

When I was done, I dried off and threw on the clothes I'd been wearing all day. I stepped out of the shower and walked over to the row of sinks where Lara was perched. "Same clothes," she said matter-of-factly.

I looked down at myself. "I didn't bring clean ones in with me."

"No matter," she said, "let's go." We went back to our room, which at that point was full. I sat down on my bed while Lara shimmied up to hers. She leaned down and looked at me. "You're okay, kid."

"I'm older than you," I said, holding back laughter.

"Maybe," she shrugged, "maybe not."

I unlocked the chest and took my book out, to read a little more before they came around for bed checks. No one paid any attention to me, and for that I felt grateful. "Lights out," Ms. Kole announced. Feet scurried around the floor, covers were thrown back and beds squeaked as the other girls climbed into them. "Random checks," she said, "per the usual." A few loud groans answered.

One girl muttered, "Same shit, different day." Another girl laughed.

"Goodnight." Ms. Kole said in a sharp voice.

I spent most of the night tossing and turning, unused to sharing a room with so many people. In fact, it was quieter than I was used to, and it made me restless. I shifted beneath the covers then decided I was too warm, so I shook them off and tried reading by the sliver of light coming through the window from the almost-full moon. It didn't help. I counted the slats beneath Lara's bunk then extrapolated that out to guess how many might be in the entire room. I made a note to myself to count them the next day just to be sure.

My mind raced and nothing would slow it down. Usually, I found the counting to be calming. It distracted me from whatever else was going on around me. Tonight though, it made me particularly frustrated. I thought about what I might do the next day. It was a weekend so I wouldn't have to worry about starting again in a new school just yet. I had no idea if any of these girls were allowed to work, or what people did here when they weren't in school or being tutored. I assumed most were in tutoring based on some of the conversations I had heard in the previous few hours.

I could hear Lara breathing deeply above me and decided

not to wake her up with questions like these. They could wait. She'd been here for a year and I had two more to go until I aged out of the system. When they had initially removed me from my mother's house, I thought that living with a foster family would be ideal. I had been placed in one of them in the past few months, but it hadn't turned out like I expected it would. In the end, a group home was my only option, aside from homelessness, so I jumped at the chance to be moved here. I wasn't regretting that decision. Yet. I mean, it had only been a few days since I found out they'd placed me, and only a few hours since I walked through the doors.

I heard the staff making their rounds. I tried to estimate how long they took between them, but there wasn't any clear pattern. Maybe it just depended on the employees' moods or when there was a commercial break. Sometimes, there would be a noise, like someone moving about, and I thought that maybe a staff person would come by to check on it, but that didn't happen.

Despite all the warnings about sneaking out after lights out, I wasn't sure how people would do that. We were on the fifth floor. We had no balcony, and in fact, our windows only opened enough to flick a cigarette through. I had seen a few girls do it in haste. I made a note to ask Lara about escape plans as well. I always liked having escape routes planned out in my head.

Before I would enter any building, even a crowded *bodega*, I'd take the time to look around and see what obstacles would be in the way. When I entered, before I purchased anything, I would walk around and look for the back exit. The law states that you need more than one egress, so it's just a matter of finding them. I discovered they're not always in logical places. Once, I found an exit hidden in an employee bathroom. I never did figure out how that was supposed to help people inside the store if an employee was actually using it.

My mind drifted into meaningless images. Faces shifted. I relived experiences, and tried to control the stories, but it never worked. I hoped that each time my brain presented a memory, I'd have a chance to do it differently, but it never turned out that way.

No matter what I did, what variable I changed, the end result was always the same. I am *She*. I am always She.

Eventually, I noticed the sky had transitioned from the blackest black to a navy blue. The sun would be coming up soon. I pulled my book from beneath my pillow and picked up where I had left off. Holding the book was primarily for comfort; that, and to let people think they were distracting me if they interrupted. But the book wasn't necessary. My sister Yvette used to play a game with me, one of the few things we ever bonded over. She would take the book and open it to any page. "Page forty-seven, fourth paragraph, third sentence," she would direct, and then giggle in delight when I would say the words she was reading there. No matter what random selection she made, I always knew exactly where to begin.

An unfamiliar authority figure flicked the light on abruptly and announced it was time to get up. "Breakfast is in thirty minutes, girls. Let's go!" None of the staff seemed genuinely friendly here. *Do they all come from the military? Do any of them have kids of their own?* I wondered if they, themselves, were ever children. The room came to life with moans and groans. I stayed put. Before I knew it, Lara was sitting on the edge of my bed. I hadn't even heard her move.

"You're stealthy," I said.

She giggled. "We should get in line. Nothing is worse than *juevos rancheros* when they're cold."

"Is there a standard menu here?"

She nodded. "Yeah, it's pretty predictable." She tugged at my arm and I followed her out of the room, down the hall and into the cafeteria. We were the seventh and eighth girls in line. This time, the staff didn't bother to ask me what I wanted. They just scooped items onto trays and passed them along to us. I grabbed a carton of cranberry juice just for something a little different.

We made our way through the maze of empty tables. Lara found one near the windows. "I saw you here yesterday," she said. "I know you like being near them." She shifted her eyes upwards to indicate the small openings.

"We can't sit here," I said, panic evident in my tone.

"Why not?" She had already ripped open her carton of milk and took a long swig from it. She wiped her face with the back of her arm and set the carton on the tray in the puddle of condensation that had formed there. The moisture soaked through the recycled paper trays from which we ate.

"Because that girl said . . ."

"Oh, Tamara? Don't worry about her. She ain't nothin'."

"I don't know her name," I said quietly. "It isn't like we were formally introduced." I scanned the cafeteria and saw the girl in question standing in line. She glared at me from across the room, and I pointed her out to Lara in an attempt to not be obvious about it. "She's there, by the second lady. She's wearing a green shirt."

Lara glanced over her shoulder and made it appear as though she was looking at the door. "Yeah, that's Tamara."

"She kicked me out of this table yesterday."

"Don't worry about her. You hadn't washed off the newbie scent yet."

"I didn't realize there was a particular smell."

"You know what I mean. Look, you've been around enough to know. There's always a Tamara. She's almost aged out and she's been here for as long as anyone knows. If there were campfires in Manhattan, we would be telling stories around them; stories about how she's older than dirt and no one knows where she came from."

"Like the ether."

Her eyes glazed over. "Yeah. Whatever that is. Anyway, she treats everyone like that at first. It's how she tests you. If you give in, she'll keep picking on you because she knows you're weak. If you fight her, she will act like she hates you for a few months, but eventually you'll be part of her inner circle."

"Then why are you here and not there?"

"I'm not political." She tore into her eggs, shredding the mess with her uneven teeth. "These things are like rocks," she said under her breath.

"But if the only two choices are to let her win or join her, how did you get out of it?"

"Because there's always more than two choices."

I realized that despite having more questions than answers, I didn't want to continue with this line of discussion. "So," I said nonchalantly, "what do people do around here on the weekends?"

"Same rules apply. We have to be in by a certain time, but there aren't really restrictions on what we can do when we're not here."

"Then what are you doing today?" I was only half-hoping for an invitation.

"Same thing I do every Saturday." She chewed loudly, with her mouth wide open.

"Well, since I've never known you on a Saturday . . ."

"Oh, I go walk the High Line."

It sounded like a well-rehearsed lie. "All day?"

"Yep."

"You walk the same mile all day?"

"Yep."

"That's it?"

"That's it." We sat in silence for a while. Then she asked, "Want to come with me?"

I shook my head. "I'll just slow you down, but thanks for the invitation."

"Well," she reminded me, "I have all day." I smiled then agreed to go. "You should really change your clothes though," she said.

We made our way back to the dorm room and I went through my locker. I found the only thing I thought would be suitable in the almost-summer heat—a long, teal tank top and black leggings. I don't wear jeans except in winter, and I absolutely do *not* wear dresses. I added a pair of flats and tied my hair in a top knot. "Let's go," I said.

She looked me up and down, "Much better. Someone might mistake you as mildly happy."

I smirked, "Don't count on it."

We stopped by the staff office and signed out. Interestingly enough, they required that we also complete the column informing them where we would be going. I could tell from the signatures before ours that no one was honest about it.

"Just know," a staff member I hadn't previously met said, "we do random checks."

"You're already understaffed," Lara said snidely. We headed out of the building and were on the street when she turned to me, "No one truly cares," she said. Talk about an understated sentiment.

"Oh, I didn't realize that." I said. She rolled her eyes. "Sorry," I continued, "I didn't know." Sarcasm at its finest.

"We have nothing to worry about today anyway. We'll be where we said we would be. Just remember it in the future."

At least now I realized how the girls managed to come back high, failing the chaotic drug tests or still getting arrested. I was never that kid so it didn't bother me much. Lara didn't seem to be that kind of girl either; if so, she wouldn't have managed to stay in the home as long as she had.

We exited the building and headed towards the train. "They give us passes," Lara said, "but they aren't unlimited, so we need to be careful about how much we use them. I really only use mine on weekends, so I almost always have extra. They're a good way to barter around the home, so keep that in mind too."

I nodded, but didn't bother to respond. I had suspected this would be the case.

We walked to the 145th street entrance. The stairs smelled of urine, and the few garbage cans in the station overflowed with trash. Frankly, this was nothing new to me. The poorer neighborhoods always had less city employees, and the ones they did have were generally not motivated to do much except take their breaks. Around here, people knew how to get to where they were going. Tourists rarely made their way this far north. If you were here, it was because you had nowhere else to go.

Because it was a weekend, the train crept into the station

after a long wait on the platform. When the doors opened, we squeezed our way inside and held on for dear life. There were no available seats in the entire car. We were used to this. At 125th street, it got a little better and by the time we arrived at Columbus Circle, most of the train had cleared.

Lara sat nearest the door, and I watched her thin, short legs swing at the hinge of her knees. She couldn't reach the floor except where her rubber soles barely gripped it at the toes. I was invisible, but much older men stared her down. She glared back at them. "Are you used to that?" I asked.

"Yeah," she said as she raised her voice. "Men are pigs. I'm barely a teenager!" They looked away, shame apparent in their eyes. She turned to me and smiled. "I actually don't care what they do, as long as they don't touch me. It's nothing new to me, but I do enjoy watching them squirm." I looked away, staring at a piece of gum that was stuck to the ground. "Doesn't this happen to you?"

"Of course not." While I knew exactly where we were going, I got up and walked away, acting like I was reviewing the subway map. It was an uncomfortable topic for me, but I wasn't ready to share *that* with her just yet. There are few things I can easily open up about, and my experience with men was not one of them.

Before I knew it, we were at our stop. I followed Lara off the train and up the stairs. I'd be out of breath before we made it halfway there, and didn't want her stuck behind me the entire time.

The sun was blinding when I finally emerged, and I rubbed my eyes with the back of my hands as we headed west. It wasn't going to be a long walk, per se, but the flats I wore were making my toes numb. I really didn't have a choice in my shoes, because I only had three pairs, and these were the lesser evil of them all. If we chose to walk the entire High Line, it would be at least a mile. That may not seem like much to the average person, but given how little physical activity I've ever found myself engaged in, it would probably end up being too much for me.

Lara spent the walk to 30th street talking incessantly. She pointed out stores and people, and yelled at cab drivers as we made our way through the streets. I laughed at her but didn't say much. Every now and then she would ask whether or not the same things annoyed me, but for the most part they didn't.

We made it to the High Line, and took the elevator up to the park. I had occasionally seen the construction process years before as I walked by, but I'd never bothered to come up here when it was finished. "Wait," I said, "can I just take in this view for a second?"

She smiled. "Of course. I mean, we have all day." She emphasized the word 'all'.

Being above the street and the traffic gave me an entirely different view of the city. All the typical noise which constantly surrounded me seemed so muted it was almost non-existent. The park itself was beautiful, but I was far more interested in seeing the city from this angle. Eventually, we began our walk toward Chelsea. We took it slow, not even because of my numb toes, but because we had so much time to waste and neither of us wanted to go back to the home until curfew.

Children ran through the park with absolute satisfaction on their faces. *What must it feel like to be that free and uninhibited?* I'd never been in a situation where I could feel that way. I was always on edge. I was always prepared for the next attack. My doctors told me it was because I had Post-Traumatic Stress Disorder. I read about it, but most of what I could find was about how many soldiers returning from wars suffered from it. There wasn't much information given to me about kids in my situation, and I was tired of hearing how my reactions to things were normal given the abnormal circumstances in which I found myself. They just gave me a diagnosis, wrote me a prescription and sent me on my way.

I drifted off into my own mind. Lara's voice was barely perceptible. After my lack of response on the first few questions or comments, she simply gave up talking to me directly. Every once in a while I would hear her say something that seemed irrelevant and I would shrug, but I still had nothing to say. I was a sponge, absorbing my environment. I wanted to breathe in every aspect of this place and use it when I needed an escape; like when Tamara would inevitably try to start an argument with me. I knew I wasn't safe.

Lara and I walked to Chelsea then continued on to SoHo. Lara wanted to explore St. Mark's Place, even though we had no money to spend, and it wasn't really the scene either of us preferred. "There are interesting characters there, at least," she said. She 'oohed' and 'ahhed' at some of the silver jewelry, but since we were broke, we eventually gave up and headed back to the train. I felt relieved, because the closer we got to the Baruch Houses, the more my anxiety kicked into high gear.

By the time we got back to the home, dinner was close to being served. We signed back in at the desk. "Did you have a good day?" one of the staffers asked me.

"Yeah," I mumbled.

"Where did you go?"

"We just walked the High Line," Lara said. The staffer eyed her suspiciously.

"That's always your answer, Lara. I'm starting to think it's just a cover for whatever it is you really do out there."

"I'm not sure I know what that means," she said in an overly sweet voice, and with what I realized was her typical sarcastic smile on her face.

We didn't bother to go back to our room, but killed time by hanging out in the community lounge. When dinner approached, we made our way through the line as quickly as we could, but we still ended up being some of the final stragglers arriving in the cafeteria. It turned out that dinner was pizza. The same kind provided at school. You know, the kind with cheese that peels off in one fell swoop, to reveal an unbearable crust laden with holes. There were no other choices, so I ate it fast enough to not have to taste it.

They also threw Little Debbie brownies on our tray. I made sure to enjoy every bite of them. At least they were familiar in a positive way. "Hey," Lara said in a low voice, "I don't like these." She had her fingers around her brownie. "I'll bring it back to our room and put it away for you for later, if you want it."

"Thanks." I felt terrible because I had nothing to offer in return. In the last twenty-four hours, this stranger had taken me under her wing, showed me the ropes, kept me entertained and essentially gave me anything she could, including what I wanted to believe was genuine friendship. "I'm exhausted," I said. "I think I want another shower."

"I'm going to stay up and watch some TV," she said, "I'll get you the *chancletas* for the shower and put this away for you, though." She paused, "Oh, and remember to ask the staff for a pair of flip-flops tomorrow. They keep a bunch of other supplies away from the girls, because if they were left out, everything would be gone." In the course of a day, the toiletry closet was almost bare. "We're professional hoarders," she said and laughed.

The quick shower felt great. I could smell myself while we were having dinner, and the metallic scent of the sweat that clung to me was unpleasant at best. I appreciated that Lara hadn't mentioned it. When I was dried off and back in a t-shirt and new leggings, I lowered myself into bed. I reached for the book beneath my pillow and melted away into the familiar story.

The last thought I had was a wish that I wouldn't wake up. I asked for this every night, but it had yet to materialize. I'd already lost faith that it would. We are dying from the moment we are born and yet, somehow, I am still breathing. *How unfair is that?*

Chapter 2

It always starts out the same. I stand on the landing of the stairs and look down. I don't see it coming, but feel a hard shove behind me. Then, in slow motion, I am falling. It never feels slow, but when I stand outside myself, it seems like it takes forever before I can feel the ground beneath me again. Where I had been on my feet, I am now on my side. I can barely breathe, but I know it's best if I just lay there—playing dead—the way my neighbor's dog used to do.

I don't bother to look up, and keep my eyes closed as the heavy footsteps make their way toward me. He rolls me over and I can feel his hot breath on my face. It smells of stale beer and unfiltered cigarettes. Sometimes, he strokes my hair in a loving manner, but we both know it's just because it's what fathers are supposed to do when their children are hurt. He never asks if I am okay. I never offer the words.

After that, everything changes. Sometimes I stay on the floor, waiting in silence. When this is the trajectory of the dream, my sister Maria typically shows up and prods me with her shoe. I feel it dig into my ribs and my nose, and feel the pressure on my hair. I hear her cruel laugh, and know how much she despises me, and it's never worse here than in real life.

At other times, I wait until he's gone, and then I run out the door. Even though I know my way through the neighborhood, it's always a maze and the streets shift around me, leaving me confused. I look for familiarity, though I never find it. Signs have changed. Lights have moved. Even the fire hydrants make no logical sense.

My mother never makes an appearance at times like these, but I wouldn't expect her to. This is just as well, because her eyes resemble a possum's. I've never seen one in real life, but I once watched a documentary in science class and their beady red eyes looked harsh as they moved through their environment. I was surprised that they were ever alive. I had, up to that point, only heard them referred to as 'road kill'. I related to them, because I felt exactly the same.

I'd wake up from these nightmares and stand in front of the mirror examining my face. I expected gouged out eyes—hollowed out eye sockets—and marks from the soles of Maria's shoe on my cheeks. Instead, I found tears. That stopped by the time I was nine, because I realized that it changed nothing.

"Get out of the bathroom, Ella!" Maria never spoke. Everything that came from her mouth was yelled and more often than not, her fists controlled the situation.

"I'm not finished. Just wait."

"You've been in there for ten minutes. You're not the only one that lives here, you selfish bitch." I turned on the faucets while she continued to bang on the door, and made noises that sounded like I was washing my face or brushing my teeth, or rinsing my hands, but in reality, I just continued staring into the mirror.

I was greeted with a face full of spit as soon as I emerged, and this happened every single time, without fail. I was convinced she just stood there the entire time, waiting to hear my fingers on the lock, while she sucked the saliva into her mouth. It didn't matter what time I got up to get ready for school, because this had become a daily routine.

When it first began, years ago, I ran to my mother and cried.

"Toughen up," she said, with an indifferent look on her caramel face. "There are worse things to get in your eye than spit." She turned her back to me and continued doing whatever it was I had interrupted. That's how I felt for the entirety of my life . . . like an interruption.

Throughout my childhood, school was my respite. My teachers, hardened by years of handling rooms full of uncontrollable kids, appreciated the fact that I was never late and actually participated in class. To pass the time, I continuously copied my homework until the penmanship was perfect. I was always able to respond to: "What are you doing, Ella?" with "Homework."

I was bullied mercilessly, both at home and at school, because of my grades, and viewed as the favorite, which couldn't be further from the truth. Homework was demanded by my classmates so they could re-write my answers in their own way. When there were tests, kids fought to sit next to me so they could strain their necks to see my paper. I always felt surprised the teachers didn't rotate the tests so we didn't all receive the same one. When I suggested it, they scoffed at the notion and said they had enough work to do. I never wanted to be a teacher.

My mother didn't care about things like attendance or report cards. I don't remember her ever coming to an open house or making an appearance for parent-teacher conferences. "They're a waste of time," she would say, "I dunno who you think you are, but you're not gonna get anywhere anyway, so you might as well stay humble." Her proud Puerto Rican accent had slightly diminished over the years, but her lack of grammar had not.

When Maria wanted help with something, she would be kind. Well, truthfully, her demeanor would be kind, but I could still see the hate in her eyes:

"Can you help me with this?" she asked sweetly, as she held out a homework assignment. As always, when I tried to help her with it, she raised an exasperated hand in the air and said, "Yeah, I don't care. Just let me know when it's done." In the beginning, I did it in the hopes it would make her realize we were in the same situation, and that there was strength in numbers. When I finally accepted that she was incapable of such reasoning, I gave her the wrong answers.

One day, she came home in a fury and threw open the door to the bedroom we shared. She waved a piece of paper in my front of my face. "What the hell is this?" she screamed, only inches from my face. I tried to contain the smile spreading across my lips. "Oh, you think this is funny? *Que una puta*!" Her fists tightened and there was no use in fighting back. Despite her being eighteen months my junior, she learned how to win physical fights by the time she was a toddler. All of this was because 'she' failed an essay. She.

When Maria slammed the door behind her, I didn't cry. I'd developed an immunity to such things. Instead, I sat on the floor and laughed. With each passing moment, my laughter became louder. Finally, my mother walked into the room. "What the hell is wrong with you? You crazy?" Like always, she didn't actually sound concerned. "I'm in the kitchen watching *mi telenovella* and I can't even think. Your mouth is like a siren. Shut up."

At home, there were no such things as silence or privacy. There never had been, and as far as I could tell, there never would be. My mother didn't call us to dinner—we knew when it would be ready by the smells filling our small apartment. If you didn't get there on time it was likely to be completely gone. My sisters shoveled the food into their mouths as quickly as they could. As usual, they didn't even bother to leave the kitchen, preferring instead to stand over the sink to eat.

My mother fixed a plate, put it on a rickety wooden table, and ate slowly while she continued to watch her soap opera. In an attempt to find some sort of peace, I took my plate to my room. There I sat, book in one hand, fork in the other, while my plate rested on my thighs. I always forgot to bring my plate back to the kitchen, and for that my sisters nicknamed me *puerca*. Pig.

"*Puerca*," Yvette said to me one evening, "I'm tired of having to clean up after you. It's no wonder you're such a fat bitch. You eat on the floor and can't even be bothered to bring your plate back to the sink. You make all of us live in filth. It's disgusting. I'm the youngest and I'm doing all the work. What the fuck do you do?" Her cherubic face always became a deep shade of red throughout her tirades.

I picked up my plate and walked out of the room. My sisters spoke like that from the time they could string words together. We'd all been influenced by our parents, cousins, and neighbors, but I didn't absorb it the way they did. Words like that weren't contained in the pages of my books, so I ignored them. Besides, when you hear something so often, it's easy to tune out. This is a skill I had perfected, and for that, it was always assumed I was stupid, despite my grades.

"You're probably blowing Mr. Rivera," Maria accused. "Blowing him under his desk so he'll give you those grades." A simple shrug would only make her angrier, but sometimes I just didn't care. My life with them had taught me to be passive-aggressive. This was our 'normal'.

My father wasn't very visible in our lives. He provided no real support, other than bringing small staples for the pantry, or insignificant and thoughtless gifts for holidays and birthdays. It was clear my mother despised him. When he rang the buzzer at the door, he'd often have someone else in the neighborhood talk into the speaker so she would let him in. Whenever he made it to the door, she would scream from behind it and refuse to release the chain. There were a few times, in a drunken state, that he broke through it. Usually though, Yvette or I would let him in.

I never got close to him. "*Qué tal, mija?*" he would ask. I'd only say a few words, usually lies, about how I was doing. It wasn't that I didn't want to talk to him, just that I didn't know what to say. I couldn't tell anyone the truth, least of all him.

In contrast, Yvette would run into his arms and immediately jump into his lap. "*Hola, papito*," she would say in a sing-song voice. Invariably, her arms would be wrapped around his neck and her face buried in his chest. Their life consisted of whispers. Secrets I could only conjure based on their obvious intimacy.

When he was home, my mother locked herself in her bedroom, and shouted obscenities about him. She almost always included slurs at Yvette. "*Puta*," she would scream, "You don't even know him!" When my sisters used this word against me, they were almost always calling me a bitch. When my mother used it against Yvette, however, she was clearly calling her a whore. Spanish is funny like that.

We all knew my mother's version of the truth, but I was the only one who believed her. The truth, according to my mother, was that our father repeatedly raped her. Maria denied it and claimed that if he had done it once, Malda would have been strong enough to leave and not let it happen again; let alone have it result in two additional pregnancies. No one but my mother knew the actual number. Regardless, even Yvette never believed anything, no matter how much the truth stared her in the face.

"Please," she said, with a bitter look, "it wasn't *papito*. He's not like that. We all know it was Tomas that did it to her." Then she rolled her eyes. Maria's follow up to this oft-repeated sentence was always, "If she's that weak, she deserves it."

I never talked about it with my mother, at least not in a detailed way, and never asked her about it. Despite us all being borne of the same situation, the reason I was so hated was because they viewed me as the weakest of them all, and easy to pick on. I had no self-esteem, and had always been overweight, so I was bullied and never stood up for myself in a direct way. *'She'* was lost in the things they deemed unimportant. Survival was the only necessity to them and thriving was a luxury for which they saw no use.

Although I never said anything, I knew the truth: I was the only one who would amount to anything, and I was determined not to continue this cycle. Even when I was young, I watched the people around us. Growing up in a housing project meant we weren't surrounded by positive role models, but that place wasn't my entire world.

One of the advantages of living in a place like Manhattan, was that a few block's walk meant an entirely different environment. Mothers in spandex pants and sneakers pushed large strollers through the streets. These weren't the frail, umbrella-like ones I saw in my buildings, but sturdy beasts with hidden pockets and plastic trays for their childrens' suction-cupped toys.

I watched people rush to work. These must have been successful people. They almost always wore suits and constantly checked their watches. They read *The New York Times* or *The Wall Street Journal*. I determined that this is how accomplished people must have become that way; they didn't get their news from a string of people outside the local *bodega*.

From a young age, I understood there was more to life than this, and the only way for me to survive was to sit down, shut up, and take what was doled out to me. I found my own ways to fight back, and I knew this wouldn't be my life forever. It simply couldn't be.

What my family didn't realize is that the more they told me I wouldn't amount to anything, the harder it made me work. The less talent they said I had, the more I proved them wrong. They never saw it, and I was always sure they never would. When I wasn't focused on school and homework, I spent the rest of my time planning how I wanted my life to be structured. I wasn't even sure what that meant, because other than dinner always being at the same time each night, this was something my family knew nothing about.

I trudged home in the snow one morning, and ice melted inside the torn soles of my shoes then soaked through my thin socks. I tapped my feet against the wall outside our door to shake off the slush, and carried my shoes inside with me, making sure not to drip anything on the floor. "Where were you?" my mother asked.

"I just went for a walk."

"Like that? It's freezing outside."

"Yeah, no one was awake so I figured I'd just go out for a bit."

"You're always walking. One of these days you're not going to come back." That was the only moment I thought my mother truly understood the reality of my life.

"I hope not," I muttered under my breath.

She scowled and made enough noise for me to know that not only had she heard me, she was unhappy with my response. "You want breakfast?" I saw the pan on the stove but decided against it.

"I might just have some toast."

"I don't understand you," she said. "You must eat when you're not home, because there's no way you could be so fat when you hardly eat anything."

I looked at her and smiled, but didn't respond. I'm not entirely sure where my sisters got their genetics, because I looked entirely different from them, with the exception of our hair. Maria was tall and athletically thin, although she didn't play sports. She spent most of her time in tight jeans, and her curly hair spilled down her back. She wore a lot of jewelry, but it was all fake. Yvette always looked like a toy doll. She had my mother's short stature as well as her flared hips. Her lips were full and she spent much of her time seductively biting the corners of her mouth.

Whenever concerned neighbors or family passed down clothes from their older children, Yvette rushed to them and dug through them before anyone else had a chance to realize they were even there. It was all so predictable. Yvette took dresses and tank tops. She wore them even throughout the cold New York City winters. Maria leaned towards the jeans and t-shirts. My mother took just about anything that was left, but only if it had buttons. I was typically left with nothing. Sometimes, Rosa, another cousin who was also overweight, would have some hand-me-downs, but those were the only things that ever fit.

My mother worked part-time in a hole-in-the-wall restaurant a few blocks from our apartment. It wasn't the kind of place that required a uniform, or the kind of place with cloth napkins. It seemed that everyone—staff and patrons alike—were apathetic. The food was mediocre, but the prices low. Even in the sweltering heat and overbearing humidity of summer, Malda would button her shirt to her neck and tighten her sleeves around her wrists. My mother always looked shapeless, and I think it was her experiences that made her prefer to look like a walking potato sack.

There were times when she would bring leftover food home from work. This was usually the type of food that was too expensive to afford on food stamps. We were used to rice, beans and unsweetened government-issued peanut butter, so when she walked through the door with *ropa vieja* or *sancocho*, the smell would immediately make our mouths water. It was like a cage fight to see who would get to it first.

Sancocho was one of my favorite meals. Full of beef, pork, *longaniza,* and chicken, it was the type of meal that would fill us up with one measly bowl. Still, that didn't prevent any of us from gorging ourselves on it. We didn't leave leftovers because then it became fair game, which really meant it was unfair because Maria would fight to the death if any of the rest of us touched it.

Yvette could usually be found warming a seat at the counter at the restaurant after school. She would sit with her chin in her hands and bat her eyelashes at Juan—the line cook. From a very young age, she understood that sex meant power, and despite wanting to believe she was inexperienced with the act, I could never be sure.

The end result was always that he would short the customers to give Yvette a plate from their order. Juan was shy, and I think it mostly had to do with his terrible teeth and thick eyebrows. None of this mattered to Yvette. As long as she got what she wanted she would look past all of the rest of it. Once a person could no longer be manipulated, she had no use for them. They were tossed to the side, confused about how she had flipped a switch and turned so cold towards them.

My mother acted like none of this was happening. I wanted to believe it was all a cosmic joke and at some point someone would let me in on the secret. One of the only ways in which I identified with my family was the constant preparedness for attack. People like us are watchful. We note everything. We keep it filed away in our minds so we know precisely what to do in any given scenario. I'm certain my mother saw this and viewed it merely as a survival tactic. In any case, it meant she had one less child to worry about feeding.

On rare occasions I would sit next to Yvette to pass the time. I always carried a book with me, and was careful to never give Yvette the sense that I'd moved into her territory, so I barely said a word to Juan. Sometimes, he would quietly put a plate of food in front of me. In those moments, I would look up and smile at him, but I still never said a word.

"*Oye*," Yvette would say as she poked my ribs. "*Él es feo*, no?" She always muttered it under her breath, making sure he didn't hear her telling me how ugly she found him. "You can have it when I'm done," she would say.

"He's a person, Yvette. Not an 'it'. He's a 'he'. You should be more careful."

"And what are you?" she would say, narrowing her eyes, "A fucking dictionary?" I would go back to my book, turning the cover just enough that she couldn't see my smirk. Such an act of defiance would have resulted in more drama. Neither Maria nor Yvette cared whether we were in public or behind closed doors; when they blew their tops it could happen anywhere. Like a freight train, their tempers were unstoppable.

It wasn't that I never got attention from men in the neighborhood, just that the vast majority of them were perpetually drunk and leering. It made me uncomfortable, not only because they reminded me of my father, but because my sisters never failed to point it out when it happened. "*Oye*," Maria would call out to them as we passed, "she's single! You better take it while you can."

Her choice of words was never lost on me. I believed that people were meant to give themselves to one another. We're not things that are meant to be taken. It never ceases to amaze me that, given our shameful beginnings, my sisters were too ignorant to understand these sorts of nuances.

I spent a lot of time with words, and enjoyed learning the subtleties of language, because words have power. Maria believed that because she could physically overtake most people, she was strong. Yvette believed that because she could manipulate people to give her what she wanted, she was intelligent. But I always knew the truth; words are what give you true power. I tried to choose them wisely, but I am—after all—human. I slip. I've had plenty of instances where I was neither the rock nor the island, just an animal trapped in a corner, lashing out with my only weapon: words.

Chapter 3

I remember that final week, the one before I was taken into foster care, with absolute clarity. I mull it over in my head sometimes, and look for some small detail I may have missed. No matter how unlikely that is, I still try.

There was going to be a dance at school. It wasn't anything formal, and was being held in the cafeteria in the late afternoon. I'd heard the girls talking about the outfits they planned to wear.

"So, what do you think you're going to do?" my friend Bianca asked me. I had a handful of girls I would talk to, but Bianca was the only one I considered an actual friend. She knew a lot about my situation; not everything, of course, but enough that I was comfortable with her. She lived two floors above me in the Baruch Houses and we were the same age, so we had known each other the longest of anyone outside our respective families.

"I'm not sure. I really don't have anything like what these girls are talking about wearing." I paused, "I thought this wasn't formal anyway." I shrugged as I said it.

"It's not supposed to be, but you know these *putas.* They'll use any excuse to dress like whores." I laughed because I knew it was true.

"How about you?" I asked.

"I don't know. It's not like I care very much. I might just borrow one of my sister's knit skirts or something. I'm sure she'll love getting it back all stretched out." Like Yvette, Bianca was on the curvy side.

I raised my eyebrow at her. "You? In a skirt?" I didn't bother to hold back my laughter. It wasn't something I had to worry about with her.

She tapped me on the top of my head. "Yeah, me. Get over it."

"I thought you didn't buy into the whole thing."

"I don't. But I don't want to be the only person that shows up in street clothes."

"You know what they say about street clothes and the girls that wear them," I mocked.

"Only you," she said. We continued walking toward home. We stopped into a *bodega* so she could get a Fanta and a bag of *chicharones*.

"I don't know how you eat that," I said. "It's not even real pork skin."

"This is Manhattan, bitch. Where in the hell is anyone supposed to roast a whole pig?" She laughed so hard she snorted through her nose. "Bitch!" she yelled. "That hurt!" She swatted at her nose and warned, "Don't make me laugh when I'm eating. I'm going to choke to death." I just laughed along with her. "Don't even bother," she continued, "you'd be so lucky as to choke to death and we both know it."

Death was something we often talked about. I never wanted to go in a violent way. Perhaps it was because of how much violence I was surrounded by on a daily basis. My ideal death would be to just not wake up. This is why I wished for it every night. I had some other ideas, but most involved drugs (which I'd never done). I once saw a movie about a guy who locked himself in his garage with the door closed. That seemed to kill him peacefully. Unfortunately, I didn't have a car, and the only garages I knew were the commercial ones which would clearly be too large to be effective.

I once read that men typically choose violent deaths. In this sense, Bianca was less feminine than me. There were enough shootings in our neighborhood, and her preferred method of moving on to whatever comes next was to get caught in the crossfire. "Think about it," she said, "no one cares about the people with the guns. It's the innocent bystanders that end up on the news. Parents that never cared are suddenly crying in front of the cameras and telling the world what a great kid they had. They tell them how much potential they had, when we all know that no one gets out of here truly alive." It was a point I couldn't argue.

When I looked at the people around me, it was clear there weren't many with potential. But worse than that, in my mind at least, was that most of the parents seemed to range from apathetic to downright neglectful. Or worse. It was never easy to tell because we all learned to swallow what was given to us. We were also taught not to complain.

"This is your life," my mother would say. "What else do you want me to give you? You're lucky I gave you that." Under the thick woolen coat of resentment in which I engulfed myself, I appreciated that despite the choices available to my mother, she opted to have us. Regardless of her sentiments towards me, and—to a lesser extent—my sisters, there was the very real possibility that we may not have even come into existence at all.

"So," Bianca said, snapping me back to the present state. "What are you going to wear?"

Clearly, I hadn't even been thinking about it. I sighed, "I'm not really sure. You know I don't care very much."

"Aaaand we both know that's a lie." I couldn't help but laugh.

"If it will shut you up, I'll go see Rosa and borrow something from her. She's usually fine with that."

"Oh, I'll come with you." She sounded far more excited than I understood. For someone who generally didn't care about anything involving social situations, she seemed awfully excited about this.

I eyed her warily, "All right, well, I'll give her a call later."

"Let's just go now. She'll be home. Where the hell else would she be?"

I turned to face her, a hand on my hip. This was a stance I had seen Maria use more times than I could count, and whenever it happened, I knew trouble was coming. "All right Bianca, what gives?"

"What do you mean?" She looked innocent, if you could call it that, but I knew her well enough to see it was all an act.

"We've known each other our whole lives. There's something you're not telling me." I squinted my eyes at her.

"I don't know what you're talking about, Ella."

"Spill it."

"Has it ever occurred to you that maybe I'm just excited there's something different going on? We're always stuck in the same routine." She rolled her eyes.

"Yeah, we're stuck. That's just our lives, but they have this dance every year and neither of us is ever excited to go."

"But we do."

This is the reason I hate arguing. I always think I'm doing so well, that I have a solid stance and there's no way I could lose. Then it just slips away; usually in five words or less. Still, I pressed: "I thought we were better than this, Bianca." This was a page from Lessons-I-Learned-From-Yvette. "We tell each other everything, and there's something going on that you're not sharing." She crossed her arms and looked away. I knew this position. "Look, whatever it is, I hope you'll tell me at some point. It just hurts that you're obviously hiding something from me. And if you were going to do that, you could at least do it well."

Bianca looked defeated when she said, "I don't really know how to tell you this. I've wanted to for a while now. I mean, I've always known."

I had no idea where this was going, and was no longer sure I wanted to. "Go on," I said.

"Fine." She looked uncomfortable. Her eyes shifted as though she was making sure no one could hear us. "I'm crushing on someone."

"That's it? That's what all this secrecy is about?"

"Yeah." She kept her arms crossed in a defensive manner.

A span of uncomfortable silence stretched between us. "So," I dragged out, "are you going to tell me who it is or am I supposed to guess?"

She shifted her weight to other foot and took a long time to answer. I looked away. Perhaps my focusing on her was making her more nervous. "Rosa." She said, at last.

"Rosa? Rosa who?"

"Your cousin."

I wish I could tell you I was surprised, but I wasn't. I'd

always suspected something, but could never put my finger on it. When she said it, I understood why she hadn't told me, and probably no one else either. Without missing a beat, I asked if Rosa knew.

"Well, I haven't said anything to her about it." She paused, "I honestly don't know. I was more concerned about telling you."

"Why would you be afraid to tell me? You know I'm not going to judge you."

"Look, we all know how people here don't approve of this kind of stuff. It's not like the *blanquitos*." She was right. It was starting to change in our culture, but like any sort of cultural shift, it was taking a lot longer than most of our generation hoped it would.

"Do you want her to know, or are you just going to keep it under wraps?"

She sighed, "I honestly don't know what to do. I was hoping you could give me some advice when I was finally ready to tell you."

"I never got any sort of vibe from her. I mean, she *is* my cousin after all." I put a lot of emphasis on the word 'is'.

"Clearly. And besides, I didn't think you were that kind of family anyway." We both laughed. "Yeah, I'm obviously not going to just walk up to her and be all like 'Hey, I'm gay and I have a major crush on you'. It's not like we're super close."

"Well, at least now I know why you were so eager to go over there to look at dresses with me." I chewed my lip the way Yvette was apt to do. "Do you want me to tell her? Do you think that would make it easier?"

"Absolutely not!" She looked extremely flustered, and punched me hard on the arm.

I rubbed the spot where her knuckles had landed. "I mean, I could ask her in an indirect way. You know, sort of feel out how it might go over."

She sighed, "Fine. Just don't do it when I'm there."

"All right, let's head over there. We'll pick a dress for the dance and I'll talk to her after you leave. Deal?"

"I'm really nervous, Ella." She didn't need to tell me.

"I know. Don't worry. The worst that could happen is that she doesn't feel the same."

"It'd be devastating."

"It's life." As soon as the words escaped my mouth, I felt terrible. I had channeled my mother. I felt embarrassed and angry with myself. If Bianca had picked up on it, she didn't say a word. We made our way back to The Baruch Houses, taking our time. Bianca dragged her heels on the pavement and they made an annoying scraping sound. She knew I hated this, but I decided to cut her some slack, given the conversation we'd just had.

Rosa lived in the same building as us, so we didn't need to be buzzed in. We took the elevator to the fourth floor and found our way to her door. The layout of the buildings was quite simple once you figured out it was just a repeated pattern, and not even a complicated one. I knocked twice and waited. Bianca blanched. I heard the creaking sound of bare feet on parquet. "Just a minute," Rosa called out.

When she opened the door, her hair was tied up in a damp towel. She had small beads of water trickling down the side of her face. I could tell Bianca was absolutely smitten when she cleared her throat and her cheeks suddenly burned hot.

"*Hola, mija*! Come in! I've been meaning to call you. I've missed you!"

Rosa and I had grown closer after spending years ignoring each other. Despite being the black sheep of our respective branches of the family tree, at least from my perspective, we were competitors, not family. This changed when I realized we were both just too afraid to get to know each other, but once we started to, the flood gates opened. Until I left home, we never looked back.

We kissed each other hello as Bianca and I crossed the threshold. "Let me just turn this down," Rosa said. "I've been using the TV to ignore chores." She leaned over the coffee table to retrieve the remote control. Once the sound was lowered and we'd all made ourselves comfortable on the couch, she asked, "So what's up? How are you?"

Bianca was noticeably, and understandably, not herself. "We have a dance next week at school, so I was wondering if I could shop in your closet." We all laughed.

"Yeah, definitely. Let's go take a look now. I've been putting some things away for you, but just haven't come downstairs to bring them."

"What have you been up to?" Bianca asked.

"Not much, to be honest. I've been trying to figure out what I want to do when school ends. I know there's no way I can go to college. Mom can't afford it, and I have no clue what I even want to do, so I wouldn't want to waste the money."

"There's always vo-tech. It's not that expensive and you can probably get a loan." I said.

"I've been thinking about it, but I mean, could you imagine me being a stylist? I don't think I'd like being on my feet all day."

"Well," Bianca said, "you definitely have the personality for it. I bet you'd have a ton of clients."

"And," I added, "nothing says you have to stay here. You'd make better money uptown."

Rosa smiled, "I know, but who the hell is going to hire a *boriqua* from *el barrio*?"

"Anyone," Bianca said. We exchanged glances, because she knew I was about to give the same response and she'd just beaten me to it.

"I don't know. I've definitely been thinking about it though. At the very least, it can't hurt to have a skill, and if I could make any money it would be better than the situation I'm in now. I'm almost eighteen," she sighed. "My mother never fails to remind me that I should be working and helping to pay the bills. But, I mean, if there aren't jobs then there aren't jobs."

Rosa was two years older than me, and once we became close I looked up to and respected her. She wasn't destined for greatness, but I felt she had more potential than most around here.

Unfortunately, she didn't see it in herself. "It's not that there aren't jobs, Rosa," I said. "It's that no one wants to hire inexperienced people."

"Well, how the hell do I get experience if no one will hire me? You know, I even went down to the restaurant and tried to get some shifts. They told me they didn't need help I thought that maybe I could fill in for *Tia* Malda, but they wouldn't even do that. I mean, she's the only waitress there. What do they do on her days off, or when she's sick?"

"Come on. We both know she works every day and has never called in sick. That woman was working until she was about to give birth and was back two days later. When she was out, they just had Juan running plates. I'm not even sure if the food was anything but microwaved on those days." I had to admit that my mother, despite her disinterest when it came to her family, had the strongest work ethic of anyone I knew. That, and the loyalty of everyone at the restaurant, was unwavering. I sometimes thought it was the only place any of them had ever worked.

Bianca took a seat on Rosa's bed and crossed her legs, then rested her elbows on her knees. Her eyes followed Rosa as we started going through the dresses on the back of her bedroom door. Rosa was flipping through them so quickly I didn't even have a chance to see them. Finally, she inhaled sharply and squealed, "This is the one! *Mija*, look." She held out a black strapless number. It had what could only be described as purple waves from the hem to just below the waist.

"It's really pretty," I admitted. "But you know how I feel about dresses, and sleeveless ones in particular."

"*Mijita*," she said, "it's spring. This is perfect. Go try it on. You'll see."

I wanted to stand my ground, but didn't feel in the right position to do so. Rosa was doing me a favor, and for that I was grateful. So, I went to the bathroom and closed the door behind me. Sometimes when I visited, I would just sit on the edge of the tub and listen to the muted sounds on the outside of the door. No one demanded to be let in. No one screamed obscenities at me. No one told me how I took up too much time or too much space.

I struggled to get out of my clothes. The humidity made my leggings stick to my thighs, but it was that way for everyone. I needed to rinse off before I tried on her dress—I could smell the salty sweat on my skin. I reached for a towel in the small plastic bin next to the sink and turned on the water. I left it lukewarm so it would cool me off a bit. Despite knowing that Rosa would have given me all the time in the world, I didn't want to burden her, so I washed and rinsed as quickly as I could.

Once I'd dried off and hung my towel on the back of the door, I put on the dress. The mirror wasn't full-length, so I didn't have a sense of how I looked. In my mind, though, it was a catastrophe. But then again, in my mind, it always was. I headed back to Rosa's room and found her sitting next to Bianca in much the same position. Bianca was showing her a braided bracelet she had made, and talking about the different colors she had on hand to make one for Rosa.

They both looked up at the same time, Rosa's hand still placed gently on Bianca's wrist. "Well?" I asked, "How bad is it?"

"What the hell are you talking about?" Bianca said, false aggravation in her tone, "You look great." Both girls smiled.

Rosa was quiet but she hugged me. "I told you, *mija*, it's perfect." She reached for her phone and snapped a few photos, then handed it to me. "Wait," she said, "let's take your hair down." I felt her rearranging it and running her fingers through it to separate the curls. "That's even better." She took a few more photos and showed those to me as well. I had to admit, the dress did look nice, but I l still felt uncomfortable with my arms on show.

"Rosa, I really appreciate this," I began, in what I hoped was a humble voice. I didn't want to seem ungrateful, but I had to tell her. "It's really pretty, but you know, I'm still really unhappy with my arms."

"Well," she said with more humor than annoyance in her tone, "I can't change your arms. I hate mine too, but I have a solution for that." She tore through a stack of clothes at the foot of her bed. It was a giant pile of entropy. "Found it!" She held up a long purple scarf. I just looked at her quizzically. "Hold on," she said as she made her way towards me. She wrapped it around my shoulders, then my arms and tucked the ends inside my elbows. She stepped back and nodded in approval. She took a few more photos, and I couldn't argue anymore. She had managed to quell my anxiety about what to wear, and how to wear it.

"You look great," Bianca said. "I'm gonna head back and get some homework done before it gets too crazy for me to think." She hugged Rosa and I goodbye and walked herself out.

Rosa turned to me, "Is she all right?"

"Yeah, she's just got a lot on her mind lately."

"Anything you can share?" As much as I loved Rosa, she was a notorious gossip. I would have to tread carefully.

"Well, she has a crush on someone and she doesn't know how to handle it."

She chuckled, "That's easy. She should just talk to them directly, you know, like maybe just ask them to hang out or something."

"I don't think she can do that," I said.

"Why not?"

"Because she thinks she *es maricona.*"

"Gay?" She rolled her eyes. "Who gives a shit? Nobody worries about that anymore."

"No? What do you think her mother would say? Or *your* mother for that matter?"

"Well, in that sense you're right. But, I mean, it's no one's business. So, spill it." Curiosity seeped from her every pore.

"I'm pretty sure I've known for a while now. It doesn't change anything for me."

"Oh my God," Rosa exclaimed. "It's you!"

I must not get defensive. This was definitely not the time for it. "It's not me, *stupida*, but it's someone we know."

"Do I even want to know?"

"You're probably better off not knowing. They say

ignorance is bliss."

"I say good for her. She's really pretty, and whoever it is would be lucky to have her."

I eyed her with suspicion. "She's pretty," I agreed. There was no inflection at the end of my sentence. There was no intent of question.

"Yeah, she is." She looked the other way, towards the door. "So, are you just going to tell me who it is already?"

"All right," I sighed, "listen, please don't say anything. Not a word to anyone."

"Don't you trust me?"

"With something like this? Come on, Rosa, you're the biggest gossip I know. I really need you to keep this under wraps, okay? It's important this time." The last time I trusted her with anything big was when I found out that Chenelle, a twelve year old from another building, was pregnant. Before I knew it, all of Baruch had heard about it. *Wildfire*, I thought. *Her mouth is like wildfire.*

"I swear, I won't breathe a word."

"Rosa," I said in the most non-inflected voice I could muster. "It's you, *mija*."

"What?" She didn't look unhappy, just extremely confused. "No." She shook her head in denial, "Stop messing with me, Ella. Don't do that. It's not funny."

"Wait," I said, totally dumbfounded, "are you upset about it?"

"I'm upset that you're screwing with me like this."

"I'm not. She just told me today."

"You think I'm going to believe that? Come on. I can't believe you'd do this. The two of you with your scheming ways. You're being ridiculous. Even if she's *maricona*, which we don't even know, she wouldn't be interested in me."

"Not if," I said. "She knows she is."

I understood the sentiment, not from my own personal experience, but I'd seen it in the world around me, and read about it. I saw the confusion on her face, and could guess her thoughts.

She would refuse to believe that Bianca was attracted to her. In her mind, it was inconceivable. Bianca was a beautiful and relatively androgynous thing. Rosa wasn't as heavy as me, and her curves were in all the right places. In our neighborhood, though, she was considered 'just right'—a living Goldilocks.

"Look, I'm not lying. Believe what you want, but you should talk to her. Even if you're not interested in her in that way, at least talk to her about it. She's absolutely terrified, and she didn't want me to tell you. I told her I wouldn't tell you directly, but you have a way of pushing me, and you know it."

"Okay." Defeat resonated in her voice, "Okay, I'll go talk to her. Let me change and I'll go downstairs and find her." She looked me up and down and said flatly, "You need to get out of that dress if you're wearing it next week." I had forgotten I was still in it so I headed to the bathroom, in a daze, to transform back into the ugly duckling.

I went downstairs, let myself into the apartment, and then trudged to my room to wait for the fallout. It would come. It always did. With everything that had happened that afternoon, I hadn't even felt the weight of the bag on my shoulder—I was already carrying the world. I sat on my bed and took out my geometry book. I have always hated math. Despite my belief that I'm logical, for something that's supposed to be so formulaic and predictable, it doesn't work that way in my mind.

Words. Words are the answer to everything.

Chapter 4

I heard the yelling and the hard footsteps before I could make out what was being said. Like a train off the rails, it came right for me. I knew that much. When my door slammed open, it felt like everything I had surrounded myself with—books, homework, and essays—was immediately scattered about the room. A tornado had arrived and I had nowhere to take cover.

When I finally realized that both of my parents were standing above me, and the raised voices were directed at me—a barrage of questions and accusations that came so quickly I couldn't respond—I knew whatever was coming next wasn't going to be pleasant. I just didn't expect it to go the way it did.

"*Usted maricona* now, eh?" my father spat out.

"I can't believe this," my mother screeched. "How do I explain this to the family? How do I even show my face? Everyone knows!"

I felt confused, and stumbled over my tongue, which was thick with dehydration and fear. "I'm not . . . wait, what? Did Rosa tell you something?"

"See?" My mother pointed at my father, whose hands curled into fists. "She knows exactly what I'm talking about. She can only know if it's true."

"So," my father yelled, "it's bad enough that you bring shame to us every day you breathe, but now this? *This*!"

A fury the likes of which I had never let out of me exploded all over the room. I stood up as quickly as I could and my eyes narrowed. "*I* bring shame to this family?" I asked. "You," I pointed to my father, my finger only an inch from his chest, "you're the one that should be ashamed! Look at what you did to her. Look at the way you created this so-called family."

Next, I turned to face my mother, "And you," I said, without stopping to take a breath, despite being winded. "You think I bring shame to this family? You may not have chosen the circumstances, but you did choose to have us. You've never wanted us. You tell us all the time how resentful you are. You should be ashamed of the way you treat us."

I felt the rush of air before the first slap fell on my cheek. The second one landed at the corner of my eye. So did the third and fourth. Then I lost count. I tried to use my hands to protect my face, but it was useless. My father held me down and my mother delivered blow after blow. "How dare you," she interjected between a string of curses. She damned me. She despised me. And if she'd had her way, she would have killed me then.

Yvette heard the commotion and came into the room. I could barely make her out through the blood that dripped down my face, and nearly blinded me. I'm not sure where her compassion came from—perhaps it was some deep-seated and previously unacknowledged admittance that we are, in fact, the same—but Yvette struggled to distract my father from holding me down.

Because it was Yvette, it worked.

As soon as I was free, I threw my mother aside and headed towards the door. My father, realizing he'd been caught in Yvette's web, tried to grab my ankle, but I shut the door behind me and moved as quickly as I could. There was no time to wait for the elevator. I instinctively ran towards the stairs. I let the door slam behind me and tried to catch my breath, panting and gasping for air. I should have had more time. There were now three doors between us, but I shouldn't have stopped. I should have kept going. That's the thing I remember from that night: the only variable that I could have affected.

I stood on the landing, and looked down. I didn't see it coming, but felt a hard shove behind me. Then, in slow motion, I fell. It didn't feel slow, but when I stood outside myself, it seemed like it took forever before I felt the ground beneath me again. Where I had been on my feet, I was now on my side. I could barely breathe, but I knew it was best if I just lay there—playing dead—the way my neighbor's dog used to do.

I didn't bother to look up, and kept my eyes closed as the heavy footsteps made their way toward me. He rolled me over and I felt his hot breath on my face. It smelled of stale beer and unfiltered cigarettes. I didn't dare look. He didn't say a word. He just made that noise, the sound of disgust, and walked away.

I didn't know where to go or what to do next. Fortunately, my mother didn't follow my father to the stairwell. I got up slowly, and my entire body felt like it was on fire. It hurt to breathe. It hurt to blink. The only thought I had was for survival. *Get out*, I told myself, *leave*. There could be no police involvement. Things that happened here were handled here.

Bianca. I pressed my fingers against the cold concrete wall and held onto the railing with my other hand. I counted the steps until I knew where I was, then opened the door and peered around the corner. This was a useless move because I could barely see anything anyway. I didn't notice anything other than the usual shadows, so I knocked on her door, my knuckles and palms dripping blood. I kept scanning the hallway. Malda would know the first place I would go.

It wasn't Bianca that came to the door. It was her mother, Galena. "*Tia*," I said. It was common to call even those you weren't related to 'aunt' or 'uncle'. "*Ayúdame. Por favor, ayúdame.*"

"Please," I begged repeatedly, "help me."

Galena stared at me, disbelief evident in her warm eyes. She blocked the doorway for only a moment, just long enough to make sure that whoever had done this to me hadn't followed. Then, lightly—as though she was afraid to even touch me—she put her hand on my shoulder and led me into the apartment. I stood there, my back to her, and heard the familiar sounds of multiple clicks of locks and the chain being secured.

My breathing felt labored. "*Calmarte, mija*. Come with me." She took a deep breath and helped lead me to the bathroom. There was no way for me to stay calm. My hands shook uncontrollably, but the severe shock kept me from crying. Galena helped me sit on the closed toilet and began running the water in the sink. She soaked a washcloth in the warm water and pressed it to my face with a gentle touch. The water ran pink when she wrung it out, even after a few minutes of these repeated moves.

She muttered prayers and lamentations to her god. The God. The one I was sure didn't exist. When my face was no longer bloodied, she said, "All I have is this," and she held up a bottle of rubbing alcohol. "I can't do it, Ella. It's all I have, but I can't do it." I nodded slowly. I couldn't do it either. "*Necesita un hospital, mijita*" she said softly. "Now."

I shook my head. I could not go to the hospital. Things like this just weren't handled that way. "*Gracias, pero no*," I responded, my voice barely able to make an escape. "Please, just let me stay here tonight," I paused, "and please don't tell Malda I'm here." She took my chin in her hand and raised it so I would look at her.

"You can stay as long as you need, but you know, *mija*, she will know where you are."

"She won't care. She never has."

"Oh no," she shook her head. "For this, she'll know. Where else would you run?" She was right. My only hope was that even if my mother knew where I had gone, she wouldn't bother looking for me. It turned out I was correct. I stayed home from school for two days. I lay in Bianca's bed, covers up to my neck, and alternated bags of *gandules* and then white corn to reduce the swelling on my face.

Bianca hadn't come home until much later that night. We didn't talk about where she had been. In fact, we never talked about it. Ever. I heard her speaking to Rosa in a low whisper later that evening and soon they were standing over the bed, brushing my matted hair away from my face. "*Lo siento*," Rosa repeated, as tears streamed down her face. There weren't enough apologies in the world for what she had caused to happen.

I didn't blame Bianca. She was a private person and kept a lot of things to herself, even though we were the closest and most solid things we had in each other's lives. I had a difficult time not blaming Rosa, and it would take me more than a decade before I was able to look back with more clarity on the situation. But in those years, I went back to loathing her. The trajectory of my life took a wild loop after that night, and I spent much of the time cursing her and wishing for terrible things to happen. I wanted her to suffer the way I had.

I still wasn't fully recovered when I went back to school. Most teachers weren't concerned and asked no questions. Ms. Ruiz, my English teacher, wasn't in that group. I had experienced stares and whispers all day, and had watched hardened teachers as they looked away from me, unwilling to make eye contact because they would then be forced to acknowledge my face.

As other kids trickled in and took seats, Ms. Ruiz pulled me aside by the elbow. "Ella," she asked, "what happened to you?" I didn't know a lot about her, but I knew that although she worked here, in a neighborhood full of depravity, she hadn't grown up here. To this extent she was *una forastera*—an outsider.

"Nothing." I shrugged.

"That doesn't look like nothing." She pointed to my black and swollen eye.

"Well, it is."

"Ella, this isn't you."

"You don't know me. You know nothing about me."

"I know you better than you think I do," she said forcefully. Her eyes held a glint of steel. "You're unlike any of the rest of them." She swept her hand out across the room, "And in some ways, you're exactly like them."

I turned on my heel and walked to my seat. I refused to make eye contact with anyone, but I heard them talking about me, trying to guess how it had happened. Most assumed it was someone at school who'd done it. For the most part, the whispers told me I deserved it.

I spent my time at Bianca's house. She refused to talk to Malda or my sisters, so instead she shuttled clothes from Rosa. I couldn't afford to be stubborn or refuse charity at that time, so I took the clothes, acted grateful, and tried to pretend that everything was normal. We all knew it wasn't, and we were certain it would never return there again.

A few days later, a knock came at the door. I was at

Galena's kitchen table, a small thing cramped in the only space she had. A drop-leaf that was barely ever able to open, and when it did there was no room to pass. The door opened and I heard hushed whispers, but continued to focus on an essay on *The Catcher In The Rye*. I was having difficulty not transforming into Holden myself.

I heard the sound of multiple footsteps making their way to the kitchen, and when I looked up, Galena was standing next to a stranger, her hands continuously wringing around each other. "We need to talk to you, Ella," she said softly.

I put my fork down. I had been eating homemade *arroz con gandules y pollo*, a rare treat. I stood up and pressed myself against the table to follow them into the living room. The swelling of my face had dissipated, and the bruises had faded from deep purple to blues and reds, but I suspected this wasn't going to matter.

By the time I got to the living room, the two adults had already sat on the couch facing the loveseat. The small coffee table was the only thing separating us; that and about three feet of space. It felt claustrophobic. My anxiety levels rose and my heart pounded in my chest. A panic attack was imminent.

"Ella," the stranger said, using an informality I found grating, "I'm here to help you." I knew this wasn't true, because I realized she was from ACS—the New York City Child Protective Services division.

"How do you think you're going to help me?" I asked.

"You're a smart girl. I've talked to Ms. Ruiz and your guidance counselor. I'm sure you know why I'm here."

"Of course I do, but that doesn't mean I'm going anywhere with you. I'm staying right where I am."

"Unfortunately, I can't allow that," she said. "The resources here are unable to continue providing for you. You'll need to come with me so we can place you in a home where you can be cared for." By resources, I knew she meant Galena, but I couldn't fault her. She had a hard time providing for her own kids and I was sure that despite not wanting to be a burden, I was.

"That didn't take long," I said. I tried not to look either of them in the eyes. I didn't want Galena to feel guilty, because I recognized that this was in no way her doing. I was also sure that if there was any way for her to have prevented this, she would have. She always treated me more like a daughter than Malda had.

"Given the circumstances, we've made sure we have a place for you. As your case manager, I had to see you first."

"I'm not leaving with someone I don't know. Do you even have a name?"

"Ms. Santiago."

"So professional."

"Well then, you can use Linda, if you prefer."

"*Qué, Linda,*" I said, my words dripping with irony, though there was nothing cute about the situation. I sighed, "I'll go get my things. Give me a few minutes." I walked slowly back to Bianca's room. Her bedroom didn't have a fire escape, and even if I managed to sneak out, I wouldn't have anywhere to go. I also knew I was incapable of remaining hidden. My survival skills were limited to getting through my 'normal', and weren't up to attempting to live on the streets for some unknown period of time.

I filled a bag with the few personal items I had, and threw in a few of Rosa's clothes—only because if I hadn't, I would have just had the blood-stained clothes I'd escaped in. In complete disregard for my character, I swiped the lone bottle of Bianca's lavender perfume off her dresser. This was perhaps one of the only feminine things about her. I'm still not entirely sure why I did it.

"That was fast," Ms. Santiago said when I returned, the bag slung over my shoulder.

"I don't have much. I'm a light traveler."

I had a chance to say goodbye to Galena, but Bianca wasn't home yet and I wasn't going to be given any time to wait. I leaned in for a long hug and she whispered, "You be safe. Don't let anyone hurt you."

"I can't promise that."

"I know, but do the best you can. You're not a victim, *mijita*, you're a survivor. Remember that." They were the kindest words anyone had ever said to me and I've never forgotten them. I remember everything about that moment. Sometimes I go back and watch it like a sad movie projecting inside my skull.

"Are you ready?" Ms. Santiago asked.

"Probably not, but we might as well get this out of the way." I heard the door click behind us, but missed the sound of the locks. I wanted to believe that Galena was staring through the peephole, waiting to make sure we made it to the elevator without incident, but also because she was sad to see me go. I never asked her about it over the years, though I have always wanted to.

There was a jitney cab waiting for us at the curb. Linda opened the car door and I slid onto the back seat. It felt soft and uncomfortably warm. She didn't tell the driver where to go; apparently she didn't need to. When we went over the Brooklyn Bridge, I stared at the metal bars surrounding us. Perhaps it was designed to make a person feel safe, but it reminded me of how trapped I was.

I had no sense of direction here. I was out of my territory. Despite Brooklyn being part of the city, it was a foreign world to me. Eventually, we pulled up in front of a brownstone. A stained glass insert was set into the door, but otherwise the house didn't look like it was in good condition. We climbed the seemingly endless steps, and then Linda rang the doorbell. A *blanquita* opened the door. She smiled and ran her pale fingers over the long, ropey chain about her thin neck. "Welcome, Ella," she said warmly.

"Hi."

"Linda, nice to see you again. Please, come in." We went into the living room and sat down on an old leather couch that sounded like a squealing pig as I shifted my weight to find a comfortable position.

Linda cleared her throat. "Ella, this is Susan. She is going to be your foster mother until we can either sort things out with your parents, or find a family to adopt you." I didn't respond. I wasn't looking to be adopted. "Susan has one child of her own, a daughter named Anne who is about eight years old. She also fosters two additional children—Jerome and Jaiden. They are twins, fourteen years old, and have been living here for almost a year."

Susan joined the conversation, "From what I hear, you're going to fit in very well here. It's just me and the kids. We're generally quiet, but we do find ways to have fun. I have a few rules that I ask everyone to follow—respect each other's space and privacy, be honest and participate. It's really important to me that everyone gels as a family." She brought her hands together and intertwined her fingers. I felt like I had officially entered The Twilight Zone. I wasn't sure how to react so I just nodded. "I'll need to wrap up a few things with Linda, but you'll be sharing a room with Anne, so feel free to head upstairs and get settled. We'll talk later about your school transition."

The stairs were easy enough to find—I'd seen them when we first entered the foyer. There was a row of shoes on a rubber mat. I hadn't bothered to take mine off. I felt the smooth wood of the banister beneath my palm, and hesitated once I was on the landing. I felt as though I would lose my balance at any moment; that I would feel the free-fall backwards until there was nowhere left to go.

It was easy enough to figure out where the room was. The layout was very simple. At the top of the stairs was a bathroom. The bedrooms were essentially located around it. I knocked on the first door to the left. I assumed this would be Anne's room because the room right next to it seemed much larger; I could only guess that would be Susan's room. The other room was situated next to Susan's and it seemed the smallest. In time, I correctly guessed it was the twins' room. I heard the patter of small feet. A petite blonde wrapped in tulle answered the door. "Hi," she said politely, "are you Ella?"

"Yes," I said with a smile on my face. I felt completely out of my element. The room had Pepto-Bismal-pink walls and a curtain around the bed. Another bed had been set up near it and I could tell it was an afterthought, but I appreciated that this little girl would give up even part of her space. The room was a mess; clothes and shoes and dolls were everywhere.

"Sorry," she said. "I was having tea."

"Tea?"

"Well, I'm a princess and I was having tea with my ladies." I looked around the room and finally understood that the dolls propped up against the wall must be the ladies she referred to.

"That sounds fun."

"Would you like some?"

My eyebrows furrowed as I thought about how to decline without insult. "Actually, I'm pretty tired. If you don't mind, I'd really like to just lie down and read."

She looked dejected, but said, "Okay. I'll be quiet."

I placed the bag under the bed and rested my head on the pillow. It wasn't long before a knock sounded at the door. Susan entered before anyone could answer. So much for respecting people's space and privacy. "I just wanted to make sure you were all settled, Ella. Linda and I decided that you will stay home for the rest of the week, so she can get your school transition completed. The high school is only a few blocks away and she'll make sure to get you into similar classes."

"I'm in Honors English," I said. "I need to stay in Honors English."

"I'm sure she realizes that."

"Well, if you talk to her, please let her know it's important." It was the only thing important to me now. Words were my power, and without them I had absolutely nothing.

"There's plenty of food in the kitchen if you're hungry. I usually try to have dinner ready by 7:00. We eat together like a family, and on Wednesday nights, I ask that everyone stay in for game night. We rotate who chooses the games. Since you're new here, we'll let you pick tonight's game." Honestly, I wanted to vomit. I felt like I'd been pulled from the depths of hell and placed into some alternate universe. Were people really so nauseatingly polite to one another?

It wasn't that Susan and her routine were bad things, it was just that I was so out of my element I wasn't sure what to believe. When you've lived as long as I have, in the way that I have, it becomes incredibly difficult to believe that anyone has anything but the worst intentions, and I just couldn't trust it. I decided to get up and see the rest of the house. Jerome and Jaiden should be home by now, and I thought they might have some insight into what it was like to actually live here.

I thanked Susan and waited for her to leave the room. "Anne," I asked, "are Jerome and Jaiden home yet?"

"I think so. Their room is at the end of the hall. Are you sure you don't want to play? The ladies like you."

I smiled, "How about if we play tomorrow when you come home from school?"

She beamed, "Yes, please." I didn't know that a human being could be so polite, but after being exposed to Susan's communication style, it made some kind of sense. I left the room and knocked on the twins' door.

"Come in," I heard a girl say. I turned the knob and pushed the door open only a few inches; just enough to peer inside without being too intrusive. "You can come in if you want." So, I did. Jaiden was tall, and I would have guessed we were the same age had it not been for Linda's earlier clarification.

"I just wanted to say hello, since I'm new here."

"Oh yeah, you're that Ella girl, right?"

"That would be me." I didn't want to be meddlesome, but I still felt guarded. Apparently, I had learned more from Yvette than I cared to admit.

"Well, welcome," she said. I couldn't tell if it was genuine. People like us have a lot of mechanisms and tactics to get us through each day. Most of my energy got directed toward self-preservation.

"You and your brother have been here almost a year, right?" Jaiden nodded. It looked like she was doing homework, so I didn't want to stay long, but I did need to quell my curiosity. "How do you like it? I mean, what's it like here?"

She looked directly at me for the first time since I'd entered the room. "It's different." Such a non-committal answer meant something more along the lines of 'just you wait and see'.

"I hear there's a game night tonight." There is safety in numbers and she likely already had her brother on her side. "I don't know how to play anything other than spades."

"We don't play card games like that. Susan doesn't like them."

"What's she like?" I decided not to sit on her bed. I understood the feeling of having what you considered to be your territory totally invaded. Instead, I opted to sit cross-legged on the floor. The discomfort would also force me to keep the conversation short.

"She's nice," she paused. "I have to get back to this. It's due tomorrow."

"Oh, anything I can help you with?"

"Nah, I've got it." She didn't bother to thank me and I didn't bother to push the issue. At least in this way, it felt more like home.

I pushed myself up off the floor and closed the door behind me. Jerome made an appearance as I was leaving. He stared and nodded at me, a gesture that in my neighborhood was taken as a greeting. "What's up?" he asked in a cool tone.

"Nothing, I was just introducing myself to your sister. She's Jaiden, right?"

"Yeah." He was chewing on a straw so his words came out slurred. He headed towards the door and opened it. That was the end of the conversation. I decided I needed to scope out my surroundings, but didn't dare venture into Susan's room—that must have been the only fire escape on the second floor though, because I didn't see one anywhere else.

All of the home needed upkeep. The paint was peeling in places, some sections of the hardwood floor were missing, and I couldn't tell if the windows had perpetual grime or if they needed to be replaced. Despite it being seasonable for spring, there were definite drafts near the frames. I made my way to the kitchen and opened the refrigerator. I scanned it, closed it, and stood there deciding what I might like. It appeared they had some things to make sandwiches. I reopened it and pulled out the cheese, ham, bread and mayonnaise as quickly as I could. I hadn't even seen Susan standing there.

"You don't need to do that," she said.

"Do what?"

"Open and close the refrigerator like that. Just keep it open until you know what you want."

I knew exactly why she had said it. I was sure she'd had the same conversation with Jerome and Jaiden when they arrived as well. We were raised to use as few resources as possible, electricity included. "Oh, I just wasn't sure what I wanted."

She looked down at the items in my hand, "Well then, you must make very quick decisions." She pointed to her right, "The table is there, and the dishes are in the cabinet next to the sink. Go ahead and help yourself, since you already seem comfortable enough here." I felt grateful she wasn't asking me to tell her about my life. Every *blanquita* I had met up to this point, always wanted to know the gritty details of *vida en el barrio,* as though they could somehow earn credibility by hearing our stories. Life didn't work that way. You either got it or you didn't. There was no in between here.

I made my sandwich and ate it at the table, which was larger than Galena's and had room to move around it. I was confused about why anyone would really use it though. It seemed extraneous. The dining room was only a few feet away. When I finished with my plate, I washed it and the utensils, but there was no drainer, so I found a dish towel and placed them upside down on it before leaving the kitchen. Later, Susan pointed out that there was a dishwasher and I could just put them in there when I was done. Of course, I couldn't admit I didn't know how to load one.

Dinner was precisely at 7:00, and that reminded me of the

relatively decent times at home. There were no elbows shoving me away from the pots and pans; in fact, Susan served everything in separate bowls and platters. I didn't understand this because it meant there would be more to clean up later. There was no eating over the sink, no fighting to get a single serving. It was calm. It was uncomfortable.

After dinner, Susan announced it was game time. I admitted I hadn't played anything except card games, so she had me check the closet to see what I liked the look of. I chose Pictionary. I liked to draw, even though I wasn't necessarily good at it. Where I was merely mediocre, Anne excelled. Despite her age, her drawings were interpretable and she was excellent at deciphering what everyone else was trying to impart. I was impressed, and I so rarely am.

I wasn't sure if it was a genuinely good time, or if the smiles on everyone's faces were simply for show. Anne's excitement was barely containable, which told me that, at least for her, it was an authentically good time. I couldn't say for certain about the rest of us.

Jerome sat with a blank look on his face for much of the night. He threw out answers in a monotone voice, and kept the straw in his mouth. At the very least, that had to be unsanitary. Jaiden participated with more enthusiasm than her brother, but I could tell she was still proceeding with caution. I got the sense she wanted to participate with full abandon, but that would probably affect her solidarity with him.

Susan clapped and cheered when someone—anyone—got a correct answer. Interestingly enough, she showed the same enthusiasm no matter who it was. I assumed she would be most supportive of Anne, but she didn't appear to have chosen favorites. It was nice to feel like part of a cohesive group. That was something I hadn't experienced outside of my friendship with Bianca. I didn't even have that with my family, save for my time with *Tia* Paola.

I went to bed early that night. Despite being restless, I didn't bother to read. Anne fell asleep quickly, even though I had the sense that she wanted to stay up and talk. She had school the next day and Susan was adamant that she get to sleep on time. I stared into the darkness and willed myself to doze. It felt like sleep would never come, but eventually it did.

The next morning, when the house was quiet, I had a chance to talk to Susan. "Do you work?" I asked her.

"Yes, usually from home."

"What do you do?"

"I'm a nurse." I was confused by the answer. She continued, "I work for an insurance company and I take calls to answer questions their patients might have." That made more sense.

"If you have a daughter, why did you choose to take in foster kids?"

"I find it very rewarding. If I can change a life, then I want to." Her response sounded like a canned answer; like something she said to the agency that approved her to take in other people's kids. *I wonder whether the part about changing lives meant for better or worse, or perhaps even both? And I am not sure why Jaiden seemed so guarded about living here.* I chalked it up to not wanting to influence my experience, but a little insight would have been nice.

Linda came by that Friday and we talked about how things were going. I told her I was wary, of course, but that everything seemed fine. She told me she had talked to my parents and they were now required to take anger management as well as some other parenting classes. *Like that will happen.* My mother would use work as her excuse and my father wouldn't even bother to provide one.

"Listen," she said, "you're old enough to decide what you want to do. I can't, in good faith, let you go back to them. But if you wanted to stay here, or if you wanted to emancipate yourself from your parents, we could go to court and request it."

"I don't know what I want," I said. It was the truth. Until now, I hadn't given it much thought. It had been less than a week since I'd arrived here. "To be honest, I don't really understand this place. I'm confused by the niceties."

"Well, it's certainly better than what you're used to." I couldn't argue her point, because she was right. She slid a piece of paper across the table. "Here is your schedule. You'll start school on Monday. I'll have Jaiden walk you there, since the middle school is across the street."

I read the paper closely and felt my throat close up. "What happened to my English class?" I asked, biting back what would have been tears if I were able to publicly conjure them.

"I'm sorry, Ella. They were full." This was inexplicable to me. We weren't in the best part of Brooklyn. This area was certainly better than the projects, but it couldn't be the kind of place where I couldn't get into a class I really needed.

"Is there a chance something could open up? It would be a waste of time for me to go to a regular class."

"There is always a chance, but I wouldn't count on it. Let's reexamine this next year." I was devastated, but there was no point in arguing about it. I would just continue with the reading list I had from my previous class, and do the types of assignments we'd already done. I didn't want to lose my words. I wondered if maybe putting up with the abuse was worth it to stay in a single class. Then I realized I was being ridiculous.

Linda had a quiet conversation with Susan and left shortly afterward. I sat in the shared room with Anne and when she asked again about tea when she arrived home, I again declined. She seemed disappointed, but not necessarily surprised. I was sure neither Jerome nor Jaiden participated. I lay in my bed and pulled out my ragged copy of *The House on Mango Street*. "Hey, Anne," I said. She looked up. "Want to try something fun with me?"

"Sure!" Her excitement was contagious.

"How well can you read?"

"I'm the best in my class."

I handed her the book. "Pick a page and then tell me the number and what paragraph you're on. Watch what happens." She flipped open the book, but didn't seem to understand what I meant. I soon realized she hadn't learned how to distinguish paragraphs. I opened the book and showed her what I meant. She struggled to pick one from a different page, so I went slowly with my words to help her keep up.

"That's awesome. How do you do that?"

"I've just read that book a lot of times. It's my favorite."

"There's a poem I really like and I memorized most of it too."

"Oh yeah? How does it start?"

She stood up and ran her hands down her thighs, as though she was smoothing out a stiff Easter dress. She cleared her throat. "There's a polar bear in my Frigidaire. He likes it 'cause it's cold in there. With his seat in the meat and his face in the fish . . ." She continued on with what I knew was Shel Silverstein. I'd read him when I was her age. When she had done, I clapped and told her she was going to be a fabulous poet someday. She beamed and went back to playing with her dolls. There wasn't much else for me to do, so I kept to myself until dinner, and then excused myself early.

I decided that over the weekend I would try to become more familiar with the layout of the land. I wanted to find the school on my own, instead of having to depend on others, and Jaiden didn't seem terribly interested in getting to know me. The truth is, I didn't want to get to know her either. The less we all knew, the safer we would be. Some of her insight would be nice though.

"Do you mind if I go for a walk?" I asked Susan after breakfast on Saturday morning.

"No, not at all. Why don't you take Anne with you?" I thought about it and realized that despite being eight, she was smart and would know her way around here better than I did. I wasn't even sure what part of Brooklyn I was now living in. Anne seemed excited to go outside and I guessed this was a rare treat for her.

She put on a light jacket and a pair of sequined boots. Her blonde hair was a greasy mess and it stuck to the sides of her face, but it didn't distract from her near perfect angles. We stood on the stoop as she zipped up her coat. I looked over and she beamed. As she grabbed my hand she yelled in excitement, “Let’s go!”

The streets were lined with trees but I wasn’t sure what kind they were. This wasn’t simply the brown and grey concrete jungle I’d become accustomed to. The overhanging branches created a broken arch above our heads. “So,” I asked, “what part of Brooklyn is this?”

“Flatbush,” she said matter-of-factly.

“Oh.” I had heard about it, but I never imagined it looked like this. There were no familiar *bodegas* or the sounds and smells of home. I was further away from my element than I had suspected. White men in black coats and large furry hats that resembled tires walked swiftly, and their white braided belts flapped in the wind. Occasionally, I would see frumpy women, all dressed similarly, wrangling several children as they walked down the street. They were the best-behaved children I had ever seen, aside from Anne.

“There's a nice park, but it’s a little far. I usually only get to go with Mom. Do you think we could go today?”

I happened to love being outdoors and a park sounded nice. “Of course, Anne. Do you know how to get there?”

She pointed ahead and in what seemed like only one breath said, “It's that way and then when we get to the big street we make a right and then a left and then it's there. It's close to an even *bigger* park!” Throughout the walk, Anne was eager to show me the things that mattered to her—her favorite house, a neighbor's cats that sat in the window all day, her school, the library. I started to feel that if this truly were an alternate universe, and I had been born to another family, I may have even been Anne.

The big street she’d mentioned turned out to be Eastern Avenue. There were no stores, just a series of very large brick homes with high steps and wide landings. “This is beautiful,” I whispered, not even realizing such a pleasant sentiment had escaped. It wasn’t something I was used to.

“It really is. I've gotten to live here my whole life. I love it. Does it make you sad that it reminds you of your home?"

I shouldn't have been surprised that she expected everyone lived like this. I had the sense that aside from exploring this place, she had probably never been anywhere outside it; or that if she had, it was only to move about in a place just like it. "Well," I said, "It's really nothing like where I used to live."

She began to badger me with a fast stream of questions for which I had no answers that would make sense to her. "But why were there so few trees?" and "Why was it so noisy?" and "Did you have a lot of friends?" I tried to answer some of the more innocuous ones, but quickly discovered that they led to additional whys and hows, the likes of which I didn't want to discuss.

We walked along the edge of what I could only assume was the park she was so excited about. It looked completely out of place in such an urban area. We made our right followed by a quick left and walked until we saw an entrance under a visitors sign. The woman in the booth clearly knew Anne. "So, who is this?" she asked her.

"This is my new sister. Her name is Ella. Isn't that pretty?"

The woman looked me up and down. "Yes, Anne, it is." She paused for only a moment and then invited us through the turnstile. As we passed through, she turned to me and said, "Just so you know, if you get here between 10:00 AM and noon on Saturdays, it's free for everyone. It's also the best time to visit." She gave me a smile. I nodded and thanked her.

Anne rushed away from me, her hand dropping from mine quickly once we had entered the gates. "Wait up," I said in a raised voice. She turned back and apologized, and walked back to me. She said she was just excited and wanted to show me her favorite place. We walked along a path beside a superbly manicured space. Trees and plants lined the walkway in a formulaic way. I read a sign that said this was the Osborne Garden, but I didn't stop to read anything about who that was or what it meant. Anne's excitement was getting the better of her and I didn't want to have to handle an antsy child in public. It wasn't something I had personally experienced, and I had no interest in having to deal with it.

Eventually, we were in front of what looked like a large glass greenhouse. “Isn't it beautiful?” she asked, staring up with wonder in her bright eyes.

“It sure is,” I agreed, despite it reminding me of an old sanitarium. I half-expected a team of nurse's aides to start bringing people out in wheelchairs, thin blankets covering their wards' fragile legs. I did have to admit the garden was beautiful and serene—all things I was unused to.

We must have spent hours there, far longer than I’d anticipated. When we finally got back to the house, Susan was pacing the foyer with both hands on her hips. “What were the two of you doing for so long?” Her eyes narrowed when she looked at me.

Anne exploded with a barrage of details about the day. How we had walked to the park. How she had shown me her favorite place. How much fun she’d had. “Don't you dare do that again,” Susan said sternly. “Next time, I'm filing a missing person's report.”

“Sorry,” I said meekly. I didn’t understand the anger. This was the safest neighborhood I had ever lived in, but also, we were only gone a few hours. No one back home would have even realized I was gone, let alone been angry about it. It didn’t take long for me to realize this had nothing to do with me. She wasn’t concerned for my safety, but for that of her daughter.

She led Anne upstairs, and eventually, I heard the faucet turn on. When I made my way upstairs, I heard Anne crying behind the bathroom door. For privacy’s sake, I kept going until I was in our room.

When she emerged, her skin was bright red. “What happened to you?” I asked.

She sniffled, “Nothing.”

Her face looked puffy and swollen and there were streaks of red painted on her thin arms and legs. “That doesn't look like nothing,” I repeated words that had been directed at me so many times in my life.

"I was bad," she said. She looked like she had been burned and scrubbed with a Brillo pad. I turned my face away and realized I had to get out of here. Quickly. Handling my own abuse had become old hat, but seeing it on another—especially a child so young—was unbearable.

I lay down quietly on my bed. Anne crawled in next to me. She started running her tiny fingers through my hair. Neither of us said a word. Her breathing deepened and I knew she'd fallen asleep. I wished I could, but the fear had taken hold and wouldn't be abated. I began to map out a plan of action. While this was certainly a better situation than I had at home, I didn't want Susan's anger to be taken out on me. If she would hurt her own child, what was to say she wouldn't damage the rest of us in her care?

I tried to close my eyes, to shift my thoughts, but it was useless. The memories crashed around me and I had no choice but to allow myself to drown in them.

The next day, I called Linda. "I need to talk to you," I said.

"What's going on?"

"I know this is going to sound crazy, but I really want to get out of here. What are my options?"

"What's wrong? Were you hurt?"

"Look, I really don't want to talk about it, but no, I wasn't hurt. I'm just not happy here. Is there somewhere else I can be moved?"

"Yes, but I'd prefer if you finish out the school year. It's only a few more months and it would be easier then." She paused. "Can you stick it out?"

I nodded, and then realized she couldn't see it. "Yeah," I sighed, "I can do that."

"Don't you run on me." Exasperation was evident in her tone.

I decided the best way to handle the situation was simply to limit my interactions with everyone in the house. I wouldn't take Anne on any more adventures either. I wasn't entirely sure what happened in that bathroom, but I was sure the less I knew, the better.

I didn't tell Susan I'd called Linda and asked to be moved, but I knew she would be notified soon. It turned out I was right. Before the week was out, Susan stood over me with her hands on her hips, demanding to know why I'd requested the move.

"I'm just not comfortable here," I said.

"Did Jerome do something?"

I looked at her, dumbfounded. I had barely had more than a nod from him since I arrived. Even on game night, if he could get away with not speaking, he didn't bother to utter a word. Jaiden was quiet as well, so I wasn't sure where this shifting of blame was coming from. "Jerome? No, we hardly speak."

"Did he . . ." she paused, "touch you?"

"No, of course not."

She folded her arms across her chest and paced the room. This wasn't going to be good. "Well, that's a relief."

I shook my head. It had nothing to do with Jerome or Jaiden, or Anne. It had everything to do with her, but I knew better than to admit it. Truthfully, it triggered a lot of negative emotions and memories to see Anne treated the way she was. It wasn't an environment I could stay in.

"So?"

"I'm having some issues with the school here," I lied.

"Why didn't you tell me? Linda or I could have handled them."

"I don't want other people to handle what's mine. Look, I appreciate all you've done with taking me in, but this just isn't where I want to be."

Her face scrunched in an unflattering way. "Fine," she said passive-aggressively as she walked away. She did a good job at acting like she was disappointed. Dinner that night was awkwardly quiet. At 9:00 PM I heard a knock on my door. Anne had taken to falling asleep in my bed, so I did my best to climb over her carefully.

"Come in," I said softly. It was Jaiden.

"How did you do it?" she asked.

"Do what?"

"Get yourself out of here. What'd you tell your social worker?"

"I lied," I said. "I didn't admit to any abuse or anything, since there hasn't been any against me."

She nodded. "Anne. I know. I just didn't think that'd be enough." She turned on her heels and walked away. I wondered if this was exactly what she had been referring to the entire time. I also started to think that either she didn't care, or was so good at hiding her concern, that she didn't bother to get away from the situation. It became evident to me that because this was as good a situation as a child in foster care could get, neither Jaiden nor Jerome wanted to jeopardize it. Even if it meant turning a blind eye to the abuse in front of them.

I had to tell Anne I was leaving, before Susan did. Given what I had seen in my short time here, Anne bore the brunt of all Susan's anger, and I didn't want her to be confused and think she'd misbehaved or caused this. I could tell that Susan would play mind games with her and I wanted her to hear it from me.

I shook her gently and she moaned. "Anne," I whispered. "I need you to wake up for a minute."

She rubbed her eyes. "Okay." She was always so agreeable. After everything I'd been through so far in my life, and as strong as I believed myself to be, Anne was infinitely stronger than me. I could stuff my feelings down with food. I could keep quiet. I could let myself be absorbed in books. But I couldn't do it with a smile on my face. The most I could muster was an expressionless mask.

I gave her a hug, to delay telling her, even if only for a moment. She hugged back hard, her thin arms around my neck. "I need to tell you something and I need you to be strong for me. Can you do that?"

Her mouth tightened. "Did she hurt you?"

I was shocked by the question, but didn't want to give it away. "No, she didn't hurt me, but I wanted to tell you that when school ends for the year, I'm going to leave." I felt her body shudder against mine.

"I know."

I pulled away. "What? How?"

"I heard you talking to Linda. I know you want to leave and I think I know why. It's because of me."

I took her by the shoulders and demanded she look in my eyes. Hers were a soft blue in the glow of the nightlight across the room. "It's not because of you," I said, "you didn't do anything wrong. I need you to know that this isn't your fault."

"Then why are you leaving?"

"Your mother," I said.

She nodded slowly, and then sighed. "I don't blame you. As soon as I'm eighteen I'm going to leave too."

"Where will you go?" I wasn't particularly curious, nor was it an offer to help. I just wanted to keep her awake for a while and give her a chance to be heard. I guessed it was something she rarely experienced. She rambled on about college and getting married and having children of her own. I didn't bother to tell her that other than college, I thought the rest of her plan was utterly ridiculous. People like us had no business raising children. Despite raising ourselves, we were destined to become what we knew. Besides, she was eight and I couldn't think of much worse than ruining a child's dream. I stroked her hair while she fell back asleep.

We never talked about it again, and there were no tears from either of us when I walked out the door for the last time three months later. We exchanged a look; one in which we both understood what the act of my leaving meant for her, and an acknowledgment on her part that it would be okay.

Since then, I've never allowed someone else to take a beating I should have taken myself.

Chapter 5

I used to dig through *Tia* Paola's photo albums when I was younger. I would take all of them out and lie on my stomach with my feet bent at the knees, swinging above me, and flip through the pages with ease—and only rarely had to ask for clarification about who someone might be. For the most part, they were all people I knew.

My favorite was a cracked, worn and faded photo with a wrinkled-faced woman in front of a palm tree. She had a scarf on her head, something I found strange as she was clearly in a tropical climate. I brought the photo to *Tia* and asked her about it. Her face softened and she said, "*Esa es mi madre*." Her mother. She never offered any further explanation or details about her, so I simply created my own.

Over the years, I had managed to compile the story, but like a sieve, so much of it fell through the cracks. Malda grew up in Puerto Rico in the 1960s, a place with sharp contrasts—teals against light beige sand, pastels against sky, and black beans against white rice. Her father was relatively non-existent and I always had the sense they all preferred it that way.

She and her sisters grew up in a small and flimsy home just outside the slums of Cataño. It barely withstood the winds of a relatively calm storm, but the heavy ones they experienced always meant for major repairs. Local homes were built on stilts to keep the floorboards above the rising tides. In pictures, I have seen my grandmother—stoic—standing against the peeling white paint on the outside of their wooden home.

My grandfather made random and generally unwelcomed appearances, and according to *Tia* Paola, he did at times provide some financial support. He wasn't steadily employed and I had the sense that he had no real skill other than drinking. The girls spent most of their lives in poverty, but they didn't feel neglected since this is what they were surrounded by. It was their 'normal'.

My grandmother was both the matriarch and patriarch of the family. She used the little bit of money she received from my grandfather to provide for the extras—a pair of shoes or a new dress for one of the girls. Malda, being the oldest, generally received the new items, and they were passed on to her younger sisters as she grew out of them. This wasn't the way it was in our home. Despite being the oldest child, I typically received things last.

My grandmother sold small arts and crafts at the port of San Juan. Although Cataño is only ten miles away, there was no direct route by foot and cars were uncommon given their cost. When the ferry—La Lancha de Cataño—was implemented in the 1950s, it opened up opportunities for those in town to travel across the bay.

My grandmother spent the nickel fare each way, her shoulders loaded with her wares, and made her way to her stall near the port before the girls were even awake. Unlike the mothers I saw in my neighborhood, my grandmother was the one gone from sunup to sundown. She was the primary provider for her family, and despite there hardly ever being enough resources to go around, she was determined to provide for them without handouts from well-intentioned neighbors who could barely afford the assistance they so frequently offered.

My grandmother was a strong woman and a great negotiator. Tourists came into port looking to buy inexpensive items from the 'natives'. These were items of little cost or consequence to them. They bought dresses and baskets, and rugs and small metal trinkets from the various vendors. They would depart the ship with soft eyes and meander through the stalls for the short amount of time they were in port. To the chagrin of the operators, rarely did they sign up for any island tours.

The flood of money helped tremendously for all who invested in a business. My grandmother scrimped and saved to come up with the small amount she needed to start her own. Neighbors offered loans, but being too proud, and frankly, too smart to be indebted to them, she always declined. She felt it was charity; a way to bring her down inside a hole from which she would never climb out.

Women enveloped in linen departed the large ships, their hats or scarves flapping in the breeze. Their hair and full make up were betrayed by the environment, and they often dabbed at their faces in a vain attempt to maintain the work they spent so much time perfecting each day.

"Isn't it darling?" an elegant woman, wrapped in a long sari, asked as she held up one of my grandmother's small woven baskets. She said it to no one in particular, as her husband was off in another stall.

My grandmother, who really did not know much more English than the basics she needed to haggle, simply responded, "Twenty cents."

The woman turned her head and looked down at my grandmother. "No, ten."

"Twenty," she insisted. This was the game she played. She didn't intend to cut the price in half, but she knew the first person to give in during a negotiation was the one that lost. There are no true compromises in situations like this. Whether or not they realized it, this was a person literally taking food from the mouths of her children.

"Fifteen," the woman responded, placing the basket back on the table, aware the gesture would make my grandmother accept. She would rather take what the tourists offered than have them walk away with nothing. Even one sale meant she had enough money to continue her business for another day; the thought of growing it, well that was another matter entirely.

Tia Paola enjoyed telling stories about growing up with *Abuela*. I never got tired of hearing them. It took me back to my roots and despite all the trauma I had experienced in my life, it reminded me that this wasn't a cycle that had to be recreated.

My grandfather, Tito, was a known gambler, drinker and womanizer. In those days, a woman didn't just throw a man out of the house. He wasn't particularly violent, at least not in the physical sense, but he did have an intimidating presence, and when he was drunk, a bitter mouth. *Abuela* was not welcoming when he showed up, but she would let him in.

It was a better situation than many of her friends found themselves in. Many nights the crashing sound of furniture and pottery could be heard around their small shack-like home. Women often emerged from their houses early the next morning with bruised eyes and swollen lips. Tito hit my grandmother once, and according to *Tia* Paola, he never did it again. I had no details on *Abuela*'s reaction, but I assumed it must have been equally violent for him to never have laid another hand on her.

As was the way, Malda was the *madrecita* of the house. Little mother. While *Abuela* worked the stall at the port, Malda was busy running the household. She swept the breeding sand and dirt from the floors with a broom that *Tia* Paola only described as 'miserable'. She scrubbed the floors on her hands and knees, and made sure to have dinner prepared for the family when *Abuela* came into view across the flat landscape.

After the dishes were done, she often sat at the kitchen table with her sisters to help them with their schoolwork. *Abuela* had as much education as most of her neighbors. It wasn't uncommon for women to have to stop attending school after only four or five years because they were needed to help family businesses. She wanted more for her children, and while they muddled through poverty with limited shoes and hand-me-down clothes, they were always fed.

For all her lack of education, *Abuela* knew the key to breaking the cycle was to continue learning. *Tia* Paola told me that *Abuela* was always after them about their grades and that Malda—of all of them—resented it the most. At that time, none of them knew anything could be different. *Abuela* spoke to them of things which they viewed her as too ignorant to know anything about.

"Years later," *Tia* Paola admitted, "I realized that even with her limited education, *mi madre* knew a lot. Life had taught it to her. She learned the basics of what she needed for the life she had—enough English to get by in a community which depended on tourists, and enough math to negotiate and make change." But there was so much more to life than that. My *Abuela* knew that too.

According to *Tia*, my mother was much the same as a child as the woman she had become. To say I knew my mother would be a misconception. I had an idea of her, but that is all. Until this clarification was made to me, I had always just assumed her experiences with my father had hardened her in many ways.

Tia told me that my mother was never a particularly happy person, and it was just assumed it was simply the result of being the first born. Responsibilities were based on birth order and my family was no exception to this cultural rule. Maria and Paola could afford to be a little careless; Malda could not.

"It was her attitude that I thought protected her," *Tia* told me. "Your mother was always the first with her finger in the air." It was a maneuver I knew well. Whenever my mother disagreed with something, she would raise her right hand and point her index finger in the air while she went on a tirade of disapproval. "And then she met your father."

Whenever *Tia* Paola brought my father into any of our conversations—which was rarely—she did so with a look of disgust on her face. I wondered if it had always been that way. My mother was the first to immigrate to the mainland and she did so to be with my father.

Manuel, my father, had grown up in Loíza approximately thirty miles northeast of San Juan. His family was large and made their living growing and harvesting sugar cane. At least that's the story he told my family after he and my mother met. In truth, his family was from a long line of *caciques*—leaders—who, during the significant political clashes of generations before theirs, managed to accumulate wealth and power. The sugar cane business wasn't entirely false; they did own some land and they did grow and harvest it. But by 'they' it was meant the people they employed.

It was a rare occasion that *Abuela* would bring the girls into San Juan. The fare for the ferry was necessary for her to earn income, but taking it just to spend the day there was a luxury she could so infrequently afford. On one of those excursions, Manuel saw Malda standing across the street and called out to her. She was with *Tia* Paola, whose hand she took in her own and began to walk away. By that time, she would have been used to tuning out the calls of the military personnel from Fort Buchanan. As is the way I know them to be, he persisted and my mother relented.

Soon, he began to make the trek to Cataño with increasing frequency. Sometimes he brought the fare to Malda so she could come alone to San Juan to see him. *Abuela*, of course, didn't approve. In addition to it taking her away from her responsibilities at home, she didn't like the idea of Malda being away—alone—with a man. For all her progressiveness in terms of caring for her family, in this she was still traditional.

"Malda," he called from outside the thin door. "Vamos!" And my mother always did go with him. Perhaps she felt guilty that he had made the long trip to see her, or perhaps she actually enjoyed his company, but for whatever reason, and against *Abuela*'s wishes, she went.

"Manuel was very romantic," *Tia* once told me. "He would bring her small gifts like a lipstick or a bottle of perfume. I can't speak for Maria, but I was always a little jealous." Invariably, she would shiver after she expressed this emotion over these interactions. "The rest of us just thought they were in love."

My mother must have been swept off her feet. There were the usual guys *en el barrio,* but in large part, she ignored them. Then, this mysterious boy from Loíza showed up and suddenly she was everywhere with him. They both knew better than to be disrespectful towards *Abuela,* so Malda was always returned early enough in the evening to not appear scandalous.

When my father decided to immigrate to the mainland, he did so with very little notice or discussion. "I am going," he told Malda. "If you want to come, I'll send for you, but I have to go first." If he ever told her why there was such urgency to his departure, she never told anyone who would have leaked it back to us.

"Your mother was depressed, *mijita*," *Tia* said. It caused arguments between her and her mother. She didn't have the motivation to help take care of her sisters and, she argued, they were old enough to fend for themselves. In truth, they were. By this point, most of the other children in the neighborhood had been removed from school and put to work years earlier. It must have felt oppressive to Malda to still have so much responsibility, especially after the brief escapes to San Juan.

Cataño was a very different environment than San Juan. While it was only separated by less than ten miles and a beautiful turquoise bay, the two places could not have been further apart socially. People that lived outside the city weren't cosmopolitan and were always viewed as poor. Only in Loíza was Manuel anything more than a farmer's son.

When Manuel left, my mother filled the void by working the stall with her mother at the port. Maria and Paola were still in school but, after much debate, it was decided they would need to start being more self-sufficient. My mother dropped out of school not long after Manuel disappeared. She was 15.

Months later, Manuel showed up outside their door and called for Malda in the lilt he only used when he wanted to charm someone. It was the same voice he used when Yvette's arms were draped around him. It wasn't the voice he used towards the rest of us.

Tia told me that *Abuela* didn't let her go quietly. She left that night with only a few personal items and told the family she was going with Manuel to Loíza. They were only there for a few weeks before they came to the mainland, but everyone suspected they had secretly been married.

I had trouble imagining my mother as a bride. She wasn't fashion forward; not in any of the photographs I saw of her back then and certainly not now. If they had been married, I envisioned my mother standing in front of the minister in a threadbare dress, and lightly scented by the dab of perfume she would have used to mark the occasion.

For all her faults, it had never really occurred to me that Manuel's family would disapprove of my mother, until *Tia* told me about the tensions between them. The families had never met, but their resolute stereotypes of each other burned in their hearts.

I am left without any details about them immediately after leaving the island. *Tia* did tell me that Malda would write infrequently, and never with any of the details that she and Maria craved. "We wanted to know what life was like here. We had never been to any place other than San Juan and the idea of living in a city like New York was more than we could imagine."

She always paused at that part of the story. Sometimes she folded her hands beneath her chin, or I caught her chewing her bottom lip. I loved hearing her tell me these stories, and listened to them repeatedly, so I would remember in painstaking detail all the parts of my history that could be even remotely documented. Not having a real name meant that I was always looking for something to transform me into something more than a whisper.

"I wrote to your mother so many times. When we were done with school, all we had was working with our mother. Neither of us envied her life and neither of us wanted to stay. We had always looked up to your mother and we wanted to be where she was." I couldn't fathom wanting to be anywhere near my sisters. Theirs was a sentiment that was totally un-relatable to me.

It took Malda years before she agreed to help her sisters immigrate to the mainland. Well before that point, things with Manuel soured and my mother moved into her own apartment at the Baruch Houses. It was there that first Paola, and then Maria, made their big move away from home. "It hurt that it took her so long to help," *Tia* said, "She had always been there when we needed her and then suddenly she vanished and wanted nothing to do with us."

As cold-hearted as I knew my mother could be, I didn't think she wanted nothing to do with her sisters. The more I unraveled about Manuel and their life together, the more convinced I was that she was hesitating in order to protect them. "She found out she was pregnant with you not long after I moved here," *Tia* explained. "I was excited about it, but she wasn't. I couldn't understand why she wouldn't be happy. Even if things with your father weren't going well, I didn't think he'd be the type to just leave his child." Clearly, he had already proven that leaving my mother—at least for a short time—was well within the realm of possibility.

Manuel made no appearance after he found out Malda was pregnant with me. "I didn't understand, *mijita*. No one knew where he was and if they did, they wouldn't tell us." The generally accepted explanation was that he'd gone back to his family in Loíza. "I begged your mother to contact him and she refused. I had to stop arguing about it to keep the peace." Well, that explains where I get that trait. I'm sure it's also part of the reason I've always had such a connection with *Tia* Paola, as those emotional strings were nonexistent elsewhere.

Perhaps it was because my sister shared a name with my *Tia* Maria, but she and I had never become close. I know that must sound silly, but it's an important part of our culture. To her credit, she was a warm woman and unlike Malda in all ways. *Tia* Maria often brought me small trinkets. I would leave them out in plain sight so my sisters would take them. For all the issues between us, I wasn't wasteful.

I had no logical reason to dislike *Tia* Maria, but I did. I wasn't outwardly rude to her, because that just isn't my nature, but I said only the minimum necessary to not appear impolite. Once the niceties were out of the way, I immediately went back to the room I shared with my sisters, or escaped into a corner if we weren't home.

It was almost always *Tia* Paola who hosted celebrations, and I made sure to get there early so I could help her cook and learn more about our family. She loved telling stories, and though she would ramble, her thoughts tumbling from her full lips, I never got bored. "You should spend more time here, *mamita*," she said. I smiled but didn't respond. I also didn't show up unannounced or without a reason, such as a family gathering.

Tia Paola had no children, and I often thought that her taking me under her wing was her way of both giving me shelter, and feeling like she had raised one and would leave something behind when she was gone. I always felt it was vain to create a child for the sake of leaving something behind when there were so many other things one could do. *Tia* Paola just laughed when I asked her why she never married or had children. "Look at this family," she said. "What do you think?"

I couldn't blame her. I had no intentions to follow in the shaky footsteps of my mother. *Tia* Paola worked as a home health aide. She'd taken the classes as soon as she had arrived. With no money, she went on public assistance and made the best of it. She took advantage of every program available to her—education, housing, food stamps. As soon as she finished school and found a job, she moved into a non-subsidized apartment not far away and removed herself from any other assistance.

She did what she needed to do to get established here. I had a lot of respect for her. Unlike Malda and *Tia* Maria, she struck out on her own and made something of herself. Even with her education, she didn't make a lot of money, and most of what she did earn went to pay the rent. She was very frugal, and from her I learned how to balance wants and needs. She taught me how to find the best deals, and where to shop so I knew I would be getting the lowest price. In short, she was truly the only positive role model I had. Everyone needs that, but I needed it more so. She was my only sanctuary at that time.

A few days before I left the foster care situation at Susan's, I called *Tia* Paola and asked if I could stop by to chat. She never refused me, even if she had other obligations. It was merely a formality and we both knew it, but it was a tradition that remained important to me. I heard the chain being removed from the door and when she opened it, she appeared a little haggard. She had been working a lot of extra hours, and it was clearly taking a toll. "*Hola, mamita,*" she said. "It's so good to see you!" She hugged me tightly and I made my way past her through the door.

She made some Bustelo and sat down with me at the kitchen table. "Okay, *mijita,*" she said slowly, "What's going on?"

I sighed but got right down to it. "I'm not happy there. I called my social worker, Linda, and asked to be moved."

"What are they *doing* to you?"

"To me? Nothing. I have no real reason to complain. Honestly, I'm being treated better than anywhere, other than here with you, of course."

"Then?" She eyed me over the edge of her cup as she brought it to her lips.

"Susan, the one that fosters us, well . . ." I trailed off. The silence felt awkward. "She takes out her anger on her eight year old daughter. I mean, it's not as bad as what I was going through a few months ago, but I can't bear to watch it." Suddenly, everything spilled from me. I wasn't the type to show weakness; I despised it, but uncontrollable tears and sobs escaped me as I explained what had been happening.

"Linda will move you." I couldn't tell if it was a question or merely a sentiment. Concern was evident in her voice.

"*Sí*," I said simply.

"Where is she going to put you?"

"She was looking for another home, but she was really honest with me and I've heard stories from other places. At this point, I think my best option is to just get out."

She sighed. "*Mijita*, I wish I could have you here, but you know I have a hard enough time as it is."

I steeled my jaw. "*Sé.*" It was Paola. I didn't need to be formal with her. "I know," I repeated, this time in English. I wasn't asking, but I couldn't explain that to her. It would make her feel worse.

"So? . . ." I knew she wanted an answer. One that would make sense to her. She was a piece of me, and she wanted to hear me say I was going to come home and live with Malda.

I coughed to clear my throat, and decided it was best to just spit it out in the fastest string of words I hoped I'd ever need to put together. "I'm going to a group home."

The ring of her mug on the glass tabletop is a sound that still haunts me. She wrung her hands then rubbed her arms, and bent her head down to them and looked like she was chanting silent prayers. Her voice was such a whisper I couldn't make out what she was saying.

"*Tia,*" I said softly, "*por favor.*"

When she finally raised her face, I could see her makeup streaking. "*Mijita,*" she started slowly, "I want better for you. I want better than that."

"Is Malda better?" I knew this was going to come out as if I were challenging her. I was. But I did my best to soften it enough that she wouldn't be offended. She stayed quiet. I watched her chew her lip and realized the gesture was so unconsciously common in this ragtag family.

We sat that way for what felt like forever. Finally, she took a deep breath and covered one of my hands with her own. "I have always hated *tu nombre,*" she said, seemingly out of nowhere. "You're a beautiful woman, not something to be discarded. You should have a proper name."

I had nothing to say. There was no response. She was right, and I knew it, but on some level I still felt it was deserved. I didn't share the sense of entitlement my sisters had. I was smart and had potential; it was the only thing I could hold onto. I just wasn't sure if I was going to get through the next two years, let alone what I would do after I aged out of the system.

Part of me longed to see Malda and my sisters. When those moments arrived, I became disgusted with myself. How could I miss the people that were supposed to love me unconditionally, and who did anything but that very thing? I tried not to dwell on it too much. When those thoughts came, I let them go rather than trying to analyze them or even sit with them. Once they'd passed, I stopped chewing my lip.

Paola launched into what felt like a history lesson and I wasn't sure if I could bear to hear it right then. I wanted to be polite, though, so I did my best to focus on my coffee and stared out the window. "We had a tough life," she said. "Your mother, especially. She wasn't nurtured and so I don't think she really knows how to do that." She took a gulp of her coffee and continued, "I'm not making excuses, *mijita*, but I'm sure she's just doing the best she can."

I knew there were no instruction manuals for life. Self-help books aside, how do you explain your roots when they were founded in quicksand? I cannot escape who and what I am, no matter how far away I go.

"When your mother came here, she was so lonely. She wasn't used to being alone. She latched onto your father and he took advantage of her in the worst possible ways."

I felt my anger flaring up, but knew better than to lose control, even here where I felt safe. "Then why did she stay? Why did she let it continue?" To blame her wasn't right, but I couldn't understand a person who chose to stay in that situation, let alone allow it to happen so many times.

"It was a different time. Your mother needed someone to hold onto, and she put up with a lot from him. I don't have to tell you, you know what she went through."

That wasn't the point. I felt sick for thinking that way. I had no idea what it would be like to be in her shoes … to have to make the choices she did. No matter how difficult my life was, I felt grateful to be here. It could have gone a very different way.

I knew what it was to be lonely; to be so alone inside your own head and not have anyone to trust. To not have anyone to love, and to hate the person you were supposed to care about the most. Sometimes I stand outside myself and try to see what is really there. I stuff so many feelings down, and come across as shy and timid and weak, but the truth is, I am anything but those things. They are survival tactics I've had to develop. I'm a walking dichotomy, and I see that vividly when I look inward.

"The first time it happened, with you, we all gathered around and tried convincing her to report it. To leave him. She absolutely refused. We told her she was desperate, that she deserved better, that this was supposed to be a better life. Still, she stayed."

My father had disappeared for most of her pregnancy. I suspected he thought she might go through with reporting it, and I imagined he would have run to get away from it. He wasn't smart enough to stay away, however, and every time my mother lifted the chain from the door, it ended in disaster.

When my sisters were born, I didn't know about things like Post-Traumatic Stress Disorder or post-postpartum depression. I watched Malda retreat even further into herself. 'Resentment' wasn't a strong enough word to describe how Malda felt about us. I didn't need to be terribly intuitive to pick up on that. When we girls were younger, we were mostly treated the same—with disdain and aggression.

Maria and Yvette used these as lessons to hone their own particular skills. I used them to retreat further, and become even more of a people pleaser than I had ever been. I was never sure if I would be like this for the rest of my life, or if I would finally find my voice when I needed it.

In the space between the assaults, my father was a gentle giant. No one ever said if it was just the booze that brought it on, or if he was using something else that pushed him over the edge on occasion. It was that distance which allowed my mother to have what I could only consider Stockholm Syndrome. She fell in love with him. She protected him. And in protecting him, she left herself completely vulnerable.

I'd heard there were at least five assaults. I assumed there had been more than that, lest Malda would be the most fertile woman on the planet. Three children later, she would still occasionally unlatch the door for him when he showed up, but fortunately for all of us, he never assaulted her again. At least not since Yvette was born.

Malda had no voice. She said very little to anyone and I rarely saw her smile, even when she was safe and with her sisters. I suppose that's another thing we have in common: we are never safe; we are always on watch.

I wasn't so young as to not recognize what was happening between our father and Yvette. She either had a sixth sense about when he would be arriving, or he was in enough contact with her to let her know it was happening. She fell right into his lap every time, and I watched with horror as he patted her head and ran his fingers along the edges of her dress. She always smiled around him, so there was never any way to confirm my suspicions that he'd been abusing her as well. I never brought it up. No one did. And Yvette never offered a word about it.

"I was so absolutely in love with you, *mijita*. I babysat you every chance I had." I knew this was true. Paola had almost every baby picture that existed of me. Most of them included her holding me, snuggling her cheek into the crook of my chubby neck. She gave me the love I had needed, and if I knew anything about that emotion, it was primarily because of her.

I stayed for dinner and before I knew it, we had both passed out on the couch. I looked at the cable box for the time but it was pointless. It was still set to a channel. It seemed late enough that it didn't make sense for me to head back to Susan's. It was also too late to call, so I just didn't bother.

We shared a pot of Bustelo and some toast in the morning, but then I had to leave. Paola had to work, and I had no idea what Susan's reaction was going to be. Well, I suspected, but hoped my suspicions were wrong. Unfortunately, that wasn't the case.

The train made me queasy. Not always, but it was how I felt on that ride. The car swayed back and forth. I had to lean back when people walked through. My head felt heavy. My legs didn't want to carry me. I trudged. I wobbled. And I took my sweet time.

I pulled myself up the stairs. My hair was a mess and my clothes were crumpled. Truthfully, I looked like I'd just climbed out of a gutter. The wind had blown strong during my long walk, so I decided to make sure there were no leaves trapped in the swarm of hair surrounding me. It had been months and I still had no key. Neither did Jerome or Jaiden, come to think about it. Hell, Anne didn't even have one. Susan really was a warden.

I rang the bell, my fingers a little shaky despite the heat of summer rapidly approaching. I heard loud footsteps and saw Susan's familiar, frightening eyes peering through the glass in the door. She pulled it open so hard I thought she may have dislocated her shoulder. "Where have you been? I've been worried sick!"

I smiled and moved past her into the foyer, while she closed the door behind me. "I'm sorry, Susan," I said with my most sincerely fake lilt. "I went to visit my *Tia* Paola and we stayed up so late talking that I fell asleep. By the time I woke up it was too late to call you, and really too late to take the train back."

Her face had turned a deep red. I could see bits of condensation forming above her lip. "I had no idea. I thought you were a runner."

"No, not at all." I didn't feel the need to point out that we both knew I wasn't capable of running. But more than that, I tried to keep those thoughts to myself lest someone else use them against me. If I act like I don't care and that things don't bother me, I keep myself protected. No one realizes the impact they have on me. I try my best not to let it show.

"Well, next time, if there is one," she rolled her eyes, "just call. I really don't care how late it is."

I nodded. I thought it interesting that rather than talk about filing a missing persons report, or at least notifying Linda, she did nothing. She'd most likely wrapped herself in her wool cardigan, despite the temperature being too warm for such a thing, and paced for only as long as she had heard me coming up the stoop. I understood enough about her to expect that was true.

Anne was asleep in my bed, but by this point, it was routine. I found it oddly soothing. She smelled of bubble gum and corn starch. An odd combination, I know, but Susan rubbed her with corn starch to ease the scrubbing she had just done. She was smart, and those of us who have that going for us are often the ones manipulating everyone else.

She never hit Anne, so there were no bruises. She never went above the shoulder or below the elbow. She never went below the knees and Anne didn't own shorts. Not a single pair. Sometimes, I would find her picking at scratches behind her ear. But unless that child worked up the courage to lift her dress and show people what her mother did to her on a regular basis, it would remain our secret.

I crawled in next to her and wrapped her blonde hair around my finger. I heard her say my name, checking to make sure it was me. I leaned over and gave her a light kiss on the cheek. She smiled and went back to whatever dream I had interrupted.

The next few weeks felt like they were in slow motion. I was no longer invited to Game Night and that was okay with me, because I had never actually enjoyed it. The awkwardness was too much to bear. Dinner was difficult enough, but to be forced to interact with people you don't care for, well . . . that was asking far too much.

By the time I left, I had a few more possessions, but not by much. Linda would send donations over for the three of us. I kept Rosa's dress and wrap, but never had the opportunity to wear them. These days they're in the very back of my closet. Sometimes I take them out to look at, but more often than not, I forget they're still there.

It's a reminder of a life I refuse to forget.

Chapter 6

Lara and I walked The High Line every Saturday. During the week, I helped tutor her. Her writing needed some work and her ability to grasp science was non-existent. Don't get me started on the courses they insisted we attend in the home. They tried teaching us the basics of household expenses and how to be professional at any job. They offered GED classes for the ones about to age out who hadn't bothered with school. They showed us how to cook basic and inexpensive meals for small families; I assumed they thought we would all be pregnant by the time we left the home.

In return for my help, Lara bartered with other girls for the luxuries we wouldn't have obtained otherwise. Real conditioner. A nail file. A pack of Twix.

I noticed a shift in how I felt. Lara made me feel empowered for the first time in my life. She was independent and fierce, and didn't hide it. Neither did she apologize for it. Her head never hung in shame, even when she thought about how she could have done everything better than she had. I had the same strength, maybe even more, but I stayed in my shell, protecting myself. Being humble around authority figures seemed to work.

My clothes fit better, and the walks we took became longer. I didn't have the aches I used to have, and wasn't as winded as I used to be. I started feeling healthier than I ever had, Twix aside, and saw that my dimples were less deep. On the negative side, hollows had formed under my eyes.

Lara had all sorts of ideas and even hid a spoon in the freezer one night. She insisted it would reduce the puffiness in my eyes. I didn't have the heart to tell her it was my losing fat, not retaining water. I let her put that freezing block of metal on my eye lid and thought I would end up with frost bite. I swatted her hand away, "Okay, enough. That shit hurts!"

She laughed as she put it on my other eye. I didn't fight it. She would do whatever she wanted anyway. The second one hurt less because she didn't hold it there as long, and because I knew the sort of pain to expect.

I refused to get on a scale, but Lara informed me, not so politely, that I'd lost at least ten pounds. Tamara laughed and pointed when she overheard it, and said, "With another hundred to go."

"Shut the fuck up, T," Lara growled.

"Or what?"

"What ya fuckin' think?" They moved closer to one another and their hands balled up into fists. I wasn't sure what to do. My default was to take what came to me, but I had never intervened in a fight between others. They were never about me, just directed at me. This was entirely different.

Lara knew better than to grab Tamara by the hair. The new girls always made that mistake, assuming she was like any other girl, ready to give in. With her short stature, Lara also knew not to bother with the face. She got a running start and jammed one foot down on Tamara's and kicked her in the shin with the other one.

When she bent down to hold her leg, Lara launched an attack on her face. A bleeding lip and torn, broken eye vessel later, Lara was pulled off and Tamara was taken to see an on-staff nurse. I never asked Lara what happened to her, what her punishment was, but she stayed quiet for a few hours after she returned to our room. She never offered to tell me either, but within a few hours, she seemed back to her old self, so I figured it couldn't have been that terrible.

A few weeks later, over something equally ridiculous, but which also had to do with Tamara bullying me, and Lara defending me, I decided it was my responsibility to at least try to get between them. I dreaded it, because despite being used to being a punching bag, I wasn't the kind of girl that particularly enjoyed pain.

This time, Tamara reached for what looked like a hair brush and she had the advantage over Lara. Being at least four inches taller meant she could grab her hair, lift her up on her toes and beat the hell out of her face with that brush, all at the same time. With one free hand, the only thing Lara could reach was a bulge in Tamara's pocket. She found a box cutter.

Her fingers scrambled, but the cuts from her nails bled

slowly. She managed to grip the cutter in her hand, stinging as it must have been, and slashed in every direction like a wild animal. I tried to move out of the way, but it cut deep into my wrist. I felt the blood, warm on my arm as it sprayed in what felt like every direction. Both girls were so shocked that they stopped and stared at me. Suddenly, Ms. Kole pulled me away and held a towel hard over the cut. Security officers took Tamara and Lara out of the room, their arms stretched behind their arching backs.

They didn't bother with a nurse. I was rushed to the hospital in an ambulance, but all I remember was being strapped in, and I felt woozy. Darkness took me quickly. When I awoke, I was so sedated my eyes felt too heavy to open. When I managed, I found Linda and *Tia* Paola standing above me. Paola had her hand to her mouth, while her eyes looked down at my arm. No one said a word.

I looked at my right arm, but could only see a thick white bandage from my hand to my elbow. "Don't move too much," Linda said. "Keep your arm above your heart." A nurse came in quickly when my movement set off an alarm of some sort.

"You're up," she said cheerfully. "How do you feel?"

"Medicated," I slurred.

"Trust me," she said, "You'll thank me later." She paused and then asked, "So, do you want to tell us what happened?"

I thought about it while chewing my lip and said in a hoarse voice, "No."

"I have to report this, Ella," I heard Linda say. She sounded like she was in a tunnel.

"Do whatever you need to do," I whispered. "Lara was protecting me."

"I'm sure, but we can't have things like this happening under the state's care."

Yeah, well, maybe you should do more thorough background checks on your foster families, I thought. I wanted to say it, but I just couldn't bring myself to do it. I didn't want to make things any worse for Anne, and didn't want to imagine her in a place like this, gutted like a fish. The medications never wore off. They attached a pump to the bed and anytime I felt anything—a twinge, a tweak—I pushed a red button that immediately made it go away. I felt groggy all the time.

Nurses came and went through my room. They changed the bandages carefully, snipping them away with scissors. They washed the wound, doused it in iodine, and patted it dry before they re-bandaged it. I constantly tried to move my fingers, to see if I could feel anything, but I barely did. It took incredible effort to get a small movement from my damaged appendage.

I wasn't paralyzed—if I was, I wouldn't have had the pain I did, nor would any amount of effort result in even the slightest result. The cut was deep and it looked like a suicidal plea; something very unlike me. I overheard whispers of nerve damage. They gave me twice daily physical therapy sessions, but my fingers were numb and so I continued to drop everything I attempted to hold.

Each day I used less of the morphine, but the numbness didn't leave. I wasn't getting particularly better at holding things. Mostly, I was upset about not knowing what was happening at the home. I knew that in the end, I would be fine. Either I would learn to live with the numbness and the horrific scar, or I would get back to where I had been. But it caused me a lot of distress and anxiety to not know what was happening with Lara.

Linda refused to give me any information about her, telling me it was confidential, even though we both knew it wasn't. Paola visited every day after work, and her thick soles squeaked on the floor. She, of course, had no information either. Paola admitted that she told Malda what happened to me, and that she'd asked if she could come to the hospital to see me.

It was the first time my mother had ever shown concern, so I didn't want to push her away. "Sure," I said. "She can visit."

The next morning, Malda walked through the door with what looked like trepidation. I hadn't seen her since The Incident in the spring. "*Como esta*?"

"I'm fine, thanks." She stayed away from the bed, choosing the chair that was placed the furthest away. Paola used to drag that chair and sit right next to my bed. She would hold her hand in mine and stroke the tops of my fingers with her thumb. Occasionally, she would ask if I could feel anything, but other than icepicks beneath my skin, I felt little.

“What happened?” The idea that I had done this to myself was incomprehensible, but telling her the truth would have likely make her feel happy about what had befallen me. The Incident had created much more stress in her life. And while it did the same for me, I felt more capable of handling it.

“I got in the way of a fight.” I looked up at the bandages and noticed that they needed to be changed soon. At least that would give us a break from what I knew would be a stilted conversation.

I caught her eyeing me suspiciously before she asked, “Why?”

She wasn’t asking why there was a fight, but rather why I had interjected myself into it. “It doesn't really matter.” I looked away, and because she birthed me, she knew I was lying.

“You gonna tell me the truth?” Her back was straight and her hands folded in her lap. There was no animation; no raised eyebrows, nor real concern shown on her aging face.

“What do you want me to say?”

“This was your choice,” she said matter-of-factly. “No one told you to leave. You must have deserved whatever happened to you in there.”

There was no arguing with her. There was no logic that would make her understand my decisions in the last year. She was used to the horrors of her life, as was I, but she was reluctant to change anything, and that’s where our similarities in this regard ended. “I guess so.” I shrugged like it didn’t matter to me.

I appreciated her coming to see me, but I was already drained. The nurses had taken away the automatic pain medications and now I was on a routine. There was no way out of this conversation with Malda. I wasn’t due for another pill for at least an hour, and I knew she wouldn’t stay that long. At least I had that to be grateful for.

“So, you're coming home then.”

There was no lilt in her voice, but in any case, this was both a question and a statement. “No, I am not coming home.” I let the words fall quickly, not really giving her time to process them as they escaped.

She stood up, took her purse from the back of the chair,

and pulled it over her shoulder. She had become noticeably thinner and more worn. I hadn't seen her since the spring, and we were even more strangers than we had ever been. "Okay," she said, with a resigned look in her eyes.

She didn't once come near the bed. Didn't offer a word, a glance, or a simple touch of comfort. I hadn't expected her to, but anyone who walked in couldn't have known we were related. Except for our eyes. I had her eyes. Dark as night and almost always looking away, avoiding direct contact. "Be safe."

Be safe. That was the only advice or sentiment she expressed. I wasn't surprised, but still, it would have been nice to have been given more than that. Surely, deep down, she couldn't believe I deserved it. Regardless, there would be no empathy, and no desire to attempt to connect with me over a traumatic experience.

Be safe. The phrase irked me. We didn't live in a safe environment. We didn't know what safety even meant, aside from the theoretical perspective. Malda knew it, and if she were a smarter person, I would have simply chalked this up to her being ironic. Malda neither knew nor understood irony, so I took this as just another slight in a long line of them.

She turned her back to me without a goodbye, or any other parting words. Be safe. It rang in my ears. My heart burned from some unidentified emotion. I wasn't angry with her, but I felt something. I had been stirred in some way. Perhaps it was my expression of the pity I knew I wouldn't receive from her.

Before I knew it, she had walked through the door and into the hall. My day nurse, Cathy, tried to stop her to give her an update, but Malda just brushed her off. When she didn't want to interact with a *blanquita*, she simply acted like she couldn't speak English. "*No habla ingles*," she would say repeatedly, until the other person just gave up. This was exactly the case with Cathy.

Despite the interaction with Malda, Cathy entered the room in a cheerful manner. Her long, blonde hair was pulled back into a loose bun. Strands flew about her face. It looked like a hair-style from one of those magazine articles that teach you how to look like you don't care, when in fact it took you longer to get ready.

"How are you feeling?" she asked, a warm smile on her face.

"I'm okay. I have some pain, but I know I can't have another pill for a while."

"Let me talk to the doctor. Maybe he'll let you have one early. You haven't been off the pump for very long and you were using it quite a bit." I felt insulted and weak, but I didn't express it.

"Okay."

She bent down and examined my arm. "Time to change the bandage," she said. "Let me check with the doctor first, so that this doesn't have to be any more painful."

"Just go ahead with it." She couldn't have known that the physical pain was nothing compared to the emotional pain I had dealt with for sixteen years. The summer was coming to a rapid close, and fall would be here before I knew it. I would be seventeen next spring, and rather than panic, it was something I was looking forward to. One more year closer to absolute freedom.

The nurse took a pair of sterilized scissors from a package and placed it on the tray next to my bed. She moved around the cabinets in the room quickly, pulling gauze and bandages, and iodine from them as she prepared to change the bandage. Every time she approached the bed with the scissors, it made me laugh. Her look of concentration came across as being prepared to attack.

She was careful, snipping slowly, not pulling the bandage off until she had soaked it with water to loosen the scabs. It felt neither pleasant to watch nor experience. In the beginning, I turned my face the other way and I had her just tell me when she was finished. I knew anyway, because I could hear the tearing of the tape before she put it over the bandage.

Within a few days, I was able to not only watch, but was also genuinely curious. Until the third day, I hadn't even seen what had happened. The memories of The Incident appeared as though I was blinking—small images at a time and completely disjointed, next to impossible to piece together. It was like the dream, the one where I fall. Only when I try to piece The Incident together, I don't hit the landing.

The first time I watched Cathy change the bandage, I wasn't sure if I could actually stomach it. As she snipped away the gauze, it sounded like she was muttering under her breath. I couldn't tell what she was saying, exactly, but it almost sounded like she was repeating a series of steps for how to do this. She soaked the bandage before peeling it off and I could feel the wetness, but not much in the way of temperature.

When it finally came off, strands of gauze still stuck to the stitches, and I wanted to vomit. I looked away briefly, but decided that for some reason, it was important to me to see the damage that had been done. A deep gouge ran from my wrist almost to my elbow. It was as if, rather than my arm swinging out of the way and deflecting at least part of the slice, Lara and I had been perfectly in sync and I captured the entire thing in one fell swoop. It was Cathy who informed me that they had to surgically repair the tendon. This, she explained, was why I felt numbness and had lost strength in both my arm and fingers. This was why physical therapy was necessary.

The wound made a perfect red stripe down the length of my arm. It didn't look at all accidental, and I was certain that once it healed, no one would believe I hadn't done this to myself. The stitches looked like bread ties running through my arm. You know, like when you first open a loaf of bread and you aren't entirely sure which direction to turn first, and how no matter what direction you choose, you'll still have to go back the other way until it finally becomes a logical spiral to unwind.

"My arm looks like a loaf of bread," I said to Cathy.

"That was random." She looked at me with her hazel eyes, and I could tell by both the look on her face and the still-high sound of her voice that she was new to this. I didn't mind. Everyone had to start somewhere, and I would rather have been a guinea pig for a good cause than see how much damage a person could take before they finally gave in, gave up, or gave out.

"My arm is so pale and the knots are all intertwined. What does that look like to you?"

She glanced at my arm and then back at my face a few times before answering, "Well," she said with a chuckle, "I've never had anyone say that before."

I wanted to ask if she had ever had a patient with this sort of wound before, but refrained. We spent the rest of the time in silence. I chewed my bottom lip and watched her methodically clean the wound and re-bandage it. I couldn't feel very much unless it wasn't a light touch. I dreaded when the night nurse would come in to handle it. I never bothered to get her name, because I always tried to act like I was asleep. She was heavy-handed and it felt less like scratches down my arm than someone jack-hammering away at it. For all my inability to feel, her careless and rough nature shook the bed and that was what caused the physical discomfort. Mostly.

By the fifth day, everyone told me I had made great improvement, and when Linda came to check on me, she told me they would be releasing me in a few more days. I would have to continue going to physical therapy, but they would find a place closer to the group home. I still had no word on what was happening to, or with, Lara. I stopped asking about it because they just gave me the same response: silence.

On the seventh day, they wheeled me out of the hospital, my arm in a sling, and Linda helped me into a car to go back to the home. I had been both happily anticipating and dreading this exact scene. As a person who wasn't remotely religious—at least not as far as The Big Three were concerned—the last thing I wanted was to be discharged on the seventh day. You know, when He created the day to rest. The irony wasn't lost on me, and though few others would connect the dots in that way, I certainly did.

We sat in silence for the entire ride back to the home. I couldn't tell if my arm was itchy, or if the nerves were just doing their now normal dance. My arm was in a sling, which I thought was overkill. It wasn't broken, but they told me immobilizing it would help the healing process, so I let them put it on. Before I left, they packed up the things I would need to take care of the wound myself, and made me do it once in front of both the nurse and physical therapy technician, to make sure I followed the instructions. It wasn't difficult, and I had moved beyond being sickened by the sight of it. At that point, it had simply become an inconvenience. At least that was what I told myself to get through it.

I attempted to go straight to my room, as soon as we walked through the door. I wanted to see Lara. I wanted to know she was all right, and I wanted her to know I was as well. Ms. Kole stopped me before I could get anywhere near the room. "Ella," she said. "We need to talk." I sighed. I'd learned early that it is never a good thing when someone in authority tells you that you need to talk. In that moment, I promised myself that if I ever had a child of my own, I would never say that. I decided that "Let's chat," sounded less dire.

I followed her into the staff office and it was easy to recognize that no one looked me in the face. Their eyes were downcast as though I was invisible. She sat at a desk and pointed at a chair off to the side of it. This was a cramped space and the staff didn't even have their own area; at each shift, they relinquished it and the next staff member took over the desk. This was evident by the fact that there were no personal items anywhere in the office. No smiling children. No spouses' arms around their necks. No family holidays or photos with Santa. Nothing.

The chair creaked beneath my weight. I had lost at least another ten pounds while in the hospital, and despite the medications making me slow and uneven, my body ached less. At least, it ached less in the places I was used to. My arm? That was another story.

"Ella," her tone was mild and almost warm. "I know you have been asking about Lara, so I wanted to talk to you first." I didn't say a word or give so much as a nod. "We moved her to a foster home this week, so she won't be back here." My mouth dried up. It was like someone had shoved a fistful of sand down my throat. I tried to cough to clear it away, but it did nothing. I just coughed and coughed.

"As for Tamara," she said. "She's still here. We couldn't place her yet, but she's in process. In the meantime, we've found some space for you in a less open setting. We'd like to keep the two of you away from each other until she is moved."

"That's fine." It wasn't fine, but there was no point in

arguing about it. They had obviously labeled Lara the trouble maker. It was she that bore the brunt of The Incident. I would carry a scar and possibly nerve damage, but once a label had been applied, it was next to impossible to remove. Even if no one else knew your secret, you did.

"This isn't a prison, so you're free to go where you want as usual. I just think you should be escorted by a staff member so we can assure that there aren't any further incidents between the two of you."

I felt like I was being punished. Why Tamara was still here and Lara had been moved was beyond me. It may not be a prison, but it certainly felt like one. And I knew the consequences that would be coming. The girls would hate me. They would blame me for Tamara being moved. No one cared too much about Lara. She was a courier and that would be the only reason they would have any negative emotion about her departure.

I took my things to my new room, which already housed a handful of misfits like myself. Only two or three, but I never bothered to ask their names. I simply didn't care. I set my locker combination: 4-1-9-7, as per the usual. I had nothing worth stealing. One of the only things I'd cared about had been taken from me.

I spent the rest of the week in relative silence. I wasn't on a hunger strike, but I didn't leave my room except to shower. I lay in bed with *The House on Mango Street* and let the words blur on the page. I had never taken LSD, but from what I'd heard, this was what it was like. Words askew on the page. The walls breathing with me. It could have been the pain medications they sent back with me, or it could have just been me losing my mind.

I retreated into myself and stayed there. I had no interest in anything. This was depression, but there was nothing anyone was going to be able to do to resolve it. Some of the girls tried talking to me, until word got back to them that I was the one involved in The Incident. Then I became a pariah.

It wasn't so much that they particularly cared that Tamara was leaving, or that Lara was already gone. Tamara made most people's lives absolute hell; except for those that sided with her, did her bidding, and made her a stronger figure in the home. It was more that they felt it was my fault, and anything that could be traced back to someone, at least in the sense that it tightened security or made their lives more difficult, wasn't appreciated. Nor should it be, really. In any case, there wasn't anything I could do about it. What was done, was done. There was no going back.

Some girl I had never been introduced to, because such things weren't customary in a place like this, but who I knew was one of Tamara's girls, approached me on the day she was being transferred. "Yo, ya better watch ya shit," she said. "Ya gonna get more than a suicide scar one of these days."

I was left unprotected. No matter how hard the staff tried to keep me safe, they couldn't be with me at all times. I felt the stitches pull and itch, and I held my good hand over the bandage. I changed them less these days, but I still wasn't healed. They told me the stitches could come out in another week. Until then, I tried to keep them protected.

I didn't say a word to the girl. No roll of my eyes, or any sign of aggression, let alone assertiveness. I simply let her attack me with her words. I didn't need fists and razors to be brought out against me.

I'd heard that, since The Incident, a lot of things were taken away. We still had freedom in terms of leaving the home, but once we entered, we were thoroughly searched and anything deemed dangerous was removed. I'm not even sure they kept them to return at some future point. Any contraband simply disappeared. None of these measures would keep me safe for very long.

I seriously considered moving back to Malda's. My seventeenth birthday was approaching. Summer dissipated into an uneventful fall. I barely felt alive enough to care. I had more than a year left. I wondered if I would be able to get through it. There was only so much introversion I could exhibit, before the other girls, and possibly even the staff, took it as my being uppity. They had made no secret of their disdain for me since the beginning. I may speak like them when I'm with them, but they know that's not who I really am. Not on the inside. Not in the places they cannot reach. Or at least the places they think they are not destroying.

These girls were physical. They were tough. They had little to no executive function except what was needed to keep them alive. This happens to people like us; I hear it is our normal. We spend our lives in a constant state of fight or flight. Many of them run and no one bothers to go after them. Once they are gone, they are gone. The only people that miss them are the ones that sided with them, but no one honestly cared about another human being in this place. At least not the way that I cared for Lara.

I knew where I was going that first Saturday. Nauseous as I was from the medications, I had to see her. I had to know she was okay. The horror stories I had heard about foster care didn't come from a figment of imagination. Besides, even if they had, these girls didn't have enough creativity to bother coming up with them.

Despite my mediocre and limited experience in foster care, I worried for Lara. While she was tough, the bad far outweighed the good. Social workers were stretched and a lot of important things were left unsaid. Foster parents were monitored and had to give reports, but they rarely, if ever, told the truth. Jerome and Jaiden were shining examples of this. Anne bore the brunt of the anger in the house and there were no social workers looking out for her. She had no one.

I had no one. Or, at least, it felt that way. I could turn to Paola, and she had reached out to me a few times when I returned. I wasn't in any sort of mood to entertain her or to be entertained. I wanted to be left alone. I wanted to run, but I had nowhere to go. Malda never appeared and I never bothered to ask Paola if she had even asked about me. I felt sure she hadn't. Especially not with the way things had been left at the hospital.

I re-bandaged my arm and signed out. "Where are you headed?" Ms. Kole asked. "You shouldn't really be out too long, given your arm and all."

"Just going for a walk downtown," I said. I wasn't exactly lying, but neither was I exactly telling the truth. I knew she knew where I was going.

"Good luck," she said.

I wasn't sure why I needed luck. I *was* sure that Lara would be there. She was there every Saturday. It always felt like yesterdays, this place in which we found ourselves. Our escape. It had become our routine and it didn't change. I knew what exit she would take from the train station, and that her long brown hair would flow behind her if there were a breeze. I knew how long we meandered up there for. I knew she would be there, and I was right.

Chapter 7

I saw Lara before she saw me. Her back was towards me, as she looked out over the city; watching the people below like the insects they were. Walking and crawling and squeezing their way through their environment like the ant farm it was. *Idiot*, I thought, *like that is not cliché at all.*

Her hair was straightened and so much longer than when she left the natural curl in it. If I hadn't seen her in profile, I may not have recognized her at all. Her lips looked inflated—like a bubble stuck out—and I noticed something I'd never seen before. She was smoking. The cigarette wobbled a bit as she brought it to her mouth and every time she inhaled, she coughed. This was something new.

My feet, heavy from the medications and from life itself, trudged along the path. In my own ears, it sounded like it drowned out the tourists and insect residents. All I could hear were my feet dragging and scraping the pavement.

She heard me over her shoulder and turned to investigate the noise. She dropped her cigarette. The hot ash created sparks as it bounced away from her. For a moment, I thought there was a flash of anger that came across her face, but when I scrutinized it—that frozen section in time—I realized it was mixed with unjustified confusion. "What are you doing here?" she asked, her face pale.

"I knew you'd be here. Why else would I have come?"

She dug her toes deep inside her sneakers. If she'd been born into a different life, she could have been a ballerina. She could have had grace and elegance. At least, she had the neck for it. "I'm really not sure what to say."

"How can you not have anything to say?" I asked. "They threw you out and kept *la puta*! How are you not fighting this?"

She reached into her back pocket and removed a box of cigarettes. She raised one to her full lips, lit it, inhaled sharply, coughed and said, "There's nothing to fight. You know that. Don't be stupid and naïve." She took another drag, coughing again. "It's not worth anyone's time."

"It's bullshit."

"Yeah, it is." She paused for what felt like forever. I couldn't find anything to say in that time frame. "Look, I don't know why you came. I don't know what you want from me."

I felt crushed. Lara didn't know why I came to see her. She didn't understand why I came looking for her. I hurt in a way I had never hurt before. Not with the abuse, or hiding my true self, not even with The Incident. "W-What?" I stammered, "What do you mean you don't know why I came? You're one of the only friends I have."

She squinted her eyes and I couldn't tell if she was glaring at me or if it truly was the sun burning her retinas. "Friend?" She scoffed and shuddered. "Yeah, well friends don't lie and get other people kicked out of the only place they ever felt was home."

I shook my head. "I don't know what you're talking about. No one asked my side of the story. They said I was in shock when they took me away in the ambulance."

"That's not what I heard. I slipped and was covered in your blood. That didn't mean a thing to you. You told them I instigated it."

I was taken aback. "Lara, I'd . . ." I took a panicked breath in. "I'd never do that. Like I said, no one ever asked me."

"Well, you should go read the report."

"What report?"

"About The Incident," she said and took another drag from her cigarette. She didn't cough this time. Perhaps she was starting to get used to it. Perhaps it was just sheer will. Perhaps she was holding it back so as to not appear weak. That was definitely one of her strengths, ironically enough. "You should go read it sometime. It's great fiction. Oh, wait," she said bitterly, "fiction isn't really supposed to be your thing, right?" She turned and walked away.

My arms went limp at my side. When I looked down, I noticed the bandage had turned a light pink. It wasn't terribly noticeable, but I didn't want to cause an uproar with the insects. I made my way back to the train, took the stairs slowly, and didn't bother to hold onto the railing. The twenty pounds, or so, I'd lost was not only noticeable, it was a major improvement in my quality of life. If there even is such a thing.

The ride seemed to take forever. I felt like everything was moving in slow motion. My peripheral vision was blurry. I felt faint, and had to force myself to stay awake. I did the only thing I knew to do in situations like this; I started a memory game. I stared to the left end of the car for a few seconds and then tried to remember the details.

There's a woman in a red coat pushing a large stroller. There's a subway map with graffiti on it. There's a boy with headphones, moving his lips. There's a child holding onto the center pole and sliding all over the place. That man over there is wearing tan shoes with a navy jacket.

I was fortunate enough to get a seat. I say this only because weekend traveling makes no difference within the city limits. You are able to get anywhere you need or want to go at any time. The train was full and I watched rugged and ragged people huddle around the bacteria-infested poles in the center of the car.

I felt tired and lonely. My body ached. Aside from the stint in the hospital, I'd been feeling better, lighter—but that wasn't being carried over right now. My mind, normally a series of organized pathways, morphed and caved in on itself. Where I had once been so meek and timid on the outside, where my thoughts—while judgmental—had not been vicious, I realized there had been an incredibly large shift towards the negative.

I think we all want to believe that the negative parts about ourselves don't exist. When this realization hit me, I wanted to deny it. I wanted to feel horrified, or at the very least, embarrassed. But those feelings didn't come. It would have been easy to chalk it up to the adrenaline that was typically higher in people like me—people that live in survival mode—and that it made perfect sense. I had to acknowledge that these changes didn't start simply with The Incident. They went deeper than that, and I wasn't sure where this shift was going to take me.

It's the not knowing that makes people fearful. This is why they tether themselves to there being a purpose … a promise of something after.

Usually, I didn't bother letting such existential things

bother me. I was a black and white cookie. The line was clearly drawn in the middle. In the middle, there was no gray. Sometimes, there was just a lot more black where the white should be. I didn't have time to waste on such frivolities as questioning life and its meaning. I had reached a point where I couldn't be fearful of what would come next. I had become so numb to the abuse, at least in the sense of the person I showed myself to be to the world, that it really did become my only expectation. Because it was my only expectation, there was no reason to be fearful.

The business of signing in and out of the home had become rote. Once I began to treat it the way I would coming home to the Baruch Houses, it clicked for me. Hide anything I knew would cause trouble. Keep my head up lest I look suspicious. Be prepared for the questions they are going to ask. This was the easy part, because less intelligent people always ask the same things.

"Well, you're back, Ella," some woman, whose name I never bothered to remember, said.

"Yeah, my arm wasn't feeling very well."

"You should probably go see Ms. Kole about it. You might need to go see a doctor."

"I'll be fine. I really just want to go lay down." I didn't wait for the rest of the questions. I hadn't even signed the book. I assumed she would do it for me, and make a note in the daily file they kept for each shift.

Once in my room, I popped open my locker and removed my book. I felt heat behind me. I held the book tightly in my left hand, knowing full well that it wouldn't cause enough damage. Not only because it was a paperback, but because it wasn't in my dominant hand. I acted like I didn't notice she was there. I didn't move. Didn't flinch. Instead, I grit my teeth and said in an aggressive voice, "If you're going to do something, Tamara, you should just do it. If not, get the fuck away from me."

I was unsure where or when this boldness developed. I'd always wanted to be able to defend myself with my words, but up to this point had found it next to impossible.

I still hadn't moved, but I felt her lean in, her breath hot on my ear. “You have no idea the things that are coming for you.” She smelled of weed and it made me even more nauseated.

I turned around and looked right into her black-as-night eyes, “None of us do.” I didn’t touch her as I walked away. In my mind, the scene would have been perfect if only there had been some sort of physical contact—a brush on the arm, my shoulder accidentally (on purpose) hitting hers. But there was none of that. In fact, afterward, it felt a little disappointing.

Do not get me wrong, I hadn’t been looking for a fight. This was largely because I knew that the only people I would win against—toddlers, the infirm, the elderly—well, they weren’t exactly the kind of people that would be appropriate to take this out on. But this . . . this defiance. This new-found defiance enhanced the adrenaline so much that I would swear I heard a fly burn out on a light bulb hanging over my head. My focus was just that intense.

Still, there was no fear.

When I left the room I bumped into Ms. Kole. I had my head down as I walked. If Tamara was going to try something, it would be aimed at my back anyway, so I decided that tucking myself in upon myself was the best tactic. “What's goin' on here?” I noticed that when she was talking to the administration, or in a few other rare instances, Ms. Kole didn’t use street talk. She enunciated. This was clearly not the time for it.

“Ain't nothin' happenin',” Tamara said as she turned to face her.

“Then go,” Ms. Kole pointed at the door, “Get outta here. You know you ain't even supposed to be over in here.” The supervisor used her body as a shield. She stood sideways in the doorway, one hand on her hip, the other pointing towards the hallway while she stared Tamara down. I was behind her, my head down but my eyes wide open. I chewed my lower lip to stop myself from laughing.

It was what I imagined watching someone hunting a shark must look like. You have a person, this flimsy Ziploc-like bag full of plasma and bone. You have a shark, predatory and muscular with teeth meant to saw through us as though it were its only purpose. At first it seems that the shark has all of the power. But the truth is, the hunter outwits the beast by locking itself in a cage, giving itself the unfair advantage of being able to shoot endlessly without fear of reprisal.

Ms. Kole wasn't terribly bright, at least not from what I had seen, but any education trumped none. She was in a position of authority here and she wasn't in the cage; she was it.

Tamara skulked by without even looking at me. When she had gone, Ms. Kole turned to face me. "You okay?" I nodded. "I don't know how she slipped by."

"I guess we can't all be everywhere all at once."

She chuckled, "Well, *we* certainly can't."

I didn't want this to turn into a philosophical debate about omnipresent beings. And besides, it was neither the time nor the place. The only opinions that mattered here were the ones held by the staff. They literally held the keys to all things—where you slept, if you ate, when you could leave, how far you could go. There were no bars, but it was still a prison.

"Listen," I said as I pulled her aside, "I'm sure I can't get the report of The Incident, but I have to admit that I saw Lara today. She's under the impression that I said she instigated it."

"That's what you told us."

"They said I was in shock. I had no idea what was being asked or what I said. I can barely remember anything." When I closed my eyes, I had flashes, but I still couldn't piece them together in any cohesive or coherent way.

"Let's talk about it tomorrow. She's out, and Tamara is on her way out. I'm not sure we can bring her back in. It really doesn't matter who started the fight. We don't tolerate that here."

"I get it," I felt defeated. "I've seen others get into fights. It happens almost daily and they aren't placed elsewhere."

"Not at this level."

I understood her then. I didn't want to admit it and I didn't want to give it away. No matter who started the fight, they were both being blamed. I had to convince Lara of this so she wouldn't continue to think I'd betrayed her. If I had, in any way, it wasn't intentional and I needed her to know that.

"Is there a way to reach her?"

"Didn't you just find her today? You know where she'll

be."

I sighed, trudged back to bed, and stared at the ceiling until I fell asleep.

Chapter 8

I was doing fine in school. In fact, I was bored. I had no real motivation to do anything as far as that was concerned, which was unusual for me. *I have one year left*, I told myself. One more year. My seventeenth birthday had come and gone with zero fanfare. I had no idea what I would do once school was finished. I'd never had a job, not even a part-time gig to provide me with some experience. I had no sense of what I wanted to do except go to college. Even then, I had no grasp on what I wanted to study. Psychology, maybe.

"I've had a lot of thinking to do lately." I was in my weekly meeting with Linda and it was the last place I wanted to be.

"About?"

"What I want to do. Who I want to be. I don't feel like I'm figuring it out, and with a year left, it's starting to bother me."

"I think this is the most honest you've ever been."

"I'm choosing to trust you."

"That's a huge leap forward. You don't trust easily."

I smiled. "It's only taken a year."

"So, what are your options?"

"I can stay in school for another year or so, which doesn't really interest me. I'm not a social creature and I don't care about things like the supposed fun of senior year."

"Haven't you made friends?"

I sighed, "I thought I did, but apparently not." I didn't want to get into The Incident again, or how it revealed the truth behind what I thought had been an actual friendship.

"Ah," she nodded as she said this, and a look of concern crossed her face. "I think you need to try harder to build a network of people you can rely on."

"Isn't family supposed to be the core of that?"

"Well, in this case, I don't think that's an option."

"At least not a viable one."

She smiled. "You're one of my favorites, you know. I'm

not supposed to say that, but you really are. You certainly keep me on my toes."

"You're going to look up viable as soon as I leave, aren't you?"

She smirked at me, "I don't need to."

"Good," I said, "I'm tired of having to dumb myself down just to communicate the basics to people around here."

"You've changed a lot since we met. You're more vocal and you're expressing different emotions now. I think this is progress. You've done a lot of work. I think you should be proud."

Why am I supposed to be proud? I was venting more, and allowing people to get under the thick skin I'd developed to protect myself. I had let people in and paid dearly for it. "I don't think it's an improvement that my thoughts are becoming more negative, or that I'm speaking up for myself. It's not been in a positive way."

"You're at least defending yourself now."

"Tell that to Lara."

"That's a different case."

"No, it's not." I wanted to scream. I wanted to pull myself out of the chair across from her, and fling it and myself against the pea green walls. It was so institutional. It was cold, and I felt a chill beyond anything I had known before.

She changed the subject. I suppose she could see the agitation crossing my face. "I think you have more than one option. What else do you think you can do?"

"Get my GED and start college immediately."

"I think that's a good solution. Have you talked to Ms. Jackson about it yet?" Ms. Jackson led the in-house education program. The Life Improvement Classes had been her idea. To this end, the only real skill I had learned was how to cook the basics. It wouldn't matter anyway; I assumed that a life of ramen noodles was in my future.

"No. I haven't decided anything, and I find the classes they run to be unhelpful, at best."

"At least you're vigilant in attending them. A lot of girls leave here, struggling, not knowing how to move forward."

"That's exactly where I am right now."

"Ella," she said sternly, more sternly than I had ever heard her speak to me, "you're one of the smartest girls here. Hell," she laughed, "you're one of the smartest people I've met."

"Then you need some new clients, or friends, or cases, or something." I sucked my teeth but sat up straight in my chair. I did want to hear more—I just wasn't sure if I was ready. Compliments made me extremely uncomfortable.

Linda didn't skip a beat while I readjusted myself. "You're doing a great disservice to yourself. I think getting your GED is a good thing."

"No one respects them."

"They're as much work as finishing high school, if not more. The education system wants to keep kids in school. They provide this as an option, but it's not really an incentive, if you know what I mean. It's harder."

"I know I could get into college with it, but–I mean, how do I explain it later? It's awkward."

"No, it isn't. When you get your diploma, no one is even going to care how you finished high school. It won't come up."

"Until reunions and alma mater letters roll in begging for money."

She laughed, "For someone who claims to not have any friends, you seem awfully concerned about social situations around high school and graduation."

"That's because high school never ends. I'm sure of it."

"Everything ends, Ella."

"I'm not in the mood for philosophy today, Linda. Nor your psychological evaluations. I'm fine."

"Will you commit to talking to Ms. Jackson?"

I hadn't made a decision about school yet, so I didn't think it was prudent to waste her time with it. "We'll see."

"That's not a commitment, Ella."

"It's all I have." I glanced at the clock. "Imagine that,

we're out of time."

Linda grimaced. I assumed it was because we hadn't come to the conclusion she wanted. "Next week, then."

"I'll bring the bells." My sarcasm had become out of control. Actually, that's not entirely true. It had always been there, I'd just done a better job of hiding it. I used to have a tight grip, not only on my reality—or personal hell—but on my interactions and thoughts. Since moving into foster care and seeing how that turned out, I felt irrevocably changed.

I wondered how Anne was doing. I knew I couldn't go back. I knew I would never see her again, but I wondered if her situation had improved at all. It was unlikely, but I still hoped. No one had the courage to stand up and protect her. I felt terrible. Of all of the people she should have been able to count on, it should have been me. I'd failed her.

I felt the same about Lara. Her notion of betrayal still burned inside me. I couldn't escape what felt like another personal tragedy in a string of them throughout my life. Where once I began to feel that things were finally making sense, the Universe took me by my heavy ankles and turned me upside down.

Speaking of heavy ankles, I continued to refuse to weigh myself, but the limited amount of clothes I owned had rapidly become too large. I thought I could borrow belts or other girls' clothes, trading them like currency the way they did habitually, but one of the skills I never bothered to learn from Lara was that of her negotiable nature. I supposed I would need to talk to Ms. Kole about it. It felt like my to-do list had become burdensome. Questions. Conversations. Decisions. But most of all, survival.

I sat with all of this until the day before my next meeting with Linda. If I walked in with limited or no progress, it wasn't going to make for a productive conversation. In fact, during weeks like that, I generally only provided one word answers. It made the conversation stilted, but at least I left feeling like I had protected myself and my boundaries.

I still didn't feel ready to address the decisions I needed to make about the next 12-18 months. So, I waited until I could catch her alone, her keys dangling from around her wrist like a warden. I didn't want to have this conversation in the staff room. Most of them made me uncomfortable. While I had never truly warmed up to Ms. Kole, I did feel a bit more at ease with her since The Incident.

"Can I talk to you for a minute?"

She stopped and faced me. "Sure Ella, what's up?" I found it nearly impossible that she knew all of us by sight and sound.

"I don't know how much weight I've lost in the last few weeks, and frankly, I don't care. However, my clothes don't really fit anymore and I'm sort of at a loss here. I have nothing to borrow and I can't afford to buy anything."

"I know we don't have anything on site," she said. "But let me call around and see what I can dig up. You're not terribly picky, right?"

I looked down at my feet, feigning humility. "Do I really look like I have a choice?"

She put her hand on my shoulder; an act I hadn't seen previously and which took me by surprise. "I'll do the best I can."

I turned to walk back to my room, but suddenly felt the urge to call *Tia* Paola instead, and used the phone in the staff office. As expected, she picked up on the third ring. She didn't have an answering machine or any sort of caller ID, so if you missed her, you just had to keep trying. I was incredibly familiar with her schedule, and as she and I were both creatures of habit, I knew I would be able to reach her.

"*Hola*," my excitement felt barely containable.

"*Aye*! *Mijita*! I was thinking about you today!" she exclaimed. "I miss you. When can you stop by for a visit?"

I thought about it. Saturday would work for her, but I really wanted to try to find Lara and talk through the nonsense. "I usually walk the High Line on Saturdays, but I can come by afterward."

"I've never been there," I heard the longing in her voice.

She was looking for an invitation. That is just how we are. Formal. Unimposing. And for the most part, completely false. She was the only one I truly trusted and felt I could count on.

"Come with me."

"I don't want to bother you."

"Why? I bother you all the time." We shared a laugh. "The weather is nice and it's a beautiful view. Just come meet me there."

"You won't take no *por respuesta*, will you?"

I giggled, "Of course not. When do I ever?"

"This is a new you, *mijita*. I can't wait to see you this weekend."

"*Sábado*," I said, "*Alrededor del mediodía*." Saturday. Around noon.

"Okay, see you then."

The fact that I'd planned this visit so close to noon meant that bumping into Lara when I was with *Tia* was highly likely. Perhaps her seeing me with someone else would make her less aggressive. Or, at least, I hoped she hadn't changed that aspect of herself.

The next day, I intentionally made myself ten minutes late to my meeting with Linda. "Where have you been?" she asked while checking the flimsy watch around her wrist.

"Busy."

"With?"

"Thinking."

"It's disrespectful and I expect more from you."

"Sorry."

"Are we back to this then?"

"Maybe."

She sighed, "How was your week?"

"Fine."

"Ella," she said with annoyance, "you say you're doing a lot of thinking. Talk to me. What's going on?"

"Nothing." I just didn't want to talk to her at the moment. I felt caught up in the excitement of seeing *Tia,* but it was mixed with strong feelings of defeat with Lara. I wasn't sure any amount of apologies or humility would win her trust, or what I still considered friendship. And even if it did, life is unpredictable, and definitely not a Disney movie.

There are no glass slippers. There are no rodents or birds doing my chores. There are no dwarves, no magic carpets and certainly no princes. There was beauty, of course, but there was certainly more beast in the mix.

"I really have nothing to say."

"Did you talk to Ms. Jackson?"

"Do you think I did?"

"No, but one can still hope."

"Can they?"

"What's gotten into you in the last week? You don't seem like yourself."

"Sure I do. It's just the me you saw for a year, not the me I've shown you in the last few weeks." I slid down in the chair and stared at a hole in the wall. It looked like there had been a picture there at some point. Maybe it was just my imagination running wild, but I decided to tune Linda out and instead create an entire story about the ghostly, unreal painting that I presumed had hung there.

"Are you listening to me?"

"No."

"What are you doing?"

"Thinking."

"Well stop thinking, Ella."

"No. I'll lose everything if I do."

"What are you thinking about?"

"Nothing."

"This conversation, if that's what you could even call it, is extremely frustrating to me right now."

"Then end it." I continued the story in my mind. *It was a woman wrapped in gauze. She floated in the water, surrounded by lilies. She had a sharp nose. Her eyes were closed and her hands folded over her chest.* I had seen this painting, which is why it was the first place my mind went, but I couldn't remember the artist or the name of the piece.

The woman looked depressed. She'd lost everything because she had no time to think. She ran out of words. She lost her independence. She could no longer stand up for herself. This wasn't the story, it was mine, but I didn't care.

Linda's voice interrupted my thoughts. "Let's try again next week."

"Sure." I moved from the chair as swiftly as I could and didn't bother to be careful with the door behind me. I let it close on its own and heard it slam when I was just a few feet away. I turned to face it and shrugged. I was depressed. I'd lost everything and I had no time to think. Not really, anyway.

Friday came and went without incident. I hadn't heard from Ms. Kole and so I had taken to wearing leggings that were making me look like I had elephant knees, wrinkled and worn because of age. I tried on everything I owned in the hopes that at least something would be worthy of keeping, but aside from a few shirts, most of it fell away from me as though it were resting on a hanger.

I could barely contain myself on Friday night. I lay in bed, and stared at the ceiling while I was on my back, or out the window when I shifted to my side. This time, I did think, instead of daydream. I tried to formulate an apology to Lara, or at least some sort of explanation for why the report read like it did.

I also felt excited about seeing *Tia*. I hadn't seen her since her last visit to the hospital, and I'd been too drugged to really enjoy it. The medications had made me so loopy that other than the flush of anger from seeing Malda, I hadn't truly experienced much emotion while I was there.

The stitches had been removed a while back, and despite the external wounds healing well, the internal scars were the hardest to handle. My tendon had been severed and even though I'd had physical therapy several times a week, I didn't see improvement. Everyone told me I was making progress, but it didn't feel that way to me.

It was what I imagine being drunk must feel like. I wouldn't know from experience, but I've certainly seen my fair share of alcoholics. They would usually be the only ones catcalling or whistling at me as I walked by. I have seen the leanness, and the wobble and the shakes. I have seen the stammering and the confusion. I felt all of those things when I tried to do anything requiring my right hand.

The numbness was still there, and the tingling sensation drove me crazy. The outward scars were itchy—one of the only sensations I could feel aside from numbness—but I had to resist the urge to scratch them. Even with my rugged and bitten nails, I didn't want to run the risk of reopening anything. They'd already warned me it wouldn't scar nicely. By that I could only interpret that it wouldn't be a flat, light scar. "You'll run the risk of it becoming keloid," the doctor told me. The only thing I took away from his words is that the scar would be ugly. *Keloid is truly an ugly word*, I thought.

It would be yet another thing to be self-conscious about. The weight may have been coming off at a pace I never imagined, and I may have looked the best I had in my whole life, but now I would be bearing the scars from an incident I had no control over. I don't like not being in control, despite my knowing it's only an illusion anyway. Like time, but no one seems to care. We all keep rushing to the same inevitability as though we have anywhere else to go.

I paired my leggings with an also-too-big long sleeved t-shirt, slipped on a pair of *chancletas,* and made my way to the staff office to sign out. I looked ridiculous with the long sleeves and flip flops, but I didn't have much choice in the matter.

"Where ya headed today, Ella?"

"Same as usual, Ms. K." I had taken to shortening her name as the other girls did. It established familiarity, and I wanted to believe it made me fit in better with the others.

"All right, you know the drill."

"Of course."

I left the home with some trepidation. On the one hand, I

felt nervous about seeing Lara. On the other, I was excited. I had worked out my version of The Truth in my head and longed to share it.

As usual, the train was packed. This was the cost of living so far uptown. It was crowded with folks from the Bronx, Sugar Hill and Morningside Heights, and I found it funny how the *blanquitas* would team themselves up as they boarded the train at their stops further south. I had lived in the city for my entire life, so had a very good sense of who would board when, and where they would leave the train.

I have never been familiar with designers. It's just not my thing, but when I saw the older woman with the large beaded necklace and the fancy suit, I knew she had come on in the Upper West Side and would either exit at Lincoln Center, or Columbus Circle. Because of the time, and the looks of her, I settled on Columbus Circle. It was close enough to the ritzy shopping I'd never have the luxury of enjoying.

I suppose people think there is safety in numbers, but I've never been one for crowds. As The Incident confirmed, safety in numbers is just a myth. It's just as easy to divide and conquer as it is to attack a single individual. At least it is if you know what you're doing.

A few kids who'd boarded the train with me in Hamilton Heights were in full swing. They were raucous, and whenever they could find enough room, they turned their music on and attempted to dance. Sometimes they only had enough space to do the robot. It would have been amusing had I not seen it almost every day, and had these particular kids not lived in my neighborhood. It was common knowledge that they were trouble, but I never bothered with the details. I just ignored them.

One time, they called out "*gordita*" as I walked past. I took it as a compliment. The –ita turned what could have been a full-on insult into just a mild one. I was only a 'little' fat girl, not a full-blown one. Then again, this was Hamilton Heights and anything that could happen here, did.

After what felt like forever, I made my way to the stop and

exited up the long flights of stairs. I wasn't nearly as winded as I remember being the first time I'd gone on this adventure with Lara. I took this as a good sign. Not only did my clothes fit better, I also breathed and moved better. Right arm excluded.

I walked to the High Line and began my search. I could rule out anyone not smoking, since watching Lara chain smoke the weekend prior told me she wouldn't have quit. Stress does that to people, I suppose. I find comfort in food, not nicotine, but to be honest I'm not sure which one is worse.

I got there at 11:00 AM, and—based on her routine—she should have been here already. I ceased eliminating non-smokers, and felt like my heart was racing. Not long after, it began to feel like a full-on panic attack. I decided I needed to sit on a bench, catch my breath, and attempt to calm myself down.

I had enough experience to know that it was all in my head. There was nothing physically wrong with me. The panic was merely a figment of my imagination. However, it was hard to get under control. I needed a distraction. The memory game was back in full swing.

I spent a full hour searching for her, but didn't see her there. I realized I hadn't set an actual location with *Tia,* and neither of us had cell phones. *Que stupida!* I told myself. How stupid. I spent the next twenty minutes searching for *Tia* and I found her, unconcerned, not at all flustered, just sitting on a bench looking out at the city.

"*Ella*," she said excitedly. "I'm so happy to see you! It's been too long, *mijita*."

"Sí, sé." Yes, I know.

"How have you been? You look good. Good, but sad."

"That's exactly how I am."

"*Pero, qué*?"

"Why?" I smiled while looking off in another direction, scanning the park for Lara. "Because the only friend I thought I had, thinks I betrayed her when she was defending me in that fight."

She sighed, "I can't say I understand, but I'm sorry she

doesn't see how you truly are. You would never do that to someone."

"Especially not her." Sometimes, I thought people would think the same of me when it came to Lara as they do about Rosa. It didn't bother me. I knew it wasn't the same, but I could see how others might think that. *Tia* eyed me suspiciously and I knew we were sharing the same thoughts. We often did that. "No, *Tia*, I'm not. It's complicated and different."

"I wouldn't care," she said. "Rosa is happy and doing well, so who cares what she does? It's her life. You kids should be happy with it." She never clarified whether Rosa was happy with Bianca or if it was just a generalization. I didn't bother to ask. Frankly, I was still too angry and hurt to care.

"Well, unfortunately, a lot more people disagree with you," I said and gave her a sullen look.

"Let me see your arm. How is it doing?"

I extended my arm and pulled up my sleeve a bit so she could see it. "It's getting better," I lied. Maybe it wasn't a full-on lie, but again, from my perspective it wasn't at all true.

She became quiet while she examined it. She traced her long, graceful fingers along the edge of the scar. She inhaled sharply when she reached the end. "*Aye mijita, lo siento*." Yes, little one. I am sorry.

"It's not your fault." I drew my arm away quickly and pulled the sleeve down. It made me uncomfortable. I wasn't one to show off such things. I didn't want to hear the questions, or feel backed into a corner trying to answer them. I'm sure it stemmed from the first time I showed up at school with welts, despite trying my best to cover them.

I've always been unhappy with my body, but the outward scars make me extremely uneasy. I don't like to talk to anyone about them. And when it's just me, in a shower perhaps, I try to ignore them and do my best to act like they're not there. In my mind, there are no dark marks from previous welts. There are no tell-tale circles from having cigarettes extinguished on me. There are no faint trails from being pushed down the stairs. There are no pockets where gravel became embedded before my body removed them itself.

If I could create my ultimate self, my skin would be the first place I would start. Interestingly enough, it wouldn't be that I would instantaneously make myself thin. I would start with my skin. I would smooth it out, the way a layman spreads grout between tiles. Slowly, evenly. I would stretch it, knowing it wouldn't leave marks, but instead, help them disappear. I wouldn't ever need to be airbrushed, but would have exactly what I wanted; a look that said I had a normal life. Except, I would have forced myself to not go through the gawky acne phase.

I didn't want this to turn into an awkward conversation, so I refocused. "Anyway, how have you been?"

When the sound escaped her throat, it sounded like 'meh'. "I'm the same. Nothing new with me really."

"And," I paused, "how is everyone else?" I don't know why I even bother to ask. It's not like it will change anything, and I'm certain they don't bother to ask after me either.

"Pretty much the same, *mijita*."

"I figured."

There was a bit of silence while we just sat on the benches. "No place to get a *churro* around here, huh?" she asked with a look of delight on her face.

"No," I laughed. I haven't had one of those in ages. In truth, I could get them anytime I wanted. Living at the top of Manhattan was much like living on the Lower East Side in that regard. I simply hadn't had the appetite for it. And with the weight coming off with no effort on my part, I didn't want to impede it in any way.

"Next time we meet, I'll bring you some."

I held my stomach and said, "*Oye*, no! I don't eat those anymore."

"Apparently not," the tone of her voice felt a bit grating on my nerves for the first time in … ever, really. "But you do look wonderful."

I wasn't sure what to say. It seemed like our conversations

had always come so easily, but this particular day, what had started with excitement and hope had turned into a massive amount of negativity. It was as though I was straddling the event horizon, and nothing I did prevented me from being sucked in. "*Lo siento*," I apologized, "I don't feel like myself today."

She smoothed her skirt over her knees. She was in her work uniform and I'd known beforehand that she wouldn't have a lot of time to meet. "Come over for dinner soon, ok? I think I understand."

"Sure thing, *Tia*." I stood up to give her a hug and it was just as warm as ever, despite the conversation seeming cool, at best. It was a different experience with her, and I was unclear as to why that was the case. It was disarming.

After we went our separate ways, I took another walk along the High Line looking for Lara. I didn't find her. In defeat, I headed back to the subway. I really didn't want to go back to the home since it was still several hours before curfew, but I had nowhere else to go and nothing seemed particularly interesting to me.

I headed back north and when I got to Hamilton Heights, I shrugged at no one in particular. I used to be good at killing time. I would lie in bed and read, or watch mindless television, or immerse myself in homework, but none of that seemed at all enticing to me.

I spent the next two hours meandering. I walked along 155th Street, passing the *bodegas* and various other shops. I watched women frying *churros* and men scraping ice for *piragua*. I passed on all of them. As refreshing as a cold drink would have been, I didn't have the desire for one.

Despite the costs of everything rising, there wasn't much in the way of inflation within my own community. I cannot remember the price of a pair of *churros* or a *piragua* ever being more or less than a dollar, and am sure that *Tia* could tell me all about it, if I was concerned enough to ask.

My feet hurt. C*hancletas* had no basis for providing arch support, and one of my pet peeves was walking around collecting the dirt of New York City on the bottom of my feet. As soon as I checked back in at the home, I grabbed my towel and a fresh pair of clothes and hit the shower. I scrubbed the bottom of my feet to get the day's grime from them.

I passed Ms. Jackson while I still had a towel wrapped around my head, so I didn't bother to stop and talk to her, even though I knew I needed to get to her before Linda did. I didn't really want another session like the last one, but at the same time, if I have nothing I want to share, then I simply won't. Linda knows that, after working with me for so long, but sometimes she just pushes more than I have the patience to handle.

I went back to my room and dried my hair between the sides of the bright yellow towel. I didn't like blow-drying my hair, because it always made it brittle and turned my curls into frizzy waves. No, it was better to do it this way and wait for it to air dry. I didn't lie down, because with all my hair swirling around me well past my shoulders, my pillow would still be wet by the time I came back to bed.

Instead, I went to the common room and took a seat away from the others. I wasn't particularly interested in talking to anyone and I had no plans to work on anything. It was just an opportunity for me to have a change of scenery, since I spent so little time in there. I sat facing the television, but not paying attention, when a girl who appeared to be fifteen or so, approached me.

She wasn't as tiny as Lara, nor did the little I had seen of her around the home indicate a similar personality. "Hey," she said. "You're the girl that got knifed, right?" I didn't respond. I uncrossed my ankles and stood up from the chair. She grabbed my right wrist, not in a threatening way, but instead it appeared to be curiosity. "So? …" she trailed off.

"So what?"

"Is it you?"

"I don't know. Is it?" I turned my arm over and showed her the thickened and darkened scar.

"Oh shit! It *is* you." It was easy to move past her. Despite her stealth, she wasn't a match for my size. "Wait," she said, "I need to talk to you." She spoke in a hushed tone, but I had no idea why it was so imperative to talk to me as though she were a Bond Girl.

"What do you want?"

"I saw Lara."

My heart felt like it stopped. Then it felt like it was beating a mile a minute. If this conversation didn't go well, I suspected I might be playing the observation game for the second time today. "And?" I tried to act nonchalant, but was certain that despite my flat tone, my body language gave me away.

"She wanted me to tell you something."

"Stop being so damn mysterious and just spit it out already. I'm done chasing her around the city. What does she want?"

"She wanted to know if you read the report."

"No." I moved past her, taking my wrist from her gentle grip. "I'm not going to."

"I'll tell her."

"Do whatever you want."

I headed back to my room and stopped caring about the pillow. I laid face down, tears coming no matter how hard I tried to stop them. It wasn't that I didn't care; clearly I did. I wanted to see her and at least set things right between us, even if our friendship was irrevocably changed. But the idea that Lara—of all the people I had ever known—wouldn't just follow the routine and ask me herself upset me.

My breath came fast and my heart pounded in my chest. I swore I would talk to Linda about the anxiety and see if there was anything they could do for me. I turned over, gasping for air and started again. *There's a plastic bag on the floor…* The memory game would save me.

My family life hadn't been all bad. I realized that long ago. There were plenty of moments, especially those, where we would laugh and tease each other. But because we were around others, the teasing was never cruel. It was actually deserved and funny.

I would sit back and watch the smoke from the grill waft above the city, carrying the smell of Adobo and Goya and Mojo. Malda almost always brought *arroz con gandules,* and when it came to the meat, everyone chipped in a few dollars so there would be enough to go around. At these times, it was about *la comunidad*—the community—and not about the individual.

The fact is, though, that the bad far outweighed the positive experiences. I have tried not to relive those moments, but they come to me in flashes. Much like The Incident, my mind has a mechanism to block certain aspects of the negative. Maybe it was selective. I'm not sure, and I never bothered to get to the root cause. I was just fine with not being able to remember the entire story.

I stand on the landing of the stairs and look down. I don't see it coming, but feel a hard shove behind me. Then, in slow motion, I am falling. It never feels slow, but when I stand outside myself, it seems like it takes forever before I can feel the ground beneath me again. Where I had been on my feet, I am now on my side. I can barely breathe, but I know it's best if I just lay there—playing dead—the way my neighbor's dog used to do.

The way my neighbor's dog used to do. Lying there, pretending to be dead. When those flashes hit me, I often wished I could do the same. I wished I could will myself into non-existence so I didn't have to feel or think, or see any of it. When I closed my eyes, I felt all of the disorientation. I didn't know what direction I was facing. In those times, the pain in my ribs was very real.

The discussion with Lara's minion, and my reliving both positive and negative memories—a roller coaster in itself—left me drained, and I had to force myself to get up and grab something to eat for dinner. The meal was a heavy one and I was in no mood. "Is there any way I can just get a grilled cheese sandwich instead?" I asked when I finally reached the server, whose name I never knew. They changed out so frequently I just never found out who they were, and none of them wore name tags.

She laughed, "Whatchu think this is? IHOP?"

"I'm not hungry enough for this." I paused. "And my stomach hurts, I can't eat this." *And really*, I thought, *there isn't an International House of Pancakes anywhere near here. Most of these people would not even get that reference. This woman is from another planet.*

She called back to the kitchen and waved me away to the end of the line to wait. A few minutes later, what came my way was not, in fact, a grilled cheese sandwich. It was just two slices of bread with a slice of rubbery cheese between them. I didn't argue. It wouldn't have made any difference. Instead, I wrapped it in a napkin and brought it back to my room.

We weren't supposed to eat in our room, but I needed to be alone. If this was my worst act of rebellion, then I was doing well for myself. I took one bite of the sandwich. The cheese—government provided, I imagined—tasted terrible. One bite. Then it was bequeathed to the garbage can.

And they work so hard to dispel the notion that this is not, in fact, a jail cell.

Chapter 9

It took another week, but Tamara finally got relocated. The staff moved me back to my old room, which felt empty without having Lara in the bunk above me. I asked to be moved elsewhere. "Listen, princess," one of the staffers said. "You get what you get. That was your bunk and it still is."

"But can't you make an exception? Can't I just go back to where I've been staying while Tamara was here?"

"Hell no. We have to do checks even more frequently. It's more work for us. Why would we move you back there just to create more work for ourselves?"

"State employees," I muttered under my breath.

"Whatchu said?"

"Nothing." I walked away. I set my locker password to the one it had always been, and moved my belongings over in one fell swoop. There still wasn't much, even though Ms. Kole had managed to dig up some donations. I had shrunk from a size 20 to a size 16. Linda told me that meant about a thirty pound loss. It was finally noticeable.

The depression worsened and the new clothes—or at least new to me—were loose again. Since they were mostly stretchy clothes—leggings, shirts that looked like maternity wear, sundresses—I didn't ask for new ones. I didn't want to appear greedy or selfish. It was why, despite my hatred of dresses, I wore them. Beggars can't be choosers after all.

Lara's minion hadn't approached me since the previous week, and after the incident with Lara hiding herself in what was most likely plain sight, I decided to skip the High Line for the first time in over a year. "Just the usual," I said as I signed out that afternoon. There were no questions asked and no one would be looking for me any time soon, if at all.

I had nowhere particular in mind to go, but as usual I found myself heading south. I just sat on the train, indecisive, until I got to West Fourth Street. I hadn't been this far from the home, other than briefly moving to Brooklyn. I wandered through the West Village. Unlike Times Square, the Village maintained its sense of individuality and perversion. I passed the stores selling bongs and bowls—for tobacco use only—of course.

Before long, I realized I'd made my way over to the East Village and was heading even further south. I was being pulled, much against my own will, to the Lower East Side. The sights and smells of familiarity washed over me, and for a little while, I almost felt nostalgic. There wasn't a lot of difference in the diversity of the community between there and the home, nor in the rhythm. I was used to the hustle, but not the women with their double wide strollers, who took their sweet time along the edge of Central Park.

The Baruch Houses came into view and I stopped. I had no idea what I was doing here. I had no expectation. I was frozen in both fear and a sense of wonder. What if I ran into Malda? What if I ran into Tomas or Maria, or Yvette? Or even worse, Bianca? Interestingly enough, the idea of seeing my father never came into play. The likelihood of him being anywhere near here was slim to the point of being non-existent.

I took a deep breath and made my way towards my old building. The outside and emergency exit doors were rarely locked, which is why residents had so many of their own chains on the doors to their apartments. I let myself in and stood in the filthy lobby for a few minutes. In truth, I shouldn't say it was filthy. It had just been cleaned, and I could tell the floors had been mopped. I never knew what they used except that it was pink and industrial, and the smell of something floral never covered up the persistent smell of poverty.

Old neighbors came and went, but no one gave a greeting, nor did I. Sometimes someone would nod their head towards me, but I generally acted like I was looking through them, not at them. I wasn't exactly sure why I was there, or what I wanted to do, but my hand froze when I touched the door to the stairwell. The last time I had touched a door here, I was a deer in headlights, injured and fleeing into the unknown. I had no desire to do it again. Instead, I turned on my heels and left the lobby.

Again, I had no idea where I was headed, but I had to leave. I walked as swiftly as I could, and went north. North. There were so many historical connotations and it dawned on me that as humans, it seemed like we were drawn to those poles. I never heard people feeling drawn to the east or west. But north or south? Undoubtedly, yes.

After what felt like forever, I was out of the Lower East Side. I felt relieved, and the sense of danger had dissipated. While the sense of security anywhere is generally false, I sincerely felt like nothing worse could happen to me. Fortunately, it didn't.

Linda once mentioned exposure therapy as an option for me. The idea of going back to the places where the worst traumas had taken place was terrifying. Even the idea of closing my eyes and putting myself back in those environments, those moments, wasn't something I was willing to do. The flashes of memories were enough. I had no intention of digging into them in such a direct way.

"Studies show that it helps," she said to me months ago.

"I don't care, Linda. I'm not doing it."

"Okay, but it's shown to be a very helpful approach for Post-Traumatic Stress Disorder."

"Linda."

"Yes?"

"No." And that ended that discussion. After having the same one for weeks, she finally gave up on the idea. I wasn't budging. I would not. I could not.

As I made my way along St. Mark's Place, I stopped to look at the various wares. There happened to be a sidewalk sale, where each store brought incredibly discounted items out of the store and practically into the streets. *Tia* had given me twenty-three dollars. She slipped the bills into my hand as we were hugging goodbye, "Take this, *mijita*, I won't accept a 'no', and it is all I have on me." So as to not be insulting, I took it without argument.

I went up the south side of the street first, examining anything that happened to catch my eye. I turned fabric around my fingers, held earrings up to my ears, and tried on bangles and rings. I didn't fit in here, but it didn't matter. No one looked at anyone else as anything other than human. It was a place for everyone and no one at the same time. The buildings and streets, and people, were generally dingy, but no one seemed to mind. The punks and the ravers and the NYU kids were cohesive here.

Most of the stores had much of the same items for sale. T-shirts with quotes from *Scarface* or band logos, tie dye dresses, head scarves, hammered metal jewelry, records. On the north side of the street, a small Tibetan store nestled amidst the bustle. I'd almost missed it. A minute, wrinkled woman manned a table outside the shop. I stopped to look over the sparse wares.

An intricately carved box caught my eye. I tried to open it, but it wouldn't budge. The wooden box had flowers, elephants, and symbols carved throughout the entire piece. I ran my fingers along the grooves, imagining that this must be what it would be like to read Braille. "Here, I show you," she said in broken English.

The woman smiled as she took the box from my hands and into her own paper-thin ones. I watched as her blue veins moved under the loose light brown skin of her hands. I was mesmerized, not only by this stranger's translucent flesh, but by her kindness. It felt genuine, not as though she needed the sale. In fact, this was the first thing I had seen her say to anyone, as no one else seemed to stop at her table.

She slid a sliver of wood on the front face of the box to the right. There was no click, but it opened to reveal a velvet-lined inner compartment. She closed it, shifted the wood to the left and showed me that it wouldn't open again. "Here," she said, handing it back to me. "You try now."

I imitated the movement of her fingers and quickly found the piece that transformed this into something more useful than just a beautiful decoration. I shifted it to the right and opened it, staring deep into the purple velvet inside. "Is royal," she said. I nodded. I knew what she meant.

"How much?"

"Twenty dollar."

"I can't pay that," I said. It would be insulting not to barter.

"What you pay?"

"Ten."

She scoffed and waved her hand at me with a toothless grin. "No, twenty dollar."

"I do not have twenty dollars," I said more sternly. "I will give you fifteen."

"Seventeen," she said. She knew how to negotiate and she drove a hard bargain.

"Fifteen dollars or I will have to leave."

She took her time before saying, "Ok, fifteen." She wrapped the box in a piece of fabric and put it inside a small unmarked bag. "Thank you," she said, and then lowered her eyes as she murmured goodbye. I did the same out of respect, but in reality, it was my typical stance. Eyes low, head bent. I knew what this was like. Servitude. Only I did it without the gratitude truly required for it.

The brown paper bag swayed on my arm and would occasionally brush against my thigh as I walked. The woven rope handle began to feel like an Indian burn in the crook of my elbow. As crazy and ridiculous as I'm certain the idea must have been, I decided to try the High Line again.

The characters on the train, particularly this far south in the city, were almost always good for entertainment. The break-dancers stayed off the trains here, despite having no problem on the extremely crowded ones uptown. I suppose they didn't want to waste their time where they wouldn't get tips from tourists. Not very many out-of-towners bothered to come this far anyway; they mostly stayed where the biggest traps were.

Other than Chinatown, I rarely saw them anymore. Well, Chinatown and The New Disney. The lights of Times Square changed from gaudy flashing legs of peep shows to Coca-Cola ads and preppy stores. Tourists could get these things back home, but the lights drew them. The lights and perhaps the architecture, but I always thought it was simply the lights.

Entertainers on the train here were typically acoustic guitarists. Sometimes there would be mariachi bands. Other times, they weren't artists at all, just regular folks with loud headphones and voices, repeating the lyrics they heard on their phones. No one used mp3 players by this point. I had neither, so I settled for whatever I could pick up on the train.

It was late afternoon by the time I was up on the High Line again. I would make one round so I could get back to the home in time for curfew. I had never been late and didn't want to start building that sort of reputation. It meant that they became stricter with you, and especially with how depressed I had been, the last thing I needed were more rules and watchful eyes. I already felt like a leper.

I walked quickly this time. I suppose it was only a half-hearted attempt at this point. I didn't expect to find Lara, and so wasn't surprised when I didn't. It had only been a few weeks, but given the changes I saw when I had recently bumped into her, I wasn't really sure that I would even recognize her. Where once I had looked for a smile and bouncing curls, I was now on the lookout for someone who could be anyone.

The sun fell behind the clouds, and although it was often cloaked behind the clutter of buildings, I appreciated it when I could see it. New York City was so overpopulated and cramped. The flood of commuters from outside the city on any given day made the streets swell. No matter, nothing was worse than on holiday breaks. It was impassible during Christmas.

Each year, I wound my way along Fifth Avenue to see the festive lights and window displays. Macy's happened to be my favorite. It filled me with a sense of wonder I didn't have the other 364 days of the year. The others felt pretentious, but Macy's was the type of place I could see myself shopping in one day. Saks? Not so much.

Just under the wire, I made it back to the home. "You're later than usual," Betty said.

I nodded. "I did a little shopping." I held up the bag for

her to see.

"Oh? What did you get?"

I removed the box carefully from both the bag, and the silky material in which it had been wrapped, and placed it in her open hands. "This is beautiful," she said. "Where did you get it?"

To avoid any inconsistencies or unexplainable incidents in my file, I told the truth. "I wanted to go for a longer walk, so I found a sidewalk sale down on St. Mark's."

She laughed, "We call them stoop sales in Brooklyn." She handed me back the box, which I promptly re-wrapped as quickly as possible.

"You know," I said thoughtfully, and played with the dead ends of my hair, "I've never had a stoop now that I think about it."

"So you know nothing about stoop ball."

"No offense, Betty, but I'm pretty sure no one in my generation does."

Her crow's feet crinkled as she laughed. She was an attractive woman despite her age. I guessed she must have been in her early 70s, and was surprised she was still here, but I'd heard she was her own institution in the home. She shook her head. "You kids still think you know everything. At least that doesn't change."

She was one of the only staff members who allowed us to call her by her first name. It was a nice change of pace for me. Though I was never one for such familiarity—and as much as I didn't like people calling me by my own name—it was comforting to know there was at least one person that knew it, and who in return, gave us girls the same respect.

"I don't suppose you've seen Ms. Jackson today?"

"She's probably in her usual spot, teaching."

"Or at least attempting to." We shared a knowing grin before I walked away. Though I had no real mementos or small personal items I planned to store in the box, it would eventually come in handy. I scanned the room before opening the lid. I didn't want anyone to see the secret lock and decide there were important things hidden inside. All I really had were the few leftover dollars from *Tia*'s generosity.

I should go see her. I know she would love the visit and it is the least I can do. Especially with her going so far out of her way for me. I decided I would wait a few days and give her a call to set something up. I ran my fingers over the carvings of the box, distracted. I felt like this could become another routine, much like *The House on Mango Street.*

I was delaying the inevitable. Linda was relentless, like a watch dog, constantly following up. She knew all her cases' triggers and never failed to harp on them. She was big on exposure therapy and this was the only way she could use it on me. I never liked it and so I was trying to beat her to this week's chase.

Ms. Jackson was alone, bent over a stack of papers and shaking her head. I saw that she was muttering under her breath, but I couldn't make out what she was saying. I knocked lightly on the door and waited. She looked up and waved me in. I kept my eyes lowered out of respect.

"What do you need, Ella?" She was terse, but I knew it was unlike her so I didn't take it personally. She was probably stressed out by the pile of paperwork on her desk. Half of the chalkboard was covered in rudimentary geometry. The other half was full of Spanish-to-English vocabulary translations.

"Linda asked me to come see you."

"I know. She told me you were going to stop by." Her look softened, "Eventually."

I stared at my feet. "She thinks I should consider taking the GED rather than being miserable for the rest of high school."

"Well, obviously I'm biased."

I was happy that she wasn't dumbing her vocabulary down for me. I enjoyed being spoken to like an adult. I felt like I had already been one for the majority of my life. I had seen and experienced more than many of the adults I had met, or found myself surrounded by, and certainly more so than many of the other girls here. Although we were all in a similar boat, I knew I was destined for a better life than most of them could even dream of. “Yeah, so …”

“The first step would be to take a practice exam. That will help me get a better understanding of where you are. I’m sure you’ll do fine.”

“When can I do that?” I wasn’t thrilled about it, but if this was going to be a workable option, I at least needed to give it a fair shake.

“I can administer it here. It will take a few hours, but you let me know when you’re ready and I’ll schedule it for you.”

“I’m ready.”

Ms. Jackson gave me a quizzical look, “Don’t you want to study at all, or try to prepare? You could sit in on one of my prep classes and see if there are any blind spots before you take it.”

“If it’s a practice exam, I’d rather just take it.”

“Your confidence is improving.” I smiled at the compliment. “I know you’re usually out on Saturdays, but that would probably be the best time.”

“That’s fine.”

She opened up what looked like a calendar. “How’s next weekend?”

I didn’t hesitate. “That works.” Then, “Is there anything I need to know?”

She smiled, “I thought you didn’t need to prepare.”

“I know nothing about it. Some sort of heads up would be helpful.”

“Take a seat.” She pointed to a chair, and barely took a breath before she started. “It’s in five sections—math, science, social studies, reading and writing. The scores for each section range up to 800 and you should aim for at least a 500 per section.”

“That shouldn’t be a problem. My grades have always been exceptional.”

“It’s testing for all four years. Ya know, everything you would have learned had you gone through the whole ordeal of high school.”

"Doesn't matter," I said matter-of-factly. "It doesn't end."

She tilted her head at me as I got up from the chair. "In a rush?"

"Isn't that all I needed to know?"

"You should get a grip on that confidence, kid. It could easily spiral out of control."

I knew what she was getting at, but it didn't mean I had to like it. "I'll see you next weekend." I exited the room but left the door ajar, the way I had found it. I stopped off at the cafeteria to get some dinner—what was supposed to be chicken parmesan—I presumed. It was something I had seen, but couldn't honestly say I had ever eaten. Even at the home. As usual, I sat alone. Lara's minion made her way over as I was getting up to leave. I sat back down.

"So," she said nonchalantly, "any update?"

"I really have nothing to say. I was in shock from the loss of blood and honestly, I don't even wanna do this. It's pointless. Clearly, we weren't friends."

"She was pissed."

"So was I."

She eyed me suspiciously. "What should I tell her?"

I stood up to leave, my tray in hand. "Whatever the hell you want." I turned on my heel. I was tired of this game. I was tired of being defeated. I was tired of being hurt. I was just … tired. Her mouth formed an 'o' but she had nothing to say. I left her sitting there.

I had nothing of interest to do. I thought about trying a practice GED test online but opted against it. I would rather have something strange and new, and different, to look forward to than to try cramming and overwhelming myself with doubts.

In starting to find myself, I discovered boredom. I had been used to loneliness, but being on constant alert meant I hadn't often experienced being bored. Oddly enough, even being here post-Incident, I felt safer than I had in a long time. These days, I even felt ambivalent about Lara's departure, but still found comfort in the fact that Tamara was finally gone.

I wasn't the type of person to wish harm to another, but did hope that Tamara's move to wherever she was, turned out to be as negative as possible. I mean, not anything like my mother's myriad experiences, but certainly worse than Lara's. As upset as I was, I didn't want anything bad to happen to *her*.

Lara. I hated myself. I didn't want to think about it, but I found my mind wandering there anyway, unable to keep the racing thoughts under any sort of control. On the one hand, I missed her. I missed her being here. I missed what I thought was our friendship. On the other, I felt betrayed. She felt that way too and I wasn't sure there would be a way to bridge either the gap or the emotions. I berated myself for not keeping them under control. I'd always been better than this, and wasn't sure why there had been so many changes in such a short amount of time.

"I heard you finally got around to seeing Ms. Jackson," Linda said as she scribbled notes.

"Yeah, I did. I scheduled my practice exam for Saturday. Are you happy now?"

"It doesn't matter what I think or feel. Are you?"

I did *not* like being challenged, but I didn't have a witty reply at hand. "I suppose."

"I heard you're just going to blindly take the practice exam."

"Do you really think it's necessary for me to study?"

"Only 70% of people pass it on their first try."

"Well then, I'll just have to make sure I'm in that 70%."

Linda had some other random topics on her agenda. Mostly my responses were limited to one word answers. Neither of us had anything of true importance to discuss. The only real takeaway I had was that if I was going to succeed at this GED thing, I should probably start thinking about a transition plan.

I had the option to stay until six months past my eighteenth birthday, but I wanted to be out of there as soon as possible. I don't know anyone who would choose this over the ability to be on their own. We all had our crosses to bear, which is why we ended up here in the first place, but I don't think any of us wanted to stay any longer than we needed to.

On Saturday morning, I arrived a few minutes early to see Ms. Jackson. "I'm as ready as I'm gonna be. When can we start?"

"Well, aren't you the chipper one this morning?"

"I had some coffee. I mean, it's not Bustelo or anything."

She laughed. "I could ask Betty to bring you some, if you wanted." I hadn't had it since the last time I visited *Tia*'s apartment. I could get it at any of the *bodegas* in the neighborhood, but why should I bother if she was willing to bring some in for me? "Let's use it as an incentive."

"That'll be easy."

She shook her head at what I assumed was in response to my cockiness, and then handed me a thick booklet and a standard bubble response form. I filled in my personal information on the top of the page. I was precise. Answers could be scored incorrectly if you weren't neat. "And, go," she said, seemingly out of nowhere.

I slid my pencil through the side of the booklet to open it and was excited to find that the first section was science. I was hoping to get the more challenging sections out of the way first. My reading and writing skills didn't need work and I could do that sort of stuff with my eyes closed, and even half brain-dead after what I knew would be a long exam.

There were a lot of questions, but I didn't need to take much time to answer them. *How would you extract table salt that had been dissolved in water? Near water, which is better: sandy or clay soil?* I moved through the sections so quickly that, despite it having precise start and end times, I used the space between for small breaks. Regardless, Ms. Jackson warned me that this would be a seven hour exam and so I needed those breaks to get up and walk around. I felt like my back was seizing from sitting for so long during each section.

Hours later, before the essay began, Betty showed up with a giant cup of Bustelo. She carried a small bag with cream and sugar in it. "I didn't know how you took it."

I smiled widely. "You're the best, Betty. Thanks!"

I sharpened my pencil and opened the blue-covered book with the wide childish lined paper. Without pause, I expounded on my definition of success. It was the better of the two options. I had no experience with good parents, so all my ideas would be theoretical at best, and I wanted to have a sound argument full of facts.

I took sips of coffee while writing, using the time to contemplate my next move. *Words are power*, I reminded myself. *Use the strongest ones you can.*

"It is not talent or luck, or fate, that determines success," I wrote. "It is dedication and hard work. Without one, you cannot have the other. Without both, you cannot be successful."

I knew that wasn't true. I had seen plenty of examples of people that were—by all societal measures—successful, but who neither had dedication nor did hard work. They sat in their miserable apartments, surrounded by dirty dishes and crying babies, and scales. They measured out poison and sold it in bags to the people they called friends. They had money, and all the things the magazines say you are supposed to want. But they chose to live in squalor, wasting their money on things that would only be stolen and re-sold.

In the end, I knew, no one reading these essays was looking for truth. They were simply looking for the correct formulaic approach and the ability to defend your own opinion. And so, I chose to take the positive and upbeat Puritan stance. One that I believed not many people had anymore.

My pencil fit neatly into the groove at the top of the desk while the steam still rose from my coffee.

Chapter 10

"It won't take long to score. Do you want to wait?"

"Why don't you just give the results to Linda? I'm sure she'll be excited about it."

"And you?"

I shrugged. "Thanks for taking the time to do this for me today." Confident or not, I was slightly worried. I wanted to do well, and didn't want there to be any doubt creeping in. I wanted to know, fully know and believe, that I was capable of this. Capable of success. Capable of moving on and putting all of this behind me. Capable of being self-sufficient. Capable of needing no one.

I hadn't needed anyone up to this point and didn't intend to ever need someone. I was broken and incomplete, and never truly comfortable in my own skin, but I was me. I wish I could say that at least I knew myself, but that was a level of arrogance even I didn't have. Truth be told, I wasn't sure that very many people knew who they were anyway, so at least I was in the majority.

After taking the exam, I found school even less challenging. It didn't help that the school year was winding down, and other than finals, there was no motivation on my part to complete anything. My reprieve had been getting back to Honors English.

I sat through my classes while imagining what it would be like to finally be free of all this. Where I had once used school as a reprieve, I now used it to waste time. I never had much in the way of talent when it came to art, but I spent much of my time doodling in the margins of my notebook, rather than answering questions when I was called upon.

The shift was noticeable, not just to me, but to those around me. I hadn't gotten close to a single person in school. I couldn't tell you anyone's name and I'm certain no one could tell you mine. I carried my bag like a mule, weighed down by books and notes, and highlighters and pens. I didn't bother to use my locker onsite. What was the point? I could be gone at any minute.

Despite my growing confidence and my attitude becoming more prevalent in the home, and with those around me, I was still the quiet and shy girl at school. I walked the halls with my head down and my bag placed securely around both shoulders.

I was never one to draw attention to myself, so in this regard I was no different. But it had become apparent, even to my most apathetic teachers, that something wasn't right with me. I had been pulling back and withdrawing into myself ever since The Incident. They had a sense of what had happened, but no details. Those were still relatively confidential. Obviously, my guidance counselor knew, but for the most part, I felt sure my teachers didn't.

Although I wasn't known for raising my hand in class, when I was called on I always had the correct response. These days, I didn't even hear my name being called. I was so immersed in my own thoughts and my doodles, as pathetic as they were, that when a teacher asked me a question, it usually resulted in them having to call my name so often they finally gave up and moved on.

No one approached me about this. Not my guidance counselor—whose name I didn't even know—nor Linda. Perhaps I should have let Ms. Jackson score my exam immediately and get the results. At this point, I wasn't going to back down though. Walking in and asking for them would be akin to admitting defeat. And I'd done that enough.

Tuesday melted into Wednesday, which blurred into Thursday. The only reason I cared at this point was because my anxiety was starting to take over, and I knew I would be meeting with Linda. It wouldn't be much longer until I knew how I had done on the exam. I was still sure I had done well, but by the same token, I was also afraid of what that meant.

If I could complete the GED exam, it would rush all of the timelines I had always kept inside my head. I never wrote such things down anywhere. I wouldn't want them found. They are mine, and so I keep them safe. Success would mean I'd need to take my SAT and figure out financial aid for school. I hadn't even given much thought to where I would want to go to college. I just knew that I wanted to go.

I also knew that I didn't want to go far. As much as certain places and smells reminded me of The Baruch Houses, and as much as I didn't want to be downtown, I also didn't want to leave New York City. It was familiar and all I had known. I'd always assumed I would go to community college, and not engage in all the dormitory living and parties. They weren't my speed, and I wouldn't fit in anyway. Besides, I had no interest.

I hadn't even given much thought to what I wanted to major in. I suppose there was just an unconscious presumption that I would go into psychology or social work. However, given how many social workers I now found myself interacting with, I realized it was something I didn't want to do as a career. I felt strongly that my experiences would give me the upper hand in helping other people get through tough times, but I also knew that dealing with apathetic, directionless children wasn't something I would find fulfilling.

"You look like you have a lot on your mind," Linda said, beaming.

"I do, actually." I sat down in the chair and noticed that the sides had even more space than usual. I supposed the weight was continuing to come off. I don't look at myself directly anymore—not in full-length mirrors or other reflections, anyway—so I wouldn't have known other than in relation to the way my clothes fit.

"I have news for you."

"I know you do." I wrung my hands together nervously, while resting my elbows on my knees.

"You don't need to be nervous. You did great."

I breathed a heavy sigh of relief. "How great?"

She smiled, "Really great, actually." She flipped some pages in what had become a ridiculously large file. My name was written neatly—if not too largely—in block letters across the top of the tab. SANTIA, ELLA. There were colored tabs and dividers, and the contents of my life were two-hole punched and housed in that monstrosity. "You scored 450 in math, 475 in science, 600 in social studies, and 750 on both the reading and writing portion. You have a lot to be proud of here."

I sat in stunned silence. I knew I'd do better on the reading and essay portions of the exam, but I didn't expect to be so close to Ms. Jackson's target scores for the other areas, let alone higher in social studies. For someone who didn't care too much about what was going on in the world around them, I'd done all right for myself.

"Don't you have anything to say, Ella? You did a great job."

"I'm overwhelmed, that's all." My teeth gripped the right corner of my mouth.

"It doesn't mean you need to make a decision right away." She paused. "There is one more thing."

I felt the muscles in my jaw tighten. "Yeah?"

"You did extraordinarily well, but I think we all had high expectations for you, and a lot of confidence that you would knock this out of the park. Ms. Jackson would feel more comfortable with your math score if it were closer to 500. The minimum for any given category is 410 and you need to pass all of the parts to obtain the certificate. She felt it was a little too close for comfort."

"What does that actually mean for me, then?"

"You're far more advanced than the other girls, so she's offered to tutor you one on one to help you get the score up."

"That's probably for the best." I was surprised to say it, given how I had started to taste the reality of finally leaving and getting out on my own, but I wanted to make sure there were no doubts. I didn't want this gnawing feeling again. Perhaps I had been overconfident. While I clearly hadn't failed, I still had so much to think about.

"You look like you have a lot on your mind." Linda said again, this time without the brilliant smile.

Of course I did. "Shouldn't I?"

"Do you feel like talking about it?"

No, I didn't feel like talking about it, but I knew I was going to have to start at some point, so I might as well. Besides, I didn't know anything about what my next steps should be. College? Living on my own? These were truly frightening realities for me—no matter how much of a dream they had always been.

"Honestly," I started, "I'm not sure what to do with myself. I want out. I want out as soon as possible, but the thought of it scares me." This was perhaps as honest as I had ever been with her.

She nodded slowly, and the faint smile passing her lips looked as though she was trying to pull it in. "It's a big deal, Ella. There's a lot to consider. What do you think you want to do next?"

"College," I paused, "obviously."

"I think that's a reasonable goal. What do you need to do to get there?"

"I need this damn GED for starters. Then I guess I'll have to start worrying about taking my SAT."

"By doing this right now, so close together, you're killing two birds with one stone. The GED is measuring whether or not you know enough to graduate high school. The SAT is a measure of how well you may do in college. The closer together you take them, the better I think you'll do.

I knew most of that and had already been thinking that's what I would end up doing. If I only had eighteen more months to go, I wanted to move fast. "Let's say," I started, "hypothetically, of course, that I pass the GED in the next few months and the SAT shortly afterwards. Then what?"

"Then you start applying to colleges and for financial aid."

"And what if I'm able to start college before I technically need to leave here?"

"Then you can still stay until that six month mark."

"And then what? I'm just on my own?"

She sighed, "Of course not, Ella. There's always a transition."

There was always a transition. There was a transition from one hellhole to another, then on to another. And now, to have my dreams within reach, it felt as though once my hands touched them, they would fall apart as well. As Chinua Achebe so accurately wrote, "Things falls apart." For me, they so often do.

I realized I was still chewing my lip, and then I looked at the clock. "There's a half hour, Linda. Time flies."

"Shit!" she exclaimed. This was an outburst I had never seen from her. I had never heard her curse or be anything other than calm and level-headed at all times. If I had to say I admired anything about her, even with all the stuff I had put her through, it was those qualities I appreciated most. "I have to be at another appointment. Next week, then?" She was already gathering up her files.

"Thanks, Linda. Really, thank you." I wanted to give her a hug. I hardly ever felt drawn to someone in that way, but I wanted to hug her and thank her tremendously. I wanted to laugh. Most of all, I wanted to laugh. It felt like it had been forever since I'd had a reason to do so. She gathered her things quickly and gave me a wave as I walked out the door.

I couldn't imagine what semblance of a life she had. She wasn't the only case worker here, and in fact, she wasn't even based here. She was a state employee. I had no idea what her case load was, but she always found time for me. If she put in this much time with me, I couldn't imagine how much she had for herself.

I never saw a wedding ring on her hand, and wondered if she had ever been married, or if she'd decided she was just too busy for such things. I pictured what could only be considered a stereotypical story of a single woman in New York City. She liked coffee. She had cats. So many cats that she worried about who would care for them all if anything happened to her.

I knew this was all a lie. I'd never seen a pet hair or piece of dander on her. Ever. She was always neat, even in this rare glimpse of being frazzled. Sometimes a wisp of hair would be out of place, and in her quick but nonchalant way, she would smooth it back to where it was supposed to be.

I rapped on the door jamb to Ms. Jackson's room. She had two other girls with her, but she waved me in without looking up. She was seated on the edge of her desk. The girls sat at desks in the front row and it didn't look like they were taking notes. Ms. Jackson's arms were crossed over her chest and she looked unhappy. Then again, she rarely—if ever—smiled.

One of the girls slid down low in her chair and I heard her suck her teeth. "That's exactly what I'm talking about, girl. You ain't got no use for nothin'. You think the world owe you somethin'? Well, it don't, and the sooner you realize that, the better off you'll be." The other girl just sat there with a look of disrespectful disregard on her face. "You two better get yo'selves together and start takin' this seriously, or you're gonna end up right where you started. You hear me?"

Neither of them said a word. Ms. Jackson's eyes looked like they could burn holes through the girls' foreheads. "Go on," she said, "Go study or somethin'." They took their sweet time and made a big show of leaving the room, but eventually they did.

Once they'd gone, she waved me over. "And how are you, Ella?" Her entire demeanor had changed in the span of a few seconds.

"I'm well, thanks. Linda said –"

She cut me off, "Yeah, I wanted to see you. We should find some time to work together."

"I have meetings with Linda on Thursday, and then Saturdays I try to get out of here for a little while. I know you run classes just about every day of the week, so," I shrugged, "it really just depends on you."

"Actually, it depends on you. Are you really going to work or are you going to waste my time like all of the other girls here?"

I felt confused. "Of course I'm going to work. I want to get out of here. I have always had goals." I was also starting to get angry. "I'm nothing like those girls!" I pointed towards the door. Towards thin air.

Ms. Jackson smiled. "Good. I just wanted to make sure."

She shifted off the edge of her desk and walked around to the other side. She bent down over what looked like a packed calendar and said, "I can see you for an hour on Tuesdays, or two hours on Wednesdays. Which do you want?"

"How many sessions do you think we'll need?"

"That depends on how hard you work. Let's start with six and see how that goes."

I didn't hesitate. "Wednesdays it is." She smiled, scrawled my name into what looked like the only open block of time, and flipped through the next few pages of weeks and added my name to those as well.

"That's all," she said, looking up only briefly. "I'll see you Wednesday. Be here at 4:00."

"Do I need to … bring anything, or can I prepare anything before next week?"

She put her pencil down and looked at me directly for what felt like the first time ever. "You're the first person to ever ask me that," she said gently. "Bring your current math textbook, your notebook and your willingness to work hard. That's all I ask. Don't waste my time," she paused. "You might want to review some of your work from Algebra 2 before you come in. That's where you were struggling on the test."

"That's fair," I said. "Math hasn't been going well for me this year."

"You're good enough," a flash of sincerity washed across her face. "I want to make you better than good enough."

I smiled but didn't say anything else. I didn't wave. I didn't make any grand exit. I simply turned around and walked out the door. I wasn't going to enjoy this process, but if anyone could help me get through it, it would be Ms. Jackson. She was tough as nails, and I sometimes wondered how the staff became involved in this work. I suspected that the menial staff jobs were held by girls that had failed in some monstrous way when they left the home, but I also knew such thoughts were judgmental and cruel. I had no idea where these women came from, and I wouldn't want someone judging me in the same way.

I need to work on that, I thought to myself. *This ego is getting out of control.*

Back in my room, I thought about everything that had happened in such a short amount of time. The Incident. The destruction of my friendship with Lara. School. This GED exam. College. Preparing to be a full-blown member of society. I was excited and terrified at the same time. Nostalgic while trying to remain aloof.

I'd developed a lack of congruence and didn't know how to get it back. Or if it would ever come back. I had always lived by a set of principles, and my inward thoughts and outward actions had matched for as long as I could remember. That wasn't the case now. Suddenly, I found myself thinking the things I hated other people saying. While I rarely, if ever, said them myself, the fact that I was even thinking them disturbed me.

Where I had always felt clumsy, I had become more agile. With my body, yes, but also with my personality. It had become more fluid, and like snow that packs to ice which melts to water and re-freezes, I wasn't entirely sure where my personality was headed. I had always believed personalities were static, but perhaps this wasn't true at all. I was sure I wasn't the exception. That notion would have been truly grandiose. No, I was just a hormonal teenager trying to find her way. That was the only logical conclusion I could come to.

It wasn't until I passed the panes of glass at the staff office that I realized my lower lip was bleeding. I pressed my finger to it and felt the stickiness. I licked my lip and tasted the bitter, metallic fluid on my tongue. This was nothing new to me. I stopped off at the bathroom to wash my hands, and then dug Chapstick out of my locker when I was back in my room. I started to feel human again.

By the time Saturday rolled around, the weather was unseasonably warm. I had become very self-conscious of the scar on my arm, and so always looked for a way to wear long sleeves. I decided that the best thing to do was to just suck it up and wear a t-shirt, since I didn't have very many options available. I paired them with jeans, which were now loose, and my *chancletas*. I had no other alternative except boots, which I only used in winter.

"*Hola*?"

"*Hola, Tia*," I said into the phone. "*Como estas*?"

"*Bueno, bueno!* Are you going to come by today?"

"I was thinking about it. You're going into work late, right?"

"*Si, mijita*. Not until tonight. Come any time."

I seriously debated whether or not to stick to my routine. I carefully weighed the outcomes. If I found Lara, there was a chance she wouldn't speak to me. Or worse, still wouldn't believe me. Or perhaps even worse than that, wouldn't care. If I didn't find her, it would haunt me all week, just like it has every week since I first saw her after The Incident.

I decided to just go to *Tia*'s and see if being there made things any less awkward. I still had a few dollars left, but was unsure what I would do with the money. I packed up the box I'd purchased the previous weekend. I wanted to show it to *Tia*. I knew that she, of all people, would understand and appreciate it. I placed the remaining singles in my back pocket, right next to my MetroCard, and put the box back into the paper bag.

"The usual, Ella?" one of the staff members asked as I was signing out.

"Actually, no. I'm going to see my aunt today." She gave me a quizzical look. "I just called her."

She sucked her teeth, but said nothing else as I signed the book. If it felt like I was signing my life away every time I left, then it felt even more oppressive every time I came back. I felt shuffled between one institution and the next. The home, the school, the home, the school. It was a repetitive and predictable schedule. The High Line had, for over a year, been my escape. Now, it had just become a reminder of something I wished I could forget.

Even though *Tia* only lived a few blocks from The Baruch Houses—in fact, I had passed her apartment building the weekend before—I felt no anxiety going there. I wasn't worried about running into people I knew—not even Malda. Everything about *Tia* had become the only safe haven I had known. Her home was tranquil, and she was even-keeled. She didn't raise her voice and when she disapproved of something, it was in relative but uncomfortable silence.

Don't get me wrong, she had a fiery and feisty spirit. When I was much younger, she had taken me shopping for a pair of shoes. A man called something out to her. I was too young to understand, but it was clearly inappropriate. The next thing I knew, *Tia* was only inches from his face and through clenched teeth told him to never speak to a woman like that again, especially in front of a child.

That was a rare occasion, however. Much of the time she seemed genuinely at peace. Her home was a sanctuary from the outside world. Though you could hear the sounds of the neighborhood outside her open window, the box fan helped turn it into white noise. She was one for simplicity, so her home wasn't cluttered. She kept herself unencumbered by limiting how many things she owned. I'd never known her to be particularly sentimental, at least not in terms of keeping items of any value.

As is common in many parts of the city, an older man sold flowers from a white bucket on a corner. He had several different kinds: single roses wrapped with greenery and baby's breath, half dozen and dozen roses, mixed varieties in both subtle and bold hues. I decided that the best option for *Tia* was a small mixed bouquet in more natural tones.

The man handed me the flowers, and the thin plastic crinkled noisily in the crook of my arm. I thought about placing them in the paper bag, but decided against it. The tips of the flowers had been in the bucket of water, and I didn't want the brown paper bag to get destroyed. Instead, I carried them the way I had seen in movies; as though I had just won an award. All I was missing was said award, the straight pearly whites, the controlled and practiced wave, and something glittery. In short, I was missing everything.

"*Gracias, señor*," I said politely as I walked away.

I hadn't felt hungry when I left the home, but by the time I knocked at *Tia*'s door, I was famished. The myriad smells I had encountered since arriving on the Lower East Side became overwhelming and now I wanted to eat everything.

On the second knock, I heard her removing the chains from the door, and before I could try for a third, her arms were around me in a tight hug. "*Mijita*! Come in! Come in!"

I went through the door and closed it behind me. I let my fingers run across the brass chains as I slid them back across the door. I'd forgotten what it was like to have this sort of privacy. Perhaps I never really knew at all, since I'd had no such thing on the door to my room at Malda's. "Whatever you're cooking smells *rico*!" I shouted from the foyer.

I heard her laugh—like the lilt of a bygone era—from the kitchen. I was sure she'd seen the flowers but, because she wasn't at all presumptuous, she wouldn't think they were for her. I placed the paper bag on the table and walked over to the stove. Tia wore an apron over a sleeveless dress, and held a thick wooden spoon in her hand. It looked like she had been making *sancocho* for days.

"How did you know?"

She laughed, "Oh *mijita*, it's all about you. I always know when you're coming back. *Usted es una paloma*." She called me a pigeon. Anyone else would have been insulted by this, but I knew she was referencing a homing pigeon, even if she didn't know the exact word to say. She wasn't comparing me to the worn, grey and white birds that seemed so out of place in the city.

I went over to the stove and wrapped my arms around her waist. "*Para usted*," I said. For you. I handed her the flowers and she appeared to be delighted. She hemmed and hawed at first, but then fawned over me as she found a vase to put them in.

"They're beautiful! You didn't have to. ...Why are you spending your money like this?" A barrage of questions and admonitions flew from her lips. I just smiled and didn't answer any of them. There would be no point. She wouldn't be so ungracious as to turn them away, but she also wanted to make it clear that they weren't expected, and of course, that I should be following her advice and not frivolously spending my money.

"I know I just saw you last weekend," she said. "But I was hoping you would come by today. Look, I willed it. I knew if I made *sancocho*, you would find your way here. *Paloma*."

I couldn't help but laugh. She and I had always been on the same page. We both recognized that last weekend was uncomfortable and awkward, and we both wanted to resolve that. In the space of her kitchen, we were transformed. It was as if last weekend had never happened. It was like so many things had never happened.

It was as though I hadn't been kicked down those stairs. Hadn't fled. Hadn't gone to foster care, or been put in a group home. As though I hadn't been torn from wrist to elbow. We were cohesive—*Tia* and I—and the rest of it fell away like so many dandelion wishes.

It smelled like she had been cooking all day. Knowing her, she probably had. *Sancocho* is one of those dishes that needs to sit on a low temperature to draw all its wonder out of the bones of the beasts within. Too little time, and you are left with a flavorless concoction that is the equivalent of a can of Campbell's chicken soup, versus taking the time to make it from scratch. There is no such thing as too much time when it comes to making my favorite dish.

"So what's new with you?" Tia asked as she gathered plates and utensils. Her voice was slightly raised over the sound of the clinking.

"Let me help you set the table."

"No, *mijita*, no. You relax."

I smiled. "And when does anyone ever get to say the same to you?"

"Oh, they say it. I just don't listen." We both laughed loudly. It was so on point. She was such a caregiver to everyone else, and sometimes I thought people—myself included—took advantage of her kindness. It was from her, however, that I learned that kindness didn't equate to weakness.

"I've had a lot of thinking to do lately."

Without looking at me, she said, "Did you come to any answers?"

I looked down at my folded hands on the table. "Some, maybe."

"Well, you have to do what is best for you, *mija*. That's what I've always told you."

"I'm just very confused."

"You? Confused? When are you ever confused?"

I smirked and tilted my head towards her, "I have my moments, *Tia*."

She finally stopped and sat across from me at the table. Instead, she folded napkins and placed them in front of the service she'd already laid out. I hadn't even noticed until now, that she'd already turned off the heat of the stove and was letting the *sancocho* steep for a little while before we would eat. The empty bowl in front of me made my stomach growl louder than I anticipated.

"You're hungry! Here, let me get you something while we wait for that to finish." She brought out some rolls and butter, and even though I took one, I went easy on the butter. "*Estás fantástica*, by the way. You must be working so hard."

I had a bit of bread in my mouth but it didn't stop me from answering, "Not really. I just haven't felt like eating, and I've been walking around a lot more."

"You have always been pretty, *mija*, but you're starting to really bloom now." I smiled at the compliment. "So why are you confused?"

"I have an opportunity to get a high school diploma without having to finish the rest of the time I have left."

"Oh yes," she scratched at her temple, deep in thought. "One of the girls at work has that. She took a test and they gave her the diploma."

"Exactly." I paused for a moment. "I took the practice test and I did very well."

"Of course you did. That's no surprise to me. You're very

smart, *mija*."

"Thank you." I took another bite of bread and waited until I had swallowed it before speaking again. "They want me to improve my math score a little bit, but I did pass the exam. I'm just worried. If I take this test and pass, I'll have to go to college sooner and move out of the home. I don't know what I'll do."

"Did you talk to Ms. Santiago?"

It had been so long since I had heard anyone call her by such a formal name. She had simply become Linda to me. "Yes."

"And?"

"She supports it. She thinks I should do it and get some college experience before I move out of the home."

"Is that what you want to do?"

"I'm not sure."

"Okay," she unfolded her hands and placed them face down on the table in front of her, at either side of her fork and knife. "Let me put it this way," she spoke slowly. "How do you get the most benefit from *las oportunidades* in front of you?"

I knew exactly what she was asking. How was I going to make the most out of the options in front of me? How was I going to be the familial anomaly of my generation that *Tia* had become of her own? I nodded, slowly, taking it in. "I will have to take out a student loan. I can't afford college." She kept her head tilted and looked at me kindly. "If I take the exam soon, I can have my high school diploma and my college entrance exams done before the summer. If I work hard, I can get into college as soon as the winter term. I have to allow enough time for financial aid decisions."

"Have you thought about what you want to do?"

The million dollar question. "I have some ideas."

"Where are you looking?"

"I haven't been. I want to stay here though, so it will probably just be a city university."

"They have many schools, *mija*."

This was true. There were at least twenty different branches of the university that I had heard of. "I'm thinking either psychology or criminal justice."

She tilted her head the other way before rising from the table and taking our bowls with her. I heard the ladle scrape along the bottom of the pot before she spoke again. "What would you do in criminal justice? *La policía*?"

"I was thinking maybe law school, or just working in the courts." I wouldn't even consider joining the police force as a real option.

"Do you think that would make you happy?"

I honestly didn't know. "Probably not."

"*Es tu vida*, you have to be happy with your decisions."

I knew it was my life. I knew I was going to bear the brunt of the consequences of my choices. I wasn't convinced that anyone truly knew what they wanted to do at this point in their life. I certainly didn't. Most of the people I'd been surrounded by were the kind that didn't seem to care about such things. More importantly, they didn't seem to want anything to change. I wasn't that person. I could find a way to change things if I was unhappy. The fact that I'd left Susan's was proof of this. The group home had its faults, but nothing in life is perfect.

"The only thing I know is that I don't want to be a social worker. I don't envy them."

We shared a laugh as she brought the now-full bowls back to the table. I let the scent waft into my nose. I remembered when I wouldn't have this moment to myself. When I would have to eat as much as I could, as fast as I could, lest I go hungry. I remembered what it felt like to never truly feel full. She eyed me, "*Comer*," she said. Eat.

I took my first bite, savoring the broth and the chunk of potato I had scooped onto my spoon. I felt the potato give way and I enjoyed the texture. This was such a different experience now. I wasn't used to home cooked meals. I was unused to anything that wasn't served in compartmentalized trays. *When I live on my own, I will not eat microwaved dinners*, I promised myself.

We ate in silence. I chewed slowly and hoped Tia wouldn't

think I wasn't enjoying the meal—that couldn't have been further from the truth. I wasn't sure how the weight was coming off, really, but whatever I was doing seemed to work. The only thing—other than walking—that had been helping was to eat slower and to leave food on my plate. I knew that wouldn't be an option here, as leaving food behind was not only an insult, it was wasteful. We had grown up in such a way that wastefulness was perhaps the most deadly sin.

When I was done, I took my plate to the sink. Tia had already packed up the food and washed the dishes. She knew not to offer me any to take back to the home. It would have been taken away before I could get to it. None of us were supposed to be above the others, but the truth is that there is an alpha no matter where you go. I hadn't been involved enough since The Incident, but if one hadn't exhibited dominance by now, there would be a new Tamara soon enough.

"What's in the bag there?" She pointed at the brown bag I'd hung on the back of the seat.

"Oh yeah. I wanted to show this to you." I removed the bag from the chair, and as I unwrapped the box from the material, I continued. "After we met last weekend, I took a walk down to St. Mark's Place. They were having a sidewalk sale and this older Asian woman had this box for sale. Take a look."

I placed it in her hands and watched the familiar movements along the carvings. I had spent so much time turning it over blindly, that I felt like I knew every crevice. *Tia* was far more 'me' than Malda, so much so that even our mannerisms were the same. Her fingers dawdled over the same spots mine did. She made a circular motion over the tip of the elephant trunk.

She placed it down on the table in front of her and smiled. "*Es muy bonito*," she said. "How does it work?" I reached across the table and showed her the secret lock and how to open it. Then I slid it back across the table to her. Her eyes sparkled when she found the latch and moved the piece to the right. Despite the box being empty, I could imagine that in her own mind, she was thinking about how beautiful anything would look against the velvet.

"What will you keep in it?"

I shrugged. "I have nothing. But I saw it and thought that if I had something I wanted kept safe, I'd put it in here."

She didn't hesitate. "I have something."

"*Tia*, no. Please. I wasn't showing this to you to get something."

"*Calmarte*." Calm yourself. She disappeared from the room before I could say anything else. I rested my head on my folded arms on top of the table. The only sounds in the room were the box fan and some neighborhood kids arguing over something. I couldn't make out what it was about.

After what felt like eons, she emerged from her room with a closed fist. "I have no nice way to give this to you. I … I've been keeping it in a drawer. I never wear them, but I was always saving it for you." She stretched her arm across the table and turned her fist palm-side up. When her fingers uncurled, they revealed a stunning pair of earrings.

"This is silver, not white gold," she started. It sounded like an apology, which was completely unfounded. "This," she said, as she turned them so I could have a better look, "is sea glass." My eyes fell on the shimmering aqua bead inside the silver filigree.

"*Tia*, I don't know what to say. I can't accept this. It's too much."

"You have to take them, *mijita*. They were *Abuela*'s, and I don't want them going to anyone else. Take them." She took my hand in her own and placed them in my palm.

"May I try them on?"

"Of course." Then, more cautiously, "But, I think you should put them away before you leave."

"Do you think they'll be safe in here, at the home?"

"The way you take care of things? If I didn't think they'd be safe, I wouldn't have given them to you yet."

I smiled and went into the bathroom to use the mirror. The earrings were small—only an inch or so long. They sparkled in the sunlight that came through the window. I moved my face from side to side, slowly, so I could take them in from as many angles as possible. With each movement, the color and shape of the sea glass seemed to change.

I decided to leave them in so that *Tia* could see them as well. "*Mijita*," she paused, "those were made for ycu to wear." There was no containing the happiness I felt at hearing that.

Something. Anything. Mine. At long last.

Chapter 11

The next six weeks seemed to fly by. My tutoring sessions with Ms. Jackson greatly improved my mathematical abilities, and my confidence in making this decision grew. The teacher didn't think I needed the full six weeks of sessions, but I decided it would be best to continue so that I had more of a buffer in the score.

I finished my junior year, and as usual, I'd done extraordinarily well. Despite the depressive state I had been in for most of the last year, I still managed to find a way to succeed when it came to my education. Ms. Jackson found the closest GED testing center and scheduled me for a few weeks after our sessions ended. I would have the opportunity to take the exam early enough in summer that, once I received my score, I would still theoretically have plenty of time to apply to colleges.

I had already been researching them. Sometimes, when I signed out on weekends, I was honest about my whereabouts. I was visiting colleges. They were informal visits. I never called to schedule a tour or meet with their admissions offices. I just wanted to get a sense of the campuses and perhaps even the other students.

I narrowed down my choice to Hunter College. This surprised me as much as it might anyone else. I could have easily opted for City College—a much closer commute from the home. But I wasn't planning on staying there. What better way to live your dream than to escape from the nightmare of your actual existence? That is, in large part, what drew me to that particular college. I felt more willing to sacrifice my time commuting to Lenox Hill on the East Side, than to continue to surround myself with the lethargy and despair I saw around me at every turn.

My interest in psychology continued to grow, and I expected to apply to their psychology program. I gave up on the idea of criminal justice. I had never truly considered social work. I watched the case loads expand, the girls become more detached, and the workers themselves become more bitter the longer they stayed in their careers.

"How do you feel about the test coming up?" Excitement was evident in Ms. Jackson's voice.

"Confident. I couldn't have done this without you. I'm sorry I wasn't more active in the time I've been here. I probably missed out on a lot."

"You're going to take away what you put into it, Ella. I just hope it's enough."

Ms. Jackson, despite it not being in her nature to be terribly encouraging, took me under her wing in those weeks leading up to the exam. I wouldn't say we became close, or even familiar, but I did notice and appreciate the shift in her attitude towards me. I supposed she had become used to, and jaded by, the girls that attended her classes. Most weren't motivated to do the work, and as she aptly pointed out, you only get out what you put in.

The night before the exam, I found sleep elusive. I was more charged than anything else. There was a sense of fear, but that was a comfortable emotion for me. Enthusiasm, well … that was different. The cloud of depression felt as though it had lifted.

My weight had become more stable, and I finally worked up the nerve to step on a scale. I estimated that I had lost forty pounds in the last year, and was down to a size 14. I looked better than I ever had, and had become more used to this body. I was still technically overweight, but I wasn't particularly interested in losing more. The shape that emerged resembled Yvette's. I'd lost enough weight to feel confident that walking back through the Lower East Side, I would be practically unrecognizable to the people who were supposed to know me the best.

While I had been easily discarded and comfortable in the shadows, I was starting to come out of my proverbial cocoon. I still had no interest when it came to dating, though I was certainly attracting more attention. I felt unsure how to handle myself, and so I mostly withdrew, kept my head down, and didn't respond. It never failed to make me smile, though I tried my best not to show it.

The morning of the exam—sleep deprived and too queasy to eat—I made my way to the high school to get this out of the way. I was told that most of my score would be available the following Monday, but that the essay portion would take longer to grade. Both Ms. Jackson and Linda encouraged me to get the score as soon as possible since they knew I would have no trouble passing the essay portion of the exam. For some unknown reason, I wanted to drag it out a little longer and expressed to them that I wasn't going to check the score until it was complete. Besides, a one week delay wouldn't mean anything significant. I still needed to take my SAT exam as well.

I grabbed a Bustelo from the nearest *bodega* on my way to the school. We couldn't bring any food or beverages into the exam room. Ms. Jackson made sure to adequately prepare me for the entire experience. She warned me that even if I finished early, I couldn't leave the room, and would have to wait for the designated breaks. Against her advice, I decided to sit for the entire exam in one day. That would be intense. A seven hour ordeal seemed worth it to me in any case, because I just wanted to get it over with.

In an attempt to savor every sip, and every moment, before what I imagined would be the torture of the day, I loitered in the hallways as long as possible. I watched them crowd, teeming with people of all ages. I was surprised by the number of people that looked to be significantly older. Then again, in this neighborhood, the fact that they were here at all was impressive.

They opened the doors to the cafeteria at precisely 7:30 AM. I could tell this test was going to be anything other than cozy. The school had no air conditioning in summer, but I was prepared for that. I'd thrown on leggings, and a tank top (for the first time in my life), and headed out the door in strappy sandals. The donations as of late had been improving and I was finally at a point where I could barter with the other girls on occasion.

"The test will begin in exactly thirty minutes," the man in the button down shirt droned in a dry monotone. "I will give you the full instructions prior to passing out the materials. Understand that the tests are rotated, so wandering eyes will find themselves with a failing score." I stopped listening. It wouldn't be applicable to me and I didn't need the warning, though I assumed many in the room did.

I dove into the test as soon as it began. It started with math, which excited me because, after all the work with Ms. Jackson, I knew it would be a breeze. I was also happy that I would get my least favorite subjects out of the way in the earlier part of the day, while the coffee was still coursing through my veins.

We didn't get breaks the way that Ms. Jackson had allowed. I suppose this was just the difference in our settings and the importance of the exams. A practice run was absolutely nothing like the real thing, and I don't think anyone—present company included—expected it to be. I reviewed my notes and began to doodle in the margins of the scrap booklet out of pure and utter boredom. By the time we got a break, my back hurt from being arched over the table scribbling away.

Nobody in the broad and dull room looked familiar to me. I suspected that none of the other girls in the group home were ready for the exam. Despite there being accommodations for disabilities, mental disorders and language barriers, I was still surprised by the lack of participation by the girls. I supposed the same could be said for me, though.

I relished in the break and didn't bother to worry myself about reviewing my notes prior to the next section. Some people looked completely ragged, frantically poring over their study materials to see if they had the correct calculations for the math portion, or cramming what looked to be another subject in an effort to glean some last minute knowledge. "Last in, first out," Ms. Jackson had told me. I wasn't surprised by what I saw. She'd said that a solid breakfast and a positive attitude would get me further than trying to overload my brain with repetitive information I'd already memorized.

The rest of the day unwound without incident. No one walked out of the exam, which I was warned could happen. Some folks couldn't take the long day or the pressure, no matter how prepared they believed themselves to be. I found that sad, given how much work it took to get here, especially for the older ones who seemed to have so much more riding on this.

These days, it seemed impossible to get even a menial job without a college degree. I couldn't imagine the type of work they would have to be doing without even a high school diploma. Whatever it was couldn't have been remotely enjoyable, satisfying or financially rewarding. I had never wanted that life for myself.

As expected, the essay was the easiest part for me. Rather than answering the most personal of questions, I opted to take a stance on euthanasia. I felt I had a unique perspective. I didn't think people should suffer unnecessarily—at least not most people—and that the decision to end one's life should be allowed. It wasn't easily defensible, and there was still a lot of controversy about taking a position like mine, but I didn't care. It was my opinion and it was my voice. It was a chance to be heard.

I dragged my feet along the concrete as I made my way back to the group home, and debated picking up another coffee, but decided against it. It was already getting late and I needed to get back before curfew. They did give me an exception since they knew I was attending the exam, but I wanted to close my eyes and try to get the scrambled images from my mind.

Ms. Jackson appeared to be waiting for me when I arrived. "How did it go?" she asked.

"I think it went well. I didn't seem to struggle. Your tutoring definitely helped." I felt enthusiastic about finally being able to move forward.

"Do you have some time to catch up?"

I suddenly became wary. My voice quivered in response, "Sure." We headed back to her classroom and both Ms. K and Linda were there. I wasn't sure what was going on, and wasn't getting a particularly warm or fuzzy feeling from this gathering.

"Now that your GED is out of the way," Ms. Jackson said, "because we're all sure you passed, we wanted to share something with you."

I was worried that they had been holding out on some information about Lara, though I couldn't determine why they would choose to gather here to tell me. "Okay." I was nervous and it showed. I chewed my lower lip.

"You mentioned to me that you were considering Hunter College," Linda said. "We all know you've been signing out to look at schools. It's not like it's a secret, even though you haven't mentioned it to any of us." I nodded. "We decided to pull a few strings."

I had no idea what this meant. "Um ..." I didn't know what to say, or what was coming next. Linda, of all people, should have known I didn't like being blindsided. "I feel like I'm about to be attacked."

"On the contrary," Ms. K. joined the conversation. "We happen to think it's excellent news."

Linda continued, "I'm not sure if you're aware, but Hunter College allows some high school students to attend classes. Ms. Jackson has some connections there, and we all recommended you. You start in the winter semester."

"What?" I was shocked. I was beside myself. What could I say? I had a barrage of questions, but couldn't manage to get the words out. My throat felt dry.

Ms. Jackson spoke next, "We know you want to get started and this was a method to get you in before taking your SATs. This way, you won't need to wait until the spring term to take some classes."

Ms. K. said, "We're all well aware that you're interested in psychology, so we signed you up for Psych 100. We thought you'd enjoy it."

I felt overwhelmed. "But how will I pay for it and when exactly do I start and I just have a million questions but don't even know where to begin?" The words came out in a rush. It was a run on sentence, and a bit of a mouthful, but I needed to spit it out as quickly as I could.

"It's all taken care of," Linda said. "We'll get you all of

the details in a few days. We need a little more time to gather the information."

"I—I …" I stammered, "I can't thank you all enough."

"No thanks needed," Ms. K. said. "We're all really proud of you and want to see you succeed. We want that for everyone, but you've shown the most potential we've seen in a good long while."

I excused myself for dinner, but didn't eat. It was simply a chance for me to get away and get back to my original goal. Now I had something else to dream about over the next few months. Sleep was difficult that night. The coffee, mixed with sheer excitement, made it impossible to keep my eyes closed.

"You're not going to believe this," I said into the phone the next morning. "They signed me up for a college class and I start this winter!"

"*Mijita*," *Tia* Paola said, "I am so proud of you!" I knew that if she were here, she would have given me the tightest hug. I missed them. Sundays weren't feasible with her schedule, but I promised I would stop by for a visit the following weekend. "Please do," she said. "You're always welcome."

Things were coming together. Finally. It felt surreal, and I was sure the other shoe would drop at any moment.

I didn't want to wait to begin my SAT preparation. Immediately after breakfast, I slipped into Ms. Jackson's classroom and asked to borrow one of her books, so I could take a practice exam. I sat cross-legged on my bunk, bent over my knees, and wrote answers down on a blank sheet of notebook paper. I read all the questions, and when I was done, I tallied up my score and found it was in the range I was hoping for: 1500 1800. I scored a solid 1750.

I felt wild as I brought the book back, and rushed into the classroom with total disregard for the other girls. I ran up behind Ms. Jackson at the chalkboard, took a spare piece of chalk, and wrote '1750' before walking out. I looked behind me and saw a smirk on her face. No one else needed to know what it meant and I'm certain that there was no explanation given.

I decided to spend some time in front of mindless television for a change. I didn't even care what the other girls chose; I just didn't want to spend more time holed up in my room with my face in a textbook. I never thought I would say that, but there it was. The truth. The honest truth was that I was no longer focused on the present; only the future.

I couldn't tell you what the girls were watching, or talking about. I sat in a chair near the window, my head resting on the wall, and looked up at the other buildings surrounding us. The sound was nothing more than white noise to me. I hadn't been to the High Line in weeks, and since my life began to turn around, I missed Lara less and less. As much as I hated to admit it, she was part of my past and I intended to carry as little of that as possible with me going forward.

The span of that week was grueling. I let the doubt sink in and take control. My mood bounced between nervousness and what felt like mania. I'd never been diagnosed with bipolar, but understood what other people probably experienced. The waiting was the hardest part, but it was all I could do.

In our usual Thursday meeting, Linda said, "So, any news yet? Have you gone to pick up your scores?"

"No, and it's killing me. I'm going to stick it out and not check until the end of next week, so that I'm sure the essay was scored."

"How are you feeling otherwise? Have you started working with Ms. Jackson, or Ms. Kole, on a transition plan? There are a lot of steps to moving towards college and getting into housing. Some of them you're able to start on now."

"Give me a for instance."

"Well, you can start working on your entrance essay for Hunter. You should start the financial aid process. You can apply for housing assistance. You can apply for food stamps. You have no income and you're about to be a college student. You'll qualify for all of it. There's plenty you can be doing in the meantime."

"Where should I start? It seems like there's a lot to do."

"Frankly, I don't think you're going to need much help

with the college requirements. It can take a while to get decisions on the other assistance, so I think you should meet with Ms. K. as soon as possible, to get that underway."

I could hardly contain my excitement. "I'll set something up with her today."

"I was hoping you'd say that."

"I can't move backwards."

"Speaking of which, have you heard from Lara?"

My face squished into a grimace. I could feel the muscles in my face tighten. It was obviously an unhappy situation for me. "No, I haven't."

"I haven't heard anything either. I asked her case worker, but she wouldn't divulge anything."

"Her minion hasn't contacted me for a while."

"Her minion?" she asked, and then chuckled.

"There was a girl here that kept asking if I'd read the report. Apparently, Lara was under the impression I'm the reason she was kicked out. Ms. K. made it clear to me that it had nothing to do with me. They recognize I was in shock when I was taken out of here, but the policy is to remove both of them."

"I'm glad you're recognizing that and have stopped blaming yourself."

Who said there was no self-blame? I thought. "That's not entirely true, but if it makes you happy, I'll let you believe it."

She changed the subject back to my transition plan. I perked up slightly, but the damage had already been done. When our meeting was over, I went at a near run to Ms. K.'s office, to schedule an appointment with her. She was making rounds, so I left her a note on the face of her monitor: PLEASE COME FIND ME. THANKS, E." I took my time with the block lettering. I wasn't known for having the best handwriting and I wanted to make it clear. She had taken to calling me 'E' as she knew how much I despised my given name.

After spending limited amounts of time in the technology room—a place where the internet was accessible, though monitored—I decided it was time to do some research. I pulled up the freshman admission page at Hunter College to get a better sense of the requirements. I had until mid-September to finish my application for the spring term, which would be the next opportunity for freshmen to begin. I had missed the February deadline for fall by miles, so this was my best option. It was okay with me, as that had been my initial intention anyway. I felt less overwhelmed by it all. The SAT exam would be out of the way by early June, which meant I had plenty of time to get the ball rolling.

It turned out the admissions essay was optional. It also appeared that at least my practice SAT score—if I could keep it in the range I expected of myself—would be more than enough to get me into Hunter. Hell, it would get me into NYU if I had decided that was where I wanted to go. I suspected I would likely get a better education there, but after spending so much time downtown, I knew it wouldn't be the place for me. No, it was better to stick to my original plan—public school with a lower national ranking be damned.

I would complete the essay regardless of whether or not it was required. It would be easy for me to finish, and perhaps it would give me a leg up on the admissions process. I was convinced I would get in without it, but thought it best to provide it anyway. After closing the browser to limit distractions, I opened a Microsoft Word window and began to respond to the first essay option. We had three topics from which to choose, but only needed to provide one.

My choice was easily made: "Tell us about a significant experience, achievement, or risk you have taken, and how it affected you." This was only a one page essay and I would be able to finish it in a matter of minutes, particularly with limited, to no, revisions being necessary. And so I began:

> *I am not your typical applicant, but I would be a great addition to your student body. At sixteen I made the decision to leave my home and enter foster care. My home situation was less than ideal and it was a risk to make a*

move like this. Foster care is a toss-up; you can get a seemingly-perfect family or you can get just another negative situation.

I was fortunate that the family that had taken me in welcomed me with open arms. I was immediately at ease which is not something that comes quickly for me. This family seemed normal or at least what I imagined 'normal' to be. Dinner was on a relatively set schedule, we bonded over Game Night, and there were two other foster children—twins, actually—with which to share the experience.

Despite this being an optimal situation, I took another risk and left foster care to enter a group home for girls. I made this decision so that I could get the support and training I needed to be self-sufficient. College has always been a dream of mine. I would be the first college graduate in my family. I would be able to have the life I had always imagined for myself; a life completely unlike the one I have lived up to this point.

Because of the experiences I have had, I have decided to focus on psychology. I am an excellent listener and believe that with the proper education, I would be able to help many people. I would like to work with at-risk children. I am certain that I would have a positive and perhaps even life-altering impact on them. Were it not for the few mentors I have found in my life, I would not be where I am today.

I am grateful for all of my experiences—the ups and downs combined. They have made me who I am and I would not change a thing.

Next to nothing I wrote had been true. I didn't want to give a sob story, but rather an encouraging one. By the same token, I didn't want my entire life to be out there. At least, not to the administration of a school that I would theoretically have no problem getting accepted into. I printed out the draft and walked back to Ms. K.'s office. She still wasn't back, so I left a copy of it on her chair and moved the note from the monitor to the middle of the page. As I was doing this, she walked in. "What's going on?"

"I wrote my entrance essay and I wanted you to see it first."

"Why wouldn't you run it by Ms. Jackson?"

"Because there's something I want you to see, and it's important to me."

She took the paper before setting herself down in her seat. She scanned it quickly and said, "Okay."

I knew she would need an explanation. "You're one of my mentors. You're one of the reasons I'm definitely moving into the field of psychology."

She smiled, "And?"

"And, of course, there's Ms. Jackson and Linda, and my *Tia* Paola. You've all been influential."

She smiled, "That's nice to hear. None of us get that very often." She paused, looking at the essay again. "This is really great. I don't even think it needs any changes, but you should run it by Ms. Jackson." She handed it back to me carefully, as though it was some fragile and irreplaceable object. "You said you wanted an appointment, what's going on?"

"Linda told me you'd be the person to help me get started on my transition. With college coming up, I'll need some help getting the other pieces in order."

"I agree. This is a perfect time to start. How about if you swing by on Tuesday afternoon—around 3:00 PM?"

"Sounds great, I'm looking forward to it!" I couldn't contain my excitement.

"Start to think about what you want to do. If you're going

to Hunter, we should look for some housing on the East side, but it's slim pickings. Once you qualify for assistance, we'll look for apartments, but Section 8 can be challenging."

"It's a start."

I brought the essay to Ms. Jackson's room. "I have something for you. You don't need to read it now." I placed the sheet of paper on her desk and sat down in the front row.

"Is this the entrance essay?"

"Yes."

"It's been a day since you met with Linda. You're really motivated, aren't you?"

"I have until September 15th to finish my application. I want to get this process done as soon as possible, but I can't wait until I earn the GED and get my SAT scores. If these are all of the pieces I can do, then I want to do them."

"You could start the financial aid and application process. You just won't have your other documentation to provide for a few more weeks."

"I'm working with Ms. K. too."

"You know you can stay for another six months after you turn eighteen, right?"

"Yes, but who would want to stay any longer than necessary?"

"I hear that, girl." We shared a laugh. "This looks good. Hold onto it. Keep the digital copy to attach to the application, and if you're really going to start then get to it."

I grinned from ear to ear as I left her office. I went back to the technology room and pulled up the online application for Hunter, and worked my way through it, entering all sorts of personal information. I left sections blank to fill in later, but attached the essay before I'd even given a copy to Linda. I knew it would be fine. I made sure not to submit it, because I would also need to apply for a subsidy, so I wouldn't have to pay the application fee. It made me feel even better knowing that I wouldn't have to do this for more than one school.

I spent the weekend doing research. I only left the home

on Sunday to take a short walk around the neighborhood. Breaking my Saturday routine was becoming my new normal. I hadn't searched for Lara in what felt like ages, and her minion still hadn't approached me. I wondered if she'd run. She said she was a runner, and no one knew that better than she and I.

I couldn't take care of myself on the hard streets of this city, or any other, to be perfectly honest. Not only was it unappealing, I just knew I wouldn't be able to handle it. Despite winter being so far away, running from the home would only set me back. I had become comfortable. Being here for so long gave me some sort of seniority with the younger girls. I didn't feel so much like a pariah, but I also didn't offer to take anyone under my wing.

Fortunately, with Tamara moving, things had significantly calmed down there. I was sure another alpha was chosen, but I didn't see as much intimidation happening. I was sure it was, but the fact that it wasn't happening to me was a welcomed change. I would have bet money—if I had any—that other girls weren't in the same boat, but it was almost as if we all had to prove ourselves in order to have relative safety. It was a key takeaway from Lara, and I never forgot it.

I sometimes felt the girls' eyes on me, burning holes through me. There were times when I felt like pieces of me were leaking through the scar in my arm. I had become a bit of a legend here, and even if it didn't result in any special treatment, it did mean I was mostly left to my own devices. The staff had warmed up to me, even if the girls hadn't. They thought me to be uppity because I was doing my best to get out in a positive way. I didn't care, and wasn't going to let them hold me back.

Had anyone bothered to ask me how I was doing this, I would have offered my advice. No one came. No one asked, and no one cared. They would milk the system as long as they could. I'd seen it throughout my whole life. Once they started breeding new versions of themselves, their benefits would only increase while their motivation and hope—if they had ever had any—would fade away. They would become resigned to what they felt was the hand they had been dealt, while completely ignoring the fact that it was their own hand that kept them down.

I had little respect for anyone anymore, but felt I had more congruence again. The depression had lifted and I hadn't seen that familiar enemy for weeks. My mind and my words were once more in alignment. I watched my attitude and mood improve with every day. I felt invincible, despite waiting for the other shoe to drop, but it was starting to seem that things were going my way. I hoped they stayed that way, but given my current trajectory, I wasn't sure they would in the long run.

By the time Tuesday afternoon came around, I was suffering from complete and total boredom. With summer here and school out, I had little to do. There was only so much I could do until I had my scores back, and the Hunter application completed. At least Ms. K. and I would be starting the other portion of the transition today.

I entered her office with some trepidation and took a seat in her guest chair. She hadn't invited me to do so, but I felt comfortable enough with her. I certainly spent enough time here. "Let's get started, I only have about 20 minutes today. Something came up." I didn't ask for clarification. "Before we do anything, I want to walk you through the process and what you will likely be eligible for."

I sat with my elbow on the edge of her desk and my chin in my palm. I had a great memory, so didn't need to write anything down. Besides, as we went through the process, I would learn more about it. She explained housing and how that works, the fact that I wouldn't qualify for Social Security benefits as I hadn't worked, and wasn't considered disabled, and the likelihood that—as part of my financial aid package—I would be required to work at least twenty hours per week. It just went on and on.

I cannot say that I was disappointed by any of it, and the idea of actually needing to work enticed me. I would need to have some cash in my pocket and working would be the only way to get that. Housing and food stamps, and Medicaid were benefits enough. A financial aid or scholarship package would be a wonderful addition, but there was only so much I could hope for. I supposed I would need to start looking for a job, but had no idea what I wanted to do, or what I would be qualified for. At the very least, an internship would help until the financial aid package came through.

We scheduled weekly appointments—a half hour each week—to get the paperwork completed. By Thursday I had a lot of things to discuss with Linda. "So," I began, "I'm meeting with Ms. K. weekly."

"That's excellent news."

"And I have something for you." It was no strain to reach across to hand her the essay. The weight loss helped but so did the fact that any of the staff with their own office space found it suffocating. I was entertained by the idea that us girls did not; we were used to tight quarters. I imagined Linda breathing a sigh of relief when she left and could finally contain herself in the sanctuary of her home. More freedom and more space were most likely her reprieve. Based on the sheer number of books in her office, I also presumed she was a reader and that her apartment had stacks of novels, which she used as end tables. At the very least, that's what I would do until I could afford bookshelves. Well, and books, for that matter.

She took her time reading the essay, and I heard a deep inhalation when she had finished. "This is really wonderful. I'm proud of you."

"You inspired me. I couldn't have done most of this without you."

"I remember the day we met. I wasn't sure how you were going to turn out, but you're one of my favorite clients."

"Clients?"

"Yeah. That's how we refer to our cases."

"So, I'm not just a case?"

"Of course not. We don't treat people that way. At least I don't."

"The staff has resorted to simply calling me 'E'."

"I know. I've heard. What does it mean to you?"

"Progress." I felt like we had run through the important things, and I didn't want to waste her time. If we could wrap up in fifteen minutes, why bother taking the extra space? I did have one more question though. "I've always been curious." My voice quivered ever so slightly. "Are you happy outside this place?"

"Funny you should ask. Yes, yes I am. Why?"

"I've been thinking a lot about moving on from here, and I have so many things I want to do."

"You'll get there. Patience is something you don't have much of, but it's going to help if you develop it." We laughed together, knowing that truer words had never been spoken. At least, not between us.

The next day I signed out. "Where are you headed today?"

"Back to school. I want to see if the test scores came in yet."

"Good luck," the staff called out behind me. I turned my back and rushed to the testing center to finally alleviate the tension. I was happy that no one had asked me about it yet. I would share the information in my own time, assuming I had a reason to be excited. I still had those doubts gnawing at the back of my mind. Well, my whole mind, actually. As of late, my thoughts had become consumed by the transition, and what it all meant. The next time I had a few dollars to my name, I would head down to Strand and start to build my literary collection. *I may not have bookshelves for a while,* I thought, *but that does not mean I cannot start getting them.* The library also had sales at dirt cheap prices, but the selection at Strand—their infamous "mile of books"—truly lured me.

I made my way to the main office. During the year, it was already understaffed, but in the summer it was far worse. There were three people ahead of me and it appeared they were also waiting for their information.

"What do you need?" the woman behind the desk asked in a rude fashion. She looked like she couldn't be bothered.

"I wanted to see if my scores came in yet."

"Your name?"

"Ella Santia."

She flipped through a stack of papers but came up empty handed. "When did you take the exam?"

I was surprised that she wouldn't know. They weren't given on a regular schedule, but only every month or two. "About two weeks ago."

She sucked her teeth and shook her head. "You've got another two weeks or so before you'll get them back."

"What?" I exclaimed, louder than I had anticipated. "I was told they would be back almost immediately."

"I don't know who told you that, but it ain't true. Come back in a few weeks and we'll check online."

"Can't you check online now?"

"You're a waste of time, child. They're not going to be available. This stack is for people that took the exam a month before you. Now go ahead and step out of line so I can help the others behind you. Come back in a few weeks."

I felt furious but it was out of my hands. There was nothing I could do to force the issue, so I walked out with nothing else to say. Even my mind was blank. I had no witty or sarcastic reply, and frankly, no desire to even give one. It wouldn't help the situation.

Dejected, I made my way back to the group home, stopping to pick up a coffee on the way. As I was heading back, I decided that it would be a good idea to stop into some places and try to fill out applications if they were hiring. Jobs weren't as scarce as I had heard they had been a few years ago, but the pickings were still slim.

My first attempt was at a local salon. I felt shy and nervous as I pushed the door open, and I heard a cacophony of noise. "Hi there."

"Hey, what do you need?"

"I was wondering if you all are hiring for reception or just general help around here."

The woman in the chair laughed and the stylist, holding a pick, laughed just as loud. "You hear 'dat, people? She lookin' for a job." They all turned to stare as if an alien had just landed in their midst. "We ain't got no reception desk. We ain't got no reason for someone to answer 'da phones and we ain't got no jobs."

"Well," I muttered under my breath, "I certainly know why."

"Whatchyu said?"

"Nothing. I said thanks for letting me know."

She sucked her teeth. "Mmm. You get on outta here now. We ain't got no use for you."

Interestingly enough, this wasn't something I took particularly personally. Business didn't seem to be moving in there. The place was mostly empty. I presumed it was their attitude that kept people away. That, and the fact that they were clearly unprofessional. Without a high school diploma, I wouldn't have many options.

Against my will, and my better judgment, I began approaching fast food restaurants. They hired high school kids. Even though I knew the wages were going to be terrible, and the stress levels of dealing with the neighborhood residents, unpleasant, I needed to at least try. As much as I would have liked to find an internship, just to gain experience, that wasn't what I really needed.

I submitted applications to McDonald's, Wendy's, and a Super Fried Chicken, but it would take time for them to review them and even potentially get back to me. In the meantime, I had the relatively bright idea of asking Ms. Jackson if she needed some assistance with her classes. I would be an excellent tutor, and the experience would certainly help.

We had become closer after our six session—math marathon—experience together. She always looked like she could use the help, so I didn't think it would hurt to ask. Obviously, I had no interest in working with most of the other staff, with the exception of Ms. K. To be honest, I wasn't entirely sure what she did, and that was part of the reason I shied away from reaching out to her about it. To help Linda would be impossible; all of her files were confidential.

To give her some space, I decided not to approach Ms. Jackson about it until later in the week. I knew that Wednesday afternoons were relatively free for her, and I thought that waiting until then would be the best option. I didn't want to burst in on her again, excitement bursting from every pore, only to be interrupting someone else's education—especially since they needed it far more than I did.

The next two days dragged. I spent most of my time either tracing circles on the concrete floor of the community room, researching jobs on the internet (to no avail, mind you), or lying in bed reading *The House on Mango Street*. There were some books in the community room, but none of them appealed to me. I had no money left, so Strand was out of the question. *Tia* Paola would be working long hours during the week, and I didn't want to be an imposition.

On Wednesday morning, immediately after breakfast, I rushed into Ms. Jackson's room before her classes began. "Good morning." Enthusiasm spread across my face and suffused my voice. I didn't even give her a chance to respond. "I know how busy you are, so I was wondering if I could help tutor the other girls? I need to get some experience if I'm going to find a job."

"You know, I've thought about approaching you about it. You've had your hands full too, so I haven't asked."

"I know I have a lot to do, but most of it's moving at a snail's pace. There's really nothing I can do in the meantime. I'm bored."

"I understand. I mean, there's only so much TV one can watch."

"So? …"

"I think it's a great idea. What subject are you thinking?"

I laughed, "The obvious."

"English."

"That's what I figured. And besides, the girls here could use quite a bit of help there."

"As can you, I assume."

She smiled warmly, "You assume correctly."

"I mean, you're always here. I have to wonder if you even have a life outside this place."

"Barely."

"Then let me help."

"You don't drive a hard bargain, ya know." I knew. I also knew that even if I landed a part-time job that summer, I would still have time to continue tutoring. And the tutoring work would mean more money, once I had some of that experience under my belt. It would be a great first step in the right direction. "So, what's happening with the exams?"

A defeated look crossed my face as I sighed. "I've got another two weeks until both results are available."

"Well, that's unfortunate."

"I thought you said it would be faster than that."

She looked annoyed. "I don't have a handle on everything. It probably just slipped my mind and came out wrong."

"When do you run the English classes, or when would be a good time for me to help with the tutoring?"

"The girls come in at any time for tutoring. Why don't you come in later, or whenever you have time? They usually sit in the back of the room."

"Approach with caution, huh?" I laughed at the notion.

"Just come see me first. I'll make the introduction."

"Sounds good. I have nothing going on, and I've been so bored. I'll check back later."

"You haven't been going out much."

"I applied to some jobs the other day. I was laughed out of a salon, but I turned in applications at some of the fast food restaurants. Maybe I'll hear back from them."

"There's a lot of competition," she said, and the snarky reply irked me. "You know that."

I did know, but I still didn't feel like hearing it. "Even though the tutoring doesn't pay, it's still a leg up. I've got about a year to go, so the experience will help."

She couldn't deny it. "True."

"I'll stop by later. At least it will get me out of bed."

"Sounds good," she said, and then put her face back into whatever project she was working on.

Selfishly, I hadn't been spending much time thinking about anyone but myself. On Saturday I would stop by to see *Tia* just to get out of here. It wasn't like I had much news to share. My weeks were disjointed. I had scheduled meetings with Ms. K. on Tuesdays, met with Linda on Thursdays, and Saturdays I spent with *Tia*. That left four other days open. I needed something to fill those voids, and I hoped the tutoring would help. It happened almost every day, and even if I didn't spend hours a day working with the girls, it would give me a reprieve from the ever increasing boredom I was experiencing.

Summer was always like this. A lot of the girls were forced into attending summer school, because they didn't bother to do the work during the rest of the year. It was disappointing, and unlike most students, the group home wasn't expected to pay for the additional time. I suppose that was a perk of being here. If not, most of these girls would fail and most likely be left behind. If they even did that anymore.

I wanted to ask Linda if she had any books she could bring in for me, but the question felt awkward. Maybe I could use the tutoring as an excuse, but the truth was that I just wanted something else to read. I wasn't experiencing the solace I used to when reading *The House on Mango Street*. It had less meaning to me, and besides, I knew the entire thing cover to cover. There was no challenge in it for me anymore.

I focused on salad and a buttered roll for lunch that afternoon. The other options didn't appeal to me, and even though this one wasn't particularly good, I wanted to stay as healthy as possible. Since losing so much weight, I felt much better. My joints no longer gave me problems, and I found that I had less colds and allergies. I remember health professionals telling me that losing weight would alleviate a lot of what I was experiencing, but when I heard such things from people that were overweight themselves, I didn't bother to listen. The hypocrisy of the world sometimes astounded me.

The incredibly long walk—miles upon miles—down to the Lower East Side would be even more beneficial than the shorter walks I'd done until now. However, when I sat down and thought it through, I realized it wasn't the best option I'd come up with for myself. Perhaps, if I exited at West Fourth Street, like I had that one time, I would get more exercise in. Lately, I'd noticed that my weight had stabilized, and I wasn't losing anymore. If it was still coming off, it must be so slow as to not see it.

"I'm back." I dragged out the word 'back', when I walked into Ms. Jackson's classroom.

"The bad news is that no one is here yet; they're all running late, per the usual. The good news is that you'll probably have three girls that are all at the same level, so having that as a first start will be helpful."

"I was hoping to work one-on-one the way we had. I got a lot out of those sessions."

She smirked, "Let's see how well you do getting through to them."

"I have an idea." I went back to my room, and after having to work the lock combination at least three times, managed to open the chest. My fingers still had some numbness, but the excitement of the afternoon hadn't helped my co-ordination either. I pulled out my ragged copy of *The House on Mango Street* and rushed back to the classroom. "Here," I said, holding it up so she could see it. "I think this might help."

"This isn't story time."

"I know, but if I can get them to read something other than textbooks, and give them writing assignments, I think it will help them."

"You're a natural teacher. I think you should consider it."

"Summers off would be nice."

"You don't have to take them. You could keep working. There's always work to be done, ya know." It was a statement, not a question. I knew it was true, but again, I didn't want to spend my life working with apathetic kids who would most likely do nothing to change their lives. From my perspective, I could change many more lives by moving into psychology.

"Thanks, but I'm really not interested."

"Don't want to work with these kids, huh?"

"Not in the least."

"Obviously, there *are* other schools. Better ones, where the kids will listen and do the work."

"Yeah, I know. But I wouldn't find that as rewarding." The girls entered the room at a slow walk, and a look of passivity settled on all their faces.

Ms. Jackson didn't welcome them. "Take your seats," she said. "I want to introduce you to Ella. She's going to be tutoring you in English."

I couldn't stop the smile from spreading across my face. "Hi you all!" I exclaimed.

Their looks didn't change. "You want us to work with her?"

"Yeah, I do. You're going to learn a lot from her."

"We ain't gonna learn shit. She can't even defend herself," the short, squat one said.

"And neither can you," I said. "You all have nothing but physical strength. I may have gotten in the way of an accident, but I can certainly defend myself." I watched her eyes as she squinted. Ms. Jackson said nothing. "Now, sit down and shut up, and let's get started." I had no idea where in the depths of my soul this courage had come from, but I wasn't going to allow myself to be treated this way by menial people.

Though they took their time, they did eventually settle down and get themselves under control. They'd brought neither notebooks, nor pens, and utterly nothing but their appalling behavior. I still had the book in my hand, so I placed it carefully on the table. "Let's get to know each other." They all rolled their eyes at the notion. "I'm Ella, and I've been here a little over a year. For the record, your best defense is intelligence, and I'm here to help you establish some of that." I waited for one of them to follow up my introduction, but no one did. Finally, I pointed to the girl directly across from me and asked her to go next.

"I'm Olivia," she said.

"Anything else you want us to know?"

"Hell no."

The other girls had nothing but their names to share. I didn't know them, so I assumed they were relatively new to the home. I recognized the toughness. It was something we all needed to resign ourselves to—not just in the beginning of our time here—but rather, the entire time. I understood, but it was hard to contain my own enthusiasm. The other two girls introduced themselves as Ana and Ximena. There were more Hispanic girls here than anything else. I never saw a *blanquita* here at all. I supposed that if they were going to go anywhere it would be to the Covenant House, where they could spend their time around people more like themselves. There wouldn't be much diversity found this deep into the jungle that is Manhattan. Regardless, because of our shared background, I hoped they might find this book to be something they could connect with.

I turned the book over when I noticed that Ximena's eyes seemed drawn to it. I didn't want to dive right into it, but rather explain how I wanted these sessions to run. They weren't going to like them, but if they gave it a chance, they would be more likely to succeed. "I'm going to start by explaining my expectations."

"Ya shouldn't even have them," Olivia said, with a cold glare. I could tell she was going to be defeatist and the hardest to break. I didn't want her to drag the other girls with her. I'd seen that too many times with other people.

"That may be true, but I have them nonetheless."

"Listen to her," Olivia spat out, "She don't even talk like us. I dunno how you think ya gonna get through if ya can't even relate."

"Relate, huh?" I was surprised she knew the word. "We're all here aren't we? I'm pretty sure we're going to relate."

"Whatever. I don't even wanna be here," she continued.

"Then leave. No one is forcing you to be here. No one is

demanding that you do well in school. No one here really even cares. You bide your time and when you're out, you're out on your own." Looks of shock came across the faces of Ana and Ximena. "Yeah, I don't take shit from people, no matter what you think."

Despite her attitude, Olivia shut her mouth, so I could at least get through the expectation portion of my little lecture. "From now on, I'd like you to bring a notebook and a pen. You're going to read, and you're going to have writing exercises. We're going to kill two birds with one stone. I don't know what your reading levels are, and frankly, I don't care. We're going to work on books that will probably take time to understand, and you're going to get through it."

I hadn't realized that Ms. Jackson was standing behind me, but once I did, I noticed that her arms were crossed. She looked angry. "Ya'll are gonna work," she said angrily. "If you ain't gonna work, then don't waste anyone's time. She's doing you and me a favor by being here. I don't want her time wasted."

I was sort of surprised by her defense of me, and my attempt to show strength and dominance in this particular situation. She wasn't exactly known for such support. Tough love? Yes. A supportive nature? No. Aside from the foul language, I was using techniques I had learned in my Honors English classes. Otherwise, I would've had no clue where to begin. While my own reading and writing had always been advanced, even in the Honors classes there were people who fell behind. These additional assignments—which I completed just for fun—helped me, and I knew that if these girls put in at least half the effort I wanted from them, they would make major advances in a very short amount of time.

The girls settled down after our respective outbursts. Ms. Jackson wasn't known for being the kindest person, but the fact that she was so direct helped whip the girls into shape. I continued, "We only have one copy of this book, so we're going to share it. You're all going to take turns reading it, one page per girl at a time. It would be best for you to take notes so you have something to refer back to."

With that, I walked up to Ms. Jackson and asked for a few sheets of paper and pens. "They're going to need these, and I've asked them to bring them next time. I'm sure the staff will give them out if they just ask."

I brought the supplies to the desk in the back of the room, but noticed Olivia had disappeared. There was no point in sighing, or getting annoyed. This was expected. I turned to Ana and Ximena without missing a beat, or commenting on Olivia's departure. "Let's get started."

Ana began first. Her voice was low and quiet, and she was struggling. "I'm embarrassed," she expressed nervously, when she was only one paragraph into the novel.

"It's okay," I reassured her. "No one is judging you."

"At least not anymore," Ana said.

I wasn't sure what she meant by that, but perhaps it had something to do with Olivia's negative attitude. At least as far as this group was concerned, she had clearly set herself apart as the dominant figure. I got the sense these three weren't a cohesive group outside of these sessions. I felt this was a good thing, as Olivia's negative energy would hinder any progress they had a chance of making.

Ana struggled to get through the rest of the page, but she did. I told her I was proud of her, and she blushed. Most people weren't proud of us girls, and even if they were, they rarely bothered to tell us. I had become more accepting of the compliments I received, but they still felt out of place.

Ximena had an easier time getting through the reading, but after an hour of them taking turns, we hadn't gotten through much of the book. "I'd like you to write a few paragraphs about what you think of this book, and to come up with some ideas for the types of books you would like to read. This is fiction, but there are some really great books based on real life out there."

"How much writing do we need to do?" Ana seemed confused.

"Maybe three to four paragraphs. That's about 12-16

sentences. I'm sure you'll find it easier than you think."

Ana left as soon as I gave them the assignment, and though she didn't look particularly thrilled about it, she wasn't coming off as totally negative either. I suspected that even though she would struggle with the short essay, she would complete it. Ximena expressed far more interest, and being further along than Ana, I thought she might become frustrated by the pace.

"Can I just work on this now and give it back to you?" she wanted to know.

I was surprised. "Sure. I can wait."

Ms. Jackson kept her voice at a high volume, but this was nothing new for her. I think she believed that if she spoke louder, it would make the information sink in better. I knew it was just going to push people away, but she was the expert here. I might have had some wonderful mentors—her included—but no one was perfect. Least of all me.

I left the book on the table as I excused myself to use the bathroom. When I came back, I found it between Ximena's hands. Her head hung low with the book close to her face. I realized she'd quickly become hooked on it. I didn't want to stop her from reading it, but I was nervous about letting her take it with her. It was my sole copy, and it was one of the only possessions I had.

When she saw me return, she placed the book back on the table, with a worried look.

"Sorry."

"Don't worry about it. It makes me happy that you're still reading it."

She put pen to paper and began scribbling away. It didn't take her more than a few minutes to hand it over to me to read.

> *In only the first few pages of this book, I already feel like I'm the main character. Esperanza comes from a poor family just like mine. She lives in an apartment with her parents brothers and sister. I've only got one brother and a sister but we had no room in our apartment either. She has dreams like the kind I hear we're supposed to want but*

no matter how much I want them I'm not sure I'm going to get them. I'm not really into reading but this book is really cool and I want to keep reading more of it. I don't know any other books I would want to read since I don't even read the ones we need to for school.

While it was certainly not the best writing I had seen, it was better than I had anticipated. I allowed a smile to spread across my face. "This is good," I said.

"Really?" There was a sparkle in her eyes, as though she had just come alive.

"Yeah. I would change a few things. If you don't mind, I'd be happy to give you some comments now. If you'd like to re-write it and hand it in in a few days, just let me know."

"That would be really great. I know Olivia and Ana don't really care what happens, but I want outta here, ya know?" She paused. "That was stupid, of course you know."

"I mean, this isn't graded or anything, but I understand the point you're trying to get across here. From this, I can tell we need to work on your grammar and boost your vocabulary. I don't talk to the other girls, so I can't say for sure, but this looks a lot better than I think most of them could do."

Her face shifted from delight to dejection, to somewhere in between. I had the sense that she appreciated the positive feedback, but that, like most of us, criticism of any kind—even the kind that is supposed to make us better people—wasn't appreciated. "Look," I continued, "Most of this can be fixed by just removing the contractions and adding some commas."

She giggled. I knew she didn't know what I was talking about. So many of these girls knew more about childbirth than they did grammar; the former was a daily part of their lives. The latter was the part that suffered.

"What I mean by that is when you put two words together to make one. Like when you wrote 'I'm'. In conversation that's fine, I'm using it right now, but in an essay you should write more formally so you would say 'I am' instead."

She nodded and smiled again. She had excellent teeth. “I think I get it. So . . .”

“So, why don't you take this with you and re-write it? If you wanted, another thing you could do, is look online to see if there are any books like this that you might be interested in.”

“That sounds like a lot of work.”

“It is. I never said this was going to be easy.” I always had a good poker face, and so I used it against her to hide that I actually cared about whether or not she would go the extra step. If she did, it meant she was serious. If she didn’t bother to do it, then at least in my mind, she was going to be as much a waste of time as Ana, or trying to get through to Olivia. Black and white cookies. There is no gray.

I felt intrigued and wanted to know more. She was the first person to express any desire to get out of here. Most of the girls just wanted to stay as long as possible, and I’d seen some try to get extensions to stay. The requests fell on deaf ears and didn’t work. Transitions were rushed, or they were placed in homeless shelters until the social workers there could find something else for them. I didn’t envy any of them, neither did I have much use for them.

“How is it that I’ve found the only other inspired person here?” Ms. Jackson asked.

“I’m sure there are more. We’re just the minority, so there’s not much to say.”

“Ain’t that the truth?” She seemed to enjoy rhetorical questions. I realized that no matter how much I wished it not to be the case, it was. And likely always would be.

Stagnation and resignation abounded.

Chapter 12

Olivia never returned and Ana's attendance dwindled away to nothing. She would show up unprepared but full of excuses as to why she never got the work done. Her reading improved only slightly, and that was only because I used those sessions to work with her. Ximena had already read well beyond where Ana was in the story, and so she spent most of that time just listening to it again. Obviously it was at a much slower speed. Sometimes her mind wandered and I would catch her drawing in the margins of her notebook. It was a commonality we had. I never mentioned it to her and I never encouraged her, but she had more skill in that area than I did. *Well*, I thought, *we cannot all be good at everything.*

Long after Ana had left the tutoring session, I turned to Ximena and asked, "What's next with you?"

"I heard you took your GED."

I nodded but gave no verbal response. It was still bothering me that even after the four week mark, no grades had been returned for either of the exams. I experienced a growing restlessness, and were it not for working with Ximena and helping Ms. Jackson prepare for her other classes, I would have had nothing to do but chew my lips and meander the city.

I still hadn't heard back from any of the fast food restaurants to which I had applied. The tutoring would help me in the long run, but it meant I had no money in my pocket in the meantime. *Tia* slipped me a little money here and there, but I always felt lousy taking it. I was old enough to be earning my own money, and that's what I should have been doing.

Everyone—Linda, Ms. K. and Ms. Jackson—all told me not to rush and not to get frustrated by the lack of responses on all fronts. It was much easier in theory than it was to live it. If a financial aid package came through, I'd be able to roll up all my expenses for the year, and I would get more money than I actually needed to pay for my classes, but it wasn't how I wanted to live. I didn't want to take out a loan to live on, just so I could be stuck with it for another ten years, or more.

I snapped back to the conversation at hand. “Yeah, I did.”

“Well, I want to do the same thing. I just have a lot longer until I get there.”

“Your reading is improving,” I said. I wasn’t known for being particularly encouraging. I had been picking up pieces of that skill, called empathy by Paola, but at the same time, sympathy was something for which I had no use. Ximena was trying to break down the wall and allow ourselves to become closer to one another, but after losing Bianca, Rosa and Lara in the last few years, I had no interest in dropping my guard. There was too much risk.

“Nothing else is,” she sighed and sounded defeated.

“I bet that isn't true. Ms. Jackson doesn't waste her time on the ones who don't show potential.”

“There are plenty of girls still in these classes that want nothing to do with them.”

“Exactly,” I said as I pointed at her. “And who does she focus on in the classes? Those girls are there, but they're never really there.”

“I never thought about it like that.”

“I didn't for a long time, either.” I was new to this encouragement thing, but I continued, “You're doing much better, and it's only been three weeks. If this is something you really want, you need to work on it all the time, not just when you're here with me or Ms. Jackson. I prepared by sitting in my room doing practice exams. You have to do the work.”

“Just like everything else.”

“Exactly. No one is going to hand us anything. Sure, they'll help us get on our feet, but that's only going to last so long. We all have to figure this stuff out for ourselves, ya know?”

She nodded. “Doesn't mean I have to like it.”

I laughed, “No one does. Not even me. I'm still waiting for those scores. Speaking of which . . .” I stopped to look at the clock. “I really should walk down and see if they're back yet.” She was amenable, and fortunately, didn’t ask if I wanted company. I most definitely did not. I never did, anymore. I had gone back to being the girl who was used to being alone. Finally, all of the drama and emotion surrounding The Incident and Lara were behind me.

Despite not being a naturally patient person, I decided that it wasn't going to do anyone any good if I kept showing up to get my scores. Instead, I used tutoring, my appointments with Linda and Ms. Kole, and visits with *Tia* to pass the time. I didn't spend time with Ximena outside of tutoring, and Ana, when she did bother to show up, didn't seem particularly interested in us getting to know one another anyway. I felt indifferent towards it.

I wouldn't be there much longer, so it didn't seem to make sense to me to even attempt to get to know people. I had the people I needed in my corner. Once I got out of there, I would be able to find other people to help me stay on the right path. Even being extremely motivated is often not enough, and I was at least self-aware enough to know my blind spots.

I didn't take the time to change my outfit, and just signed out of the home with my usual excuse, then bounded down the street. Even the smell of coffee didn't distract me. I didn't stop to chat with the guys who called out to me. Instead, I kept my head down, and my eyes watched as my toes came back into view with each step. I cannot say I was used to the catcalling. It was a relatively new, and more frequent, experience for me, but at that point in my life, it wasn't unappreciated either. I'd spent so long being ignored, that even the slightest hint of interest felt dangerous. I wasn't yet sure what I was capable of.

Given how late in the afternoon it was at that point, I wasn't surprised by the line that snaked through the office and down the hallway. I made my way to the back of the line and just stood there, taking in all of the details of my surroundings. The layout of the school was straightforward, and spread out much like the Baruch Houses—all of the classrooms surrounded a core that held the lockers and stairs.

I imagined that in places outside of this city, kids didn't know what it meant to walk up so many flights of stairs in the sweltering heat of summer, with no air conditioning. Instead, I presumed that they attended schools with low buildings, spread out across acres of land. I didn't know what an acre looked like, and I was certain I would never have a need to know.

It felt like it took forever to get closer to the desk. The woman manning it was obviously exhausted and frustrated. "Come back in a week." The line shifted. "Come back in two weeks." She droned on in a flat and monotone voice. I could tell she'd been saying the same thing to almost everyone in the line. I hoped I would be the exception to this rule, considering I'd already heard it a few weeks ago.

By the time it was my chance to approach the woman I'd chewed my bottom lip repeatedly. It was ready to split and bleed at any moment. I just hoped it would hold out until I got out of here. "I'm here to see if my scores have come back yet."

"Name?"

"Ella Santia." She clicked around on the keyboard. This was a different woman than the last one I had talked to, so at least she wasn't flipping through paperwork and was instead looking for them online. She was silent through the process but eventually I heard the printer start to warm up. She didn't say anything to me as she handed me two sheets of paper.

"Thanks," I said quietly as she handed them to me. The papers looked translucent. Before I could even walk away, she called the person behind me. I stood off to the side trying to decide if I was going to look at them now, or if I would wait until I got back to the group home. My desire to be the first to know was staggering, but so was my nervousness. I decided to fold them neatly and put them in my back pocket. I wasn't going to read them.

My mind raced for the entire walk. I bounced from considerable confidence to an utter lack of any. I moved my feet lethargically, one in front of the other, in a vain attempt to slow down time. I was only fooling myself, but had gone beyond the point of caring. In the depths of myself, I knew I had nothing to fear. I was on my path, and at least for now, I was invincible. My time had come. I shook the thoughts away as I signed back in at the staff office.

"That was quick," the staffer said.

"Yeah." I didn't say anything else. Her look told me that she was curious, but I offered no explanation. I heard the click of the pen behind me as I walked away. I wasn't sure what to do. My meeting with Linda wouldn't be for a few more days, so she wouldn't be on-site. Ms. Kole was probably doing her rounds, and Ms. Jackson would be in the middle of a class.

In the end, I decided to see Ms. Jackson. I quietly entered the room and took a seat in the very back row. She saw me and nodded, which I knew was a sign of acceptance. As silently as possible, I sat, chin in hand. She was teaching a finance class. I had taken this one and found it very helpful. Because I still had no income, there were a lot of things that didn't apply to me, but understanding how to budget, or write a check, would be helpful. As far as I knew, Malda didn't even have a bank account, let alone have any interest in showing my sisters or me what we needed to know as far as this was concerned.

As expected, there were no questions. Most of the girls didn't take notes. They just sat through it, biding their time. I remember being that girl. I remember sitting through some of the Life Improvement courses just wishing they would end. I don't know why I bothered to attend most of them, except for the fact I knew I would have been kicking myself later if I needed to know something, and discovered that I didn't.

Culinary. Finance. Resume writing. Interview training. These were topics that would help us. I recognized that. But there were softer skills that needed development, and unfortunately those were the toughest things to make stick. I had learned enough from Yvette that manipulating the weaker would come easy for me. I didn't have to depend on her technique—her sexuality—to have people want to help or do things for me. I didn't have Maria's strength, especially now, so physically overpowering people to get my way wasn't an option for me. *No,* I thought, *I have to just take what I learned here and apply it the best I can.*

Everyone wants to follow a success story. I suspected that, at the very least, Linda wouldn't desert me once I'd aged out of the system. I expected that Ms. Kole and Ms. Jackson would keep the same stride, plugging away day after day, in a job attempting to get through to girls who didn't want to help themselves. I was sure I would be welcomed back to check in from time to time, but I'd never have this kind of access to them again.

Ms. Jackson wrapped up the lesson twenty minutes after I had arrived. I didn't get any special treatment, and I did try to keep my barging through closed doors to a minimum. Unlike the usual, she didn't start in on papers or reviewing her schedule. She sat on the edge of her desk and asked, "So, what's up?"

"Oh, nothing." I pulled the folded papers from my pocket and reached out to hand them to her. I positioned myself further than arm's length away. I didn't like to be in what I considered personal space. "Just this."

She raised an eyebrow at me and reached from the desk to take it from my hands. They were shaking and I tried to calm myself. I felt light-headed, so I took a seat in the chair directly in front of her. "You look nervous."

"Shouldn't I be?"

"I don't think so."

"I have a dozen or more reasons to be nervous. If it's bad news, I have to start over. If it's good news, then I have to work harder."

She opened the papers. I watched the top start to fold in on itself, but she didn't pay any attention to it. "So," she began slowly, "Do you want the good news or the bad news?"

I couldn't stop my face from falling. It never made sense to me why people bothered to ask that question. I don't know anyone that ever wants good news followed by bad. "Give me the bad news first."

She took her sweet time before answering. "You're going to have to see Ms. Kole and start truly working through your transition plan." I shouldn't have been, but I was still confused.

"You passed both. You're on your way." She didn't say it as though it was an exclamation or a proclamation, just any other statement of fact. I was unsure what to say. I was unsure what I really needed to do next. "Don't you wanna know the actual results?"

"Hit me." I felt weak.

"For your GED, you scored a total of 3,000. 500 each on math, science and social studies; 750 on the reading comprehension and writing."

"When will I have my actual diploma?"

"That could take some time. I wouldn't count on having it right away, but you can submit these scores to Hunter with your application and they'll accept them."

"And now the drumroll," I said in an effort to be sardonic—normal.

"Don't be a smartass."

I smiled. "I'm just nervous."

"I already gave you the bad news. What else could there be?"

"Just *do* it already!"

"You maintained an 1800." She said it slowly. Eighteen. Hundred. My score had remained the same. Still, it was more than good enough to get into Hunter. I could probably get into NYU with that score, but the thought of failure was so intimidating that I pushed the notion from my mind completely.

I nodded. "Well, now I have no idea what I'll do with myself."

"You'll start college in the winter term, like we discussed."

"I don't mean that." She crossed her arms over her chest and stared at me. Presumably we had another ten minutes or so before her next class would begin, but some of the more ambitious-looking girls were already starting to trickle in and take seats near each other. Still, they were far away from our discussion. "I just mean, now this is all so real, I have to get the financial aid package together and wait for information about housing, and all sorts of things. I'm not even sure where to begin."

"Work with Ms. Kole. She'll get you through that."

"And what am I supposed to do with the rest of my time? I'm tutoring a few days a week, I have my meetings with the staff, visits with my *Tia,* and just nothing else to fill my time."

"Haven't heard back from any of the jobs yet, I guess?"

"No. I don't even have physical therapy anymore. I have no reason to stay and no reason to leave. I can't spend the next few months with my face in the same book I've been reading since I was a kid."

"Think about what else you can do in the meantime."

"Like?"

"Like," annoyance became readily apparent in her voice. "Go do something with yourself. Get out, find something to do, somewhere to go, meet people. Stop moping around here like you've done for the last eighteen months or so." I was surprised by what I felt was a personal attack. I had no response, other than to get up from the seat. "Where are you going?"

"To go *do* something with myself." I stormed out of the room like a child, but I didn't care. I made my way down the hall at speed, and threw myself face down onto my bed, my face buried in my pillow. No sound escaped my throat. I couldn't cry or scream, or anything else to get the anger and frustration out. All I could do was lay there and hear her words repeat on the inside of my skull. *Go do something with yourself. Do something with yourself. With yourself. Yourself.*

That's what it all boiled down to in the end. Myself.

Once I'd calmed down, I made a list. I used to do this all the time, but it'd fallen by the wayside. Lists helped me focus, and prevented me from getting anxious about what needed to be done.

Transition housing
A job
Financial aid application
More tutoring sessions with the girls
Perhaps taking over a class of my own
Write a resume
Read more

I kept things general enough so as to not disappoint myself. Leaving room for interpretation was one of my passive-aggressive ways of getting things done. This way, I didn't have to admit that I failed. I could always just clarify it later. *What I meant was, I would consider taking on a class of my own, but later couldn't decide on one. When I said I would read more, what I really meant was to just finish a few chapters in a book.* These are the lies I told myself to make myself feel better.

The next day, before my session with Linda, I decided to go to the library. I didn't have identification, other than the card I needed for the reader at the group home. I had no mail of my own, and certainly no utilities, so I was unsure if they would actually let me borrow books. I was tired of my reliance on the one book I owned. It was time to broaden my horizons.

Perhaps it was because it was mid-summer, or perhaps it was just the nature of the neighborhood, but the library was completely empty. "I'd like to apply for a card, please."

The woman at the counter didn't look up from her book. It was flat against the desk, so I couldn't see what was keeping her from any sort of decency. While not lifting her eyes from the pages, she slipped a sheet in front of me, and in a voice that expressed her disinterest in her work, instructed me to fill it out.

I had to borrow a pen which appeared to be an annoyance to her, but I honestly didn't care. I stood off to the side, so as to not appear nosy, and began completing the application. I took in my surroundings and chided myself for not having done this earlier. I hadn't even bothered to use the library at school.

I filled out everything I could, and skulked over to the

woman. Again, without looking up, she took the paper from my hands and said in a flat voice, "Identification."

It wasn't a question. It was clearly a statement. Being a librarian must be a lonely and miserable career. Despite my love of books, this wouldn't be something I could tolerate on a daily basis.

I handed her the card and took a step back. My bra strap had slipped through the side of my tank top and I nudged it back in, as I was doing so, she said, "This isn't proper identification."

"I live at the group home down the street and it's all I have."

Her look held no sympathy. "Bring back a note, or a school report card, or something else. I need to be able to verify an address." She reached her hand out to me with my card and went back to reading her book.

I retrieved it and glanced at the clock on the wall behind her. The second hand didn't seem to have moved at all. Time is the illusion over which we have no control. I wouldn't have time to go through the entire process or even peruse the shelves. I liked to take my time. I loved the smell of the paper, particularly in old editions. We may not have control of time, but its passing is noticeable.

I was running a few minutes late to my meeting with Linda, but she didn't look particularly upset about it. "I was wondering if you would show up," she said. She looked like she was working on another case anyway.

"Sorry, I went to the library, but they wouldn't give me a card. Apparently, I don't have enough identification."

"Ms. Kole can help you with that. Just ask." I made a mental note of it. "I heard there's all good things happening for you."

"Oh?" I wanted to play dumb just to hear her compliment me. It was so rare that I ever had any sort of positive things said about me, that I wanted to grab hold of every opportunity I had.

She smiled, "Your GED and SAT scores were impressive."

"Impressive for me, or impressive for a girl with my

background?"

"Impressive."

"I wouldn't be pushing if I didn't want the truth."

"Then," she paused, appearing to collect her thoughts. "Both."

I didn't say anything in response. Sympathy isn't what I'd been looking for, and frankly, I'd been hoping she was just going to allow the results to rest on my own efforts. Maybe I hadn't wanted the truth after all. I wondered how many other people might be taking credit for the work I had put in. *You are being resentful*, I reminded myself.

"You have nothing to say?"

"Not to that, no." *What did she expect me to say?* I wasn't exactly thrilled at that particular moment. "I have a lot to do. Did you need anything else?"

She eyed me suspiciously. "What else do you need to do? Continue with the antisocial behavior you've been exhibiting as of late?"

"Perhaps, yes. Perhaps, no."

"Which is it?"

"No. I have a list."

"Of?"

"Things I need to get done, obviously. Sitting here isn't on the list."

"So, what is?"

"Linda," frustration crept into my tone, "I have to find a job and housing, and apply for financial aid. I have to start preparing for college. I'm not sure what you think I'm sitting here doing."

"You've made significant progress. Can't you just take a breath and let it sink in?"

"You've been doing this long enough." My agitation grew. "You know it doesn't work that way."

"Nothing says it can't change."

I was done. I had nothing left to say to her that week. I felt annoyed, and knew there would be no resolution until I could sit calmly and think more about what I actually wanted to say to her. There was no part of me that was ungrateful for all she'd done for me, but sometimes those sessions turned into battles. To me, they were wars that needed to be waged and won; if for no other reason than to prove that I could win them.

I don't always win the battle, but I'll be damned if I don't win this war. Life is the most important fight of all.

Chapter 13

"What have you been doing with yourself, E?"

Ms. Kole was always a challenge, but I was prepared for her today. I knew what to expect. It wasn't the blinded roller coaster that dealing with Linda happened to be. "Not a whole lot," I admitted. It was true. I had my list, but nothing had been crossed off.

The library was a failed attempt, even on the second try. I had been tempted to just grab any book near the door and take off. The apathetic woman at the counter wouldn't have bothered to chase me. Regardless, I'd only stolen a handful of things in my life, and a book was already one of them.

"Well then, let's fix that."

Every step I took towards independence, while exhilarating, was mixed with the taste of fear. Fear, to me, has always been metallic. The tinge of blood on my lips when I had chewed through them. The bitter air of the neighborhood on my tongue. The one time I held my hands to my face after a particularly grueling subway ride. Metal. Filthy metal and fear. In this city, it was what surrounded me; surrounded all of us.

We went back to working on the housing application. Because I wasn't able to stay there beyond that six month mark, I needed to line something up. The luxury of relaxing, and simply hoping for the best, wasn't open to me. There was important work to be done. Now, if only I could motivate myself to do it.

I'd never been a procrastinator, but as of late, I had become despondent. I thought that passing the tests and being able to move forward, at least as far as school was concerned, would mean I would be happy. Just like I thought losing weight would make me happy. That leaving my family would make me happy. I was wrong, and I couldn't find ways to make myself happy anymore. Perhaps I'd been lying to myself in those brief moments of rationality and calm.

The silence was disjointed, broken apart by the sound of Ms. Kole's fingers on the keys as she completed the application.

Then she switched to her mouse and clicked. "All done," she said.

"And now we wait."

"And wait."

"And wait." I smiled, but it was false. It was just to appear endearing. Charm had never been one of my skills, but I'd learned enough from Yvette to muddle through it. As of late, I'd become more curious about how the family was doing. I never bothered to bring it up with *Tia* during our visits, and she had never offered any information. I assumed they still didn't ask about me. Sometimes, I would catch myself off guard, and expound on their apathy.

"I was wondering," I started, "if you could help me write a resume. We've submitted the housing application, and I only needed my scores to complete the financial aid package. I have a few other things on my list, but I feel like I'm getting through them."

In truth, I was making progress, but I didn't want to tell Ms. Kole that. I wanted to keep some boundaries amongst the people I surrounded myself with. I wanted to see how fast the news would travel. Because of the structure, case workers often met with the in-house staff for updates. It bothered me to think there was no such thing as true confidentiality. It only fed into my trust issues.

"Sure, I can help with that." She pulled a book off her shelf and handed it to me. "Read this and bring me a draft when you come in next week."

I thumbed through the pages and saw that it had quite a few templates I could use to get started. "Okay."

It was nearly time to tutor Ximena, so I didn't return the book to my locker. I'd given her a written assignment at our last session and I was in a hurry to read it. Her skills had dramatically improved in the short time we had been working together, and I wanted to continue being an inspiration to her. Despite her best efforts, she couldn't convince the other girls to work with me. I didn't mind, because it meant I could focus on her. After my experience with Ms. Jackson while preparing for my own exams,

I realized the incredible value that came from this approach to tutoring.

Ximena showed up early and always wanted to stay late. I usually stayed there with her, assisting with the assignments I'd provided, and helping her revise first drafts before she resubmitted them to me. Until now, I hadn't seen someone as passionate about learning as I was. She was a close second. *Ego*, I reminded myself. *Ego*.

Her face lit up when I walked into the room. "What's that all about?" I asked in an attempt at nonchalance.

"Oh nothing. I'm just excited for you to read my latest essay. I really expanded on what we talked about the other day." I was impressed. Rarely did anyone, even Ximena with all of her motivation, go above and beyond what was required. The bare minimum is what helped most people get by, and I was used to that being the only amount of effort exerted.

She slid the notebook across the table to me and I scanned it quickly. It was definitely an improvement from where she had started. I'd asked her to think about Esperanza's goals and compare them to her own. What she turned out was inspiring. It made me want to help her all the more. "This is really good," I told her. I was afraid to give too many compliments, because people like us don't take them well, and often end up feeling like they are disingenuous.

"I have a question," I began. "And if it's too personal, just tell me you don't want to answer it. You don't have to."

Her eyes narrowed. She was on the defensive. I had to phrase it that way though, because one of the worst things you could do to a girl like Ximena was to make her feel backed into a corner. "Okay." The word came out slowly with a long exaggeration on the 'ay'.

"What are you doing tomorrow afternoon?"

She smiled, her face awash in relief. "I'm coming here for a finance class Ms. Jackson's giving, but that's in the morning. I don't have anything in the afternoon. Why?"

"I was thinking it might be time we got out of here."

She laughed. "I'm out of here all the time. You're the one that holes herself up in her bunk and doesn't talk to anyone." I was curious about where she spent her time, since it felt like I'd wasted so much of mine, but I resisted the urge to ask. "What did you have in mind?"

I let myself look thoughtful, as though I didn't already have a response in mind before posing the question. I was almost always prepared, especially if I was the one asking the quietly perfected question aimed to lead one to the answer I wanted them to give. Yes, it seemed I had learned more from Yvette than I really cared to admit. "I was wondering if you'd like to come to Hunter with me, and check out the campus."

"What's Hunter?"

I was only mildly surprised that she didn't know. This told me that, for all of her effort, she was still focused solely on putting one foot in front of the other, rather than looking up the hill to see what the path entailed. "It's a local college. I'm going to start there in the winter, but I thought it might be encouraging if we went together."

She smiled, "Yeah, that sounds like fun."

"Have you thought at all about college?" Now, I felt genuinely intrigued to hear what her answer would be. It could have gone either way.

"At all, yes. As a real thing that can happen for me? No."

That wasn't just an honest answer, it was a brutal one. She was smarter than she appeared, and as such, I was finally able to connect with her. "It's a real thing."

The silence between us felt like an eternity. She gathered her things and got up from her seat. "I'll see you tomorrow afternoon." I just nodded in her direction.

I went to the technology room and stared at the blinking cursor on the white screen. I had the resume book laid out next to me, and found a sample that looked basic. That would be all I needed. I had nothing of consequence to write, and in fact, I wondered if I even needed a resume after all. *If I cannot get hired to work at a fast food restaurant with no experience, what is a piece of paper that says I have tutored English going to do for me?*

I don't know how long I sat there, but eventually I gave up. As I passed Ms. Kole's office, I placed the book on her desk, but I didn't leave a note. There wouldn't have been anyone else looking for it. In fact, I wondered if she would ever have come looking for it if I hadn't returned it.

I missed dinner that night, and sat in the community room instead, blankly staring into space. I was the strange one. I was the one people left alone. No one knew what I was capable of, and the scar on my arm had become intimidating. I was potentially a loose cannon, and girls like that stayed loners.

I tried mapping out the campus in my head. I thought about the things I could show Ximena to convince her that if this is what she wants, it is possible. In all our time together, I didn't know much about her, and vice versa. We remained guarded, despite the essays she wrote. In them, I generally asked for her reactions to the readings, or to tell me about a time when she found herself in a similar circumstance. We both knew there was nothing confidential in this place and so neither of us ever gave away too much.

She approached her work with cautionary enthusiasm—excited to be making progress, but holding back because she didn't need any more weapons aimed at her. The loose cannon. I didn't have a whole lot to go on, so I decided I would just get us there and we would meander the campus, and if she had specific questions or interests, I would do the best I could to help. This particular adventure was about her, as mine was well underway.

That night, I tossed and turned, and counted the slats in the bunk above mine. I never bothered to learn the name of the girl who'd taken over Lara's space. *Lara's space?* I thought. *No one here has claim to anything.* I was already awake when the staff made their morning rounds. If I had slept at all, it could be counted in minutes, not hours.

I felt exhausted and moved slowly. My stomach gurgled, reminding me I needed to eat. Food had become a formality—

something I needed solely for survival, and no longer for my comfort. I wasn't sure if I'd had any comfort since The Incident, but at least I hadn't resorted to letting food fill that void.

It would have been so easy to backslide until I recognized myself again, but to do so meant I would have to admit defeat. I never knew who I was, and always dreamed about transforming into someone else. Now I'd made that metamorphosis, I stopped dreaming about the distant future. *There is both solace and grief in spending this much time alone*, I thought.

As hungry as I was from skipping dinner the night before, I kept my breakfast simple. I took a single serving size box of Special K and a banana. I brought the banana back to my room to take with me when we left. A few weeks previously, one of the girls had wanted to trade one of my shirts for her messenger bag. I felt that I'd made out in the deal, because it was an off-the-shoulder top that I rarely, if ever, wore. I didn't have much use for the bag, but took it because I anticipated needing it to carry my textbooks around when the winter term began.

I didn't give much thought to my outfits anymore. I still didn't like my arms, and I was still self-conscious about the scar, but for the most part, I just threw on whatever was in the top layer of my locker. They'd been predicting a heat wave would start soon, so I opted for a maxi dress with spaghetti straps. It would be too warm to wear a shirt over it. I bent down and wrapped the strap of my sandal around my ankle. I should have been used to not being out of breath by such a simple task, but every time I wasn't gasping for air, I felt confused.

Ximena stood alone outside the staff office. She still had a notebook in her hand, and was talking to one of the women inside. "We're going to Hunter today," she said indifferently. From this distance, I couldn't make out what the woman asked her, but her response immediately put me on guard. "Oh, I dunno, she wants to show me around, I guess."

I doubted if I should go through with this. I was the one about to expose all her vulnerability in this situation. Hunter was *my* thing, and I was sharing it with someone against my better judgment. In that moment, I just wanted to get out. If I stayed anywhere in the home, Ximena would find me, and perhaps even chide me for disappearing. Unfortunately, I couldn't leave without her seeing me. I swallowed the lump in my throat and approached them. "Hi," I said.

"Hi," Ximena said. "You ready to go?"

"Sure."

We signed out, one right after the other, in the black binder with sheet upon sheet of lined paper documenting our every move. The sun blinded me as we stepped outside. *Trade something for sunglasses*, I reminded myself. Neither of us said anything until we reached the subway entrance.

"Thanks for doing this," she said and smiled.

"Oh, anytime," I said cautiously. Before we reached the turnstile, I paused. "Look, if you're not interested in going, we don't have to."

"Of course I want to."

"Oh." I stared at my toes peeking out beneath my dress.

"Why?"

This was the time to be honest. "I heard you talking to the staff, and it sounded like you'd rather not go do this." I left out the 'today or any day' that remained floating in my head.

"Oh that," she said and laughed again, "I don't like to give too much away. Of course I'm excited. You're the only positive thing that's going to come out of this place."

I appreciated the compliment, but still felt wary. "I'm not sure that's entirely fair."

"Don't you think if anyone really ever got out of there alive, it'd be all we'd hear about?"

I hadn't considered that before. "I guess I never thought about that." She reached in her back pocket and swiped her MetroCard through the reader, and I heard the familiar click of the turnstile as she went through. I paused for a moment, acting as though I couldn't find my card. I dug through my bag to buy me time to quiet the nagging insecurities which raced through my mind.

"Finally," I said as I pulled the card from my bag and ran it through the reader. I didn't have to turn sideways to get through the turnstile anymore, but out of habit I still did. "Let's go."

"So what's the plan?" she asked.

"I didn't have one in mind. I just thought we'd go down there and check it out, and then you could write about it for your next assignment."

"Of course, this is about *work*," she emphasized the word 'work' in true dramatic fashion. She rolled her eyes then laughed. Had it not been for her laughter, I would have mistaken her comment and facial expression as sarcasm. *You used to be so good at reading people*, I reminded myself.

"It's not that hot out yet," I said matter-of-factly. "I was thinking we could just take the train to Lincoln Center and cut across the park."

She looked thoughtful for a moment. "That's like a mile, ya know."

I smiled, deep in thought. A mile had changed my life irrevocably

.

Acknowledgments

Anyone that says a novel – even fiction – is ever truly a work of one's own creation is not telling the truth. An inordinate amount of time and energy was poured into this work by a number of people without whom it would never have come to fruition.

First, to Eileen: You have inspired me in more ways than you will ever know. Thank you for sharing your trials and tribulations with me over the last thirteen years. Yours and Ella's stories are forever entwined and I am so grateful for our friendship.

To Grace: Thank you for being one of my strongest supporters. You kept me churning out pages and your willingness to read, provide feedback and non-stop encouragement is the real reason that this – above any other novel I've started to write – was actually finished.

My Team: Chantal, Constance, Harmony, Jen, Jessi, Lori and Susan. You all have been my beta-readers, editors, sounding board, researchers, designers and marketing gurus. I could not have done any of this without your contributions.

Last, but not least, for Brian: Your steadfast love and encouragement has helped me believe that anything is possible. All my love, now and always.

Author Photo © Dominic Chow, 2014

Lisa Mauro is a novelist and blogger. When she's not breaking pivot tables during her day job in the pharmaceutical industry, you can find her watching *The Office* on repeat. She lives near Boston, MA with her better half, Brian Sfinas. You can visit her at www.lisa-mauro.com